THE
FIRST
THING
ABOUT
YOU

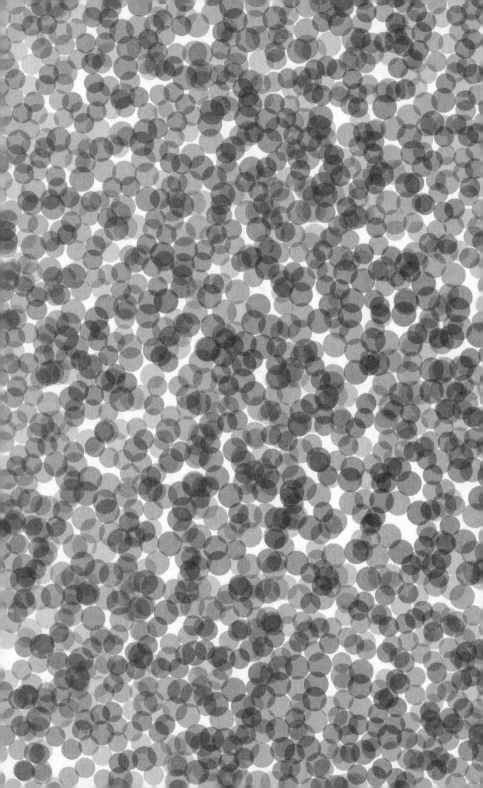

THE FIRST THING ABOUT YOU

CHAZ HAYDEN

CANDLEWICK PRESS

Copyright © 2022 by Chaz Hayden Weiner

First edition 2022

Library of Congress Catalog Card Number 2021953239
ISBN 978-1-5362-2311-8

22 23 24 25 26 27 LBM 10 9 8 7 6 5 4 3 2 1

Printed in Melrose Park, IL, USA

This book was typeset in Palatino.

Candlewick Press
99 Dover Street
Somerville, Massachusetts 02144

www.candlewick.com

For my mom, who is the most selfless person I know.
Thank you for putting up with me. I love you.

FAR

NEW JERSEY PIZZA

THE DAY BEFORE I MOVED to New Jersey, I told my only friend that I was okay with never seeing him again. *Friend* is a pretty generous word to describe us, but I wanted to feel like I was leaving something behind.

I'd always had a knack for burning bridges. This, I believed, was a trait I inherited from my mom, who knows how to get on with life.

But lots of people come and go with little regard for the people they're leaving. My nurses almost never look back. And I can't let that bother me, because (a) most of them don't think two thoughts about me in the first place and (b) I need to keep the revolving door turning to avoid a lapse in my care.

That's not to say my parents aren't capable of taking care of me; I wouldn't have been alive and starting my sophomore year of high school without them. But they can't do it every second of every day, so we hire nurses who are reliable enough to attend school with me and make sure I don't die on their watch.

On the first day in our new house, I sat watching a pre-season football game with my brother, Ollie, who was wearing a sweatshirt from the University of Virginia—his future college and the lacrosse team he'd be playing for the following year. He was sitting next to a stack of boxes on the couch we'd dragged across the country.

Our parents walked in, each looking more exhausted than the other. Mom's hands were placed firmly on her hips, which actually wasn't a sign of her being mad. She was about to ask us a question or tell us to do something.

"We're ordering pizza for dinner, okay?" she said. "I'm tired, and there's nothing in the house to cook anyway."

"I hate pizza," I said. "It's gross."

"Too bad, Harris. I'm not running to the grocery store at ten o'clock just to buy you chicken nuggets. You can deal with pizza for one night." She walked away, leaving no opportunity for a rebuttal. To argue with my mom, I had to be faster.

"Dude, we're in New Jersey. Some of the best pizza in the country is right here," Ollie told me.

I ignored him.

Dad lingered behind. "Ollie, can you get up and help a little? Pick up those boxes and bring them into your room?"

"Why didn't the movers unpack everything?"

"It doesn't matter. I asked you to do something."

Ollie dragged his body off the couch, picked up two boxes, and stomped down the hall toward our connecting bedrooms. Dad followed with the rest of the boxes.

I sat alone in an unfamiliar place.

Our house back in San Diego hadn't been big enough for my family, the several nurses who are always coming and going—not to mention the four hundred pounds of metal strapped to my ass. Someone always seemed to be in the way.

The new place seemed pretty good so far. Ollie and I had our own mini wing on the main level. Next to our bedrooms was a huge bathroom with a roll-in shower large enough for me to do donuts in with my wheelchair. Trust me, I'd tried.

You wouldn't believe how difficult it is for real-estate agents to understand what *wheelchair accessible* means. My parents probably spent more time explaining that than driving cross-country. Like, no, the house can't have stairs.

The kitchen filled up with the sounds of my parents arguing and ceramic plates clanking, until it was decided we'd use paper instead. Tensions between everyone were higher than usual. Turned out moving was pretty stressful.

I pulled up to my end of the table, which we'd brought from back home. Thank God for something familiar. My mom picked up the slice of pizza in front of me and shoved it into my mouth. My disability makes it difficult for me to lift my arms and feed myself. Even small things like a piece of cereal or a plastic spoon pose a challenge. I used to have the muscles to eat independently, but over time I've lost them.

But to be honest, having someone feed you is pretty cool. Despite the occasional mess in my lap from people dropping food, I usually feel like a king being fed by servants. Except those servants are my parents, my brother, or a nurse.

"Are you excited to start at your new schools?" Mom asked.

"We're not five years old," Ollie responded. "We're in high school. No one's excited."

I swallowed my first bite of pizza. (I'm a very slow eater.) "I'm pretty excited. New people means no one knows me. I can reinvent myself. Maybe they won't notice my wheelchair."

"They're strangers, not blind," Ollie said.

"Either way, I'm glad we left California. I never want to think about that place again."

"Hey, don't be like that," Dad said.

"Be like what?" I asked. "I was miserable there. I had no friends, it was always hot, and it's not like I could go to the beach. Besides, I had at most three good nurses in the last fifteen years."

"What about you, Ollie?" Mom asked, clearly giving up on me. "Your new lacrosse team is way better than the one in San Diego."

"I don't know. Coach introduced me to some of the guys on the team during my tour yesterday. They seemed like jerks."

"Maybe they think you're a jerk," I added.

"Shut up."

"Guys, stop," our mom ordered. "What makes you think they're jerks?"

Ollie shrugged. "None of them would talk to me."

"Why not?"

"Probably because they know I'm better than them. They're pissed off I'm on the team."

"Well, the season doesn't start for a few months. You have time to make friends."

"I don't need to be friends with them. I'm not there to make friends. I'm there to win a championship and then leave for Virginia."

While my brother vented about whether he needed friends to play a team sport, Mom pivoted back to me. "I got a call from the nursing agency here. They have a few people who are interested in going to school with you, Harris."

"Are they young?" I asked.

"I told them you prefer younger nurses. We'll see."

"I prefer young and beautiful, but I'll settle for young."

"You'll settle for what they send," my dad said.

"Yeah, why do they have to be young?" Ollie asked. "They're there to take care of you. You don't have to date them."

Mom raised a cup of water to my mouth. I took a sip from the straw and then another bite of pizza.

"Harris needs a contemporary with him," Mom said. "How would you feel if an old fuck followed you around school all day?"

Ollie shrugged. "Honestly, I wouldn't care." Then he secretly flipped me the finger from across the table.

Our dad rejoined the conversation. "Clare, don't let Harris be too picky. Otherwise you'll end up at school with him every day."

"I don't mind. Harris and I have a great time together, and either way, I'm going with him for the first few days."

The discussion ended with no counterarguments. Of course, it wasn't ideal for my mom to be with me at school, but it wasn't the worst. She was pretty cool for a mom, and not having to worry about a new person following me in a new school was comforting.

After a few bites of New Jersey pizza, I didn't see what all the fuss was about. If that claim to fame was crap, what were the odds Jersey's nurses would be any better?

THIS PLACE COULD BE DIFFERENT

THE FIRST DAY STARTED OFF like any other, even though we were in a strange house. My mom woke me up, turned off the breathing machine I use while sleeping, and started my nebulizer treatment. The only difference between waking up in New Jersey and in San Diego was that my dad wasn't around to help. He was already out the door to catch his train to the city. Mom was on her own.

Mornings are hectic when Mom has to go to school with me, since we both need to shower and get dressed and none of it can be done simultaneously, considering that one of us requires assistance in all phases. So she left me lying in bed while she got ready first.

Another thing that hadn't changed: there's always a moment in the middle of the morning chaos when Ollie pops into my room, bagel in hand, and turns the TV on to *SportsCenter*.

"Why are you already dressed?" I asked.

"My school is almost an hour away. The bus picks me up in five minutes."

"Oh. Are you nervous?"

Ollie shrugged. His eyes were focused on the top ten plays from the previous week. "Not really. It's just a new school. Plus the lacrosse team is way better than the trash in California."

There were two reasons my family had moved to New Jersey. The primary reason was that our dad got a higher-paying job at some stuffy investment bank in Manhattan. And once high schools on the East Coast got wind of our potential move, they came calling. My brother was kind of a rising lacrosse star in San Diego, and promises of scholarships and exposure to the best colleges sealed the deal. We became Jersey people.

"Are you pissed Mom has to go to school with you?" Ollie asked.

"Not really. She's done it before, and Mom is actually pretty cool when she has to be."

"You're not going to make any friends with Mom following you around. That instantly makes you the weird kid."

"Maybe I want to be the weird kid. You're just jealous Mom isn't going to be with you."

Ollie was clearly getting impatient with me, although he was never fully disgusted with me. Instead, his contempt was more like amusement. I might have even heard a chuckle. He shoved the last bite of bagel in his mouth and stood up to leave. "Whatever. I gotta go. See you later."

"I love you!" I yelled as he walked away.

"Yeah, love you too," he mumbled from the hallway.

I was alone again, surrounded by the walls of my new bedroom, which were freshly painted the shade of blue the sky takes during a cloudless rain. For as long as I can remember, blue has always been my favorite color. It's not a particularly emotional color, but it's dependable whenever I don't feel well.

I thought about colors a lot, actually. Especially when I was about to meet anyone new. It was always the first question I asked them. A person's favorite color says a lot about who they are.

No doubt Ollie would say that caring about people's favorite colors makes me weird. It's not that I *want* to be the weird kid, really. It's just that I've always been the weird kid and figure I always would be.

But then I thought about this move and how I kept telling myself that this was my chance to finally start living a real teenage life. From movies, I'd gathered that meant going to parties and breaking rules. But based on my brother, being a teen just meant playing a sport well and hanging out with your parents and younger brother. I wanted something in between those two lives. I thought maybe that'd be my sweet spot. Maybe what I really wanted was just a friend—a real one.

Since I'd spent most of my childhood in and out of the hospital, it had been difficult to form friendships with kids my age. Illnesses and surgeries would exile me for months, and I thought it was easier not to get too close to anyone in case I didn't come back. When I did return to school, everyone always seemed the same—innocent and carefree. Everyone except me.

Around the time I turned ten years old, the frequent bouts of pneumonia slowed, and I had the opportunity to actually connect with my classmates. But I never did. I couldn't start fresh. Everyone already knew who I was—the kid in the wheelchair who got sick all the time—and they were unwilling to learn more, no matter how much effort I put in.

I wanted all of that to change. Moving to New Jersey meant I could actually start fresh, make friends, stay out late, go to parties, and feel what it's like to be a teenager. But for any of that to happen, I needed a way to assess the kids I would be meeting, to know who might be good friend material and who would be a jerk or a flake. I needed my colors.

The steam from my breathing treatment billowed up in front of my face. I took a few deep breaths of the medicine, trying to clear the congestion that always accumulated in my chest overnight, while two talking heads on ESPN argued about LeBron James versus Michael Jordan.

ALL HIGH SCHOOLS
ARE THE SAME

IMAGINE BEING A MONSTER TRUCK stuck in bumper-to-bumper traffic. You know you'd be tempted to drive over the other cars. Well, that's what it's like to maneuver my wheelchair through a crowded high school hallway. I could simply drive at full speed, running over feet and backpacks along the way, but that would mean spending the day feeling guilty. Politely asking people to move is out of the question—they wouldn't hear me. My horn sounds like a microwave attempting suicide, so that's a no. The only option is to weave through the gaps, hoping I don't get nailed in the head with a backpack or a butt.

Mom was behind me, acting as my caboose. An opening appeared on the right, and I took it. My wheelchair burst through the gap like a running back. I pretended the other students were my offensive line, setting up the perfect block so I could trailblaze into the end zone untouched. I shifted to the left. In my head, I was making spectacular spin moves and juking defenders, but in reality, I was a fifteen-year-old recklessly driving a wheelchair down a hallway, followed by a neurotic mom who could barely keep up.

We reached my locker. "Do you have the combination?" I asked.

"Yeah, it's on your class schedule." Mom dropped my backpack on the floor and began digging through the compartments. She pulled out a folded piece of paper. "Seven, six, four." Her fingers spun the lock.

While she unloaded my crap into the locker, I watched the other kids rushing through the busy hall. I felt like I was in the way, and I kind of was. I was parked alongside my locker, but my wheelchair blocked the two in front of me as well. At any moment, the students those lockers belonged to could appear, and then we'd begin the awkward dance of shuffling back and forth while smiling apologetically.

My mom attached a plastic tray to my wheelchair, which allowed me to carry books and look at worksheets in class. "Homeroom starts in five minutes. After that, you have physics, trig, and English."

"Mom, I know how school works and how to read a schedule."

She ignored me and plopped a three-inch binder onto my tray. "This is your morning binder. We'll come back for your afternoon one before lunch."

A girl with brown hair held back by a green headband swooped in next to me and reached for her locker, bumping into the back of my wheelchair, which was barely in her way.

At my old school, there had been times when a student,

arms full of books, would see me in front of their locker. I would start to move, but they would say that it was all right and they could just come back later.

I would rather someone tell me to get out of their fucking space than pretend I'm not a burden. This girl did the next best thing and just went about her business.

I pulled away from the wall to make room. "Where are you going?" Mom asked. "Homeroom is the other way."

"I know. I'm just moving so this girl can reach her locker."

My mom looked up. "Oh, excuse us." She grabbed the joystick on my wheelchair and yanked it forward, driving me even farther away. My head jerked back from the sudden movement.

"No worries," I heard the girl say.

Then she was gone.

Homeroom felt the same as it had back in San Diego. I don't know why I'd expected it to be different from state to state, but I was hoping that maybe in New Jersey they handed out fresh bagels and schmear. If anything, it was the complete opposite. The room was sweltering and smelled like rancid cream cheese.

"Is it too hot for you in here?" my mom nervously asked. "I'm gonna ask the teacher to turn up the air."

"No, I'm fine. Don't make a big deal about it. We're in here for less than ten minutes. Let's just find somewhere to sit."

A commonly overlooked benefit of being able-bodied is choosing where to sit. If a seat is open, you take it. For me, it's more complicated and depends on the location of the door. If the door is in the front, I sit in the front. If the door is in the back, I sit in the back. If the door is on the side, then I block everyone's entrance and exit and pray to God there won't be an emergency.

At the far end of this room, near the window, was an open desk. I could barely squeeze my wheelchair past the teacher's desk to reach the spot. One of the windows was cracked and letting in cool air, which I didn't point out to my mom, since that would just make her worry about drafts.

Mom sat at the actual desk, and I parked next to it. I always find it strange that whoever helps me sits where the students sit, while I'm kind of just there, observing. Either way, we never have to ask for an extra chair; my assistant uses the seat intended for me, and, well, I bring my own.

An older man sauntered in, holding a messenger bag that had seen better days.

"For those of you who don't know me, my name is Mr. Wormhole," he said with no enthusiasm whatsoever. Also, his last name was Wormhole. What the hell kind of name is Wormhole? "We'll be spending every morning together. Please attempt to be on time. I don't appreciate tardiness."

If he talked any slower, he'd make us all tardy to our next class. He droned on about some additional homeroom rules, which I didn't hear, because as soon as he started, the brown-haired girl from the hall walked in.

Wormhole didn't look pleased that she was late.

"And who are you?" he asked.

"Nory Fischer."

"You're in the wrong room. This homeroom is for last names J through M."

"I was just in the guidance office, and they told me to come here. Something about the other classes being overfilled."

Old man Wormhole appeared to have a mini stroke and whispered a few expletives aimed at the school principal, Dr. Kenzing, most of which were louder than I think he intended. After he caught his breath, he instructed Nory to find a seat and not to blame him if there was a fire and she got trampled by his class, which was at capacity. Lucky for me, the only open desk was next to mine. Well, technically it was next to my mom's, but close enough.

"The school has implemented a new homework buddy program," Mr. Wormhole said. "I'm giving you all the rest of the period to find a classmate with a similar course schedule and swap phone numbers."

My mom whipped out my schedule and slapped it on my tray. "Go find someone."

"No, this is ridiculous. I don't need help with homework."

"You miss a lot of school when you get sick, and it would be nice to have someone to give you your work. Take this as an opportunity to make a friend."

"Oh my God. Can you stop being a mom for one second?" I whispered. "Besides, I can't even drive around this tiny room, and everyone is huddled in the back."

"So move up to the front, and someone will come over." She turned my chair on and gave me an unneeded shove on the back of my arm.

I faced the classroom and watched the students chatting and laughing at Instagram posts. I hated that I was frozen and couldn't seem to approach any of them. I could barely look in their direction. Traveling almost three thousand miles had not changed me.

Then I saw Nory, who looked like she was reorganizing critical documents in her bag, which was clearly empty. I thought that was funny. Our eyes met for half a second—long enough to acknowledge that we were both without a homework buddy.

"Should we exchange numbers?" I asked.

"I'm taking all honors."

"Same. I may be in a wheelchair, but I'm actually pretty smart."

Nory quickly looked down at her desk and then back at me, trying to find her words. "Oh, I didn't mean it like that."

"It's fine. So what do you say? Can I get your number, and we can move on with our lives?"

"Sure." Nory smiled. She scribbled her number on a torn piece of notebook paper, reached across the desk, and placed it on my tray.

Her outstretched hand didn't hover in the air, waiting for me to grab the paper, which I couldn't do without assistance. I didn't have to tell her where to put the paper or hate my mom for pushing me into an uncomfortable situation and myself for not being able to get a girl's number without help. It was just me and Nory, no third party necessary.

Nory adjusted her headband. "Is green your favorite color?" I asked.

Nory made the expression everyone made when I asked the question: a furrowed brow and curled lips. "Does it matter?"

"Well, I mean . . ."

Then the bell rang, and everyone rushed out of homeroom. Nory pushed past my wheelchair instead of waiting for me to move. Which was probably a good thing, since I wasn't sure I *could* move.

Most of my childhood memories link up to significant

medical events that occurred around the same time. "When I was diagnosed" or "the year I had my back surgery" became a way to track time instead of typical milestones, like learning to crawl or taking a first step or catching a football for the first time.

On that day, I was supposed to have a typical milestone—my first day at a new school. But I don't remember it as just any first day. I remember it as the day I met Nory Fischer.

NOT ALL BATHROOMS
ARE CREATED EQUAL

BEING IN A WHEELCHAIR HAS PERKS that include but are not limited to skipping lines, early entry to concerts and sporting events, free stuff, and access to people who can grant special privileges. At school, those people are the janitors and security guards—often ignored, but usually the ones who have the power to close down an entire bathroom.

Most handicap stalls in public bathrooms really aren't accessible at all. Sure, they might have a couple of grab bars on the wall or an elevated toilet, but try to fit a wheelchair in that space. Spoiler alert: it's impossible.

My preferred option is a single-use bathroom, but the only one in the entire school was in the nurse's office on the first floor, the complete opposite side of the building from where I needed to be. The school had not yet designated a bathroom for me to use, so the next logical step was for my mom to hunt down a janitor and have him lock a bathroom for ten minutes. He claimed it was one that was rarely used.

"That girl from homeroom seemed nice," my mom said once we were set up in the locked bathroom. "What was her name?"

"Nory."

"And I knew you'd be fine getting her number by your-self. You just need to stop being so afraid."

I ignored her and inhaled my breathing treatment. My wheelchair was parked outside the stalls, next to the sinks. I had just finished peeing.

"You should text her later and get to know her."

"I don't know. I think her favorite color is green."

"So what? You've known people who like green."

True, but none of them had been my friends. "Green and blue are too similar. We don't blend well."

"Seems like you've never blended with anyone, so I don't think that's a valid excuse."

"Either way, people who like green are very independent. She won't want to be slowed down by my disability. You saw the way she stormed out of homeroom."

My mom sighed. "And Nory confirmed that her favorite color is green?"

"Not exactly."

"Then I still think you should text her later. Maybe you'll find out that red is actually her favorite color."

I sighed, because my mom had never understood my favorite color theories. "I think this is done," I said, referring to the breathing treatment.

"No, it's not. Stop rushing. The janitor is outside watching. No one is coming in."

"I don't want to be late for lunch. All the tables will be filled, and I'll have to eat alone."

"We'll find a table. And lunch is an hour. You have plenty of time to finish your neb and eat."

"An hour's not long enough. I'm a slow eater. You know that."

"Fine." Mom reached into the backpack and turned off the oxygen tank running the nebulizer. "In other news, we're staying a little late today to go over your IEP with the accommodations team. Your old school sent the one from last year, and I already spoke with Ms. Maszak on the phone."

I rolled my eyes.

"Don't start, Harris. I just want to make sure everyone is on the same page."

"What page? I'm in a freaking wheelchair. They can see that."

Ms. Maszak was the accommodations manager at my new school. I'd had one in San Diego, Mr. Delty, a large, hairy older man who wore too much cologne and insisted on making my middle school years a living hell by taking every opportunity to single out the "special" kid. Needless to say, I hated him.

"These are the things I've done your whole life, Harris." Mom was annoyed. "I've met with teachers, filled out paperwork, gone over your accommodations. It's not fun, but someone has to do it, and before we moved, you said you wanted to take more control. That means advocating for yourself and going to boring meetings."

When we left the bathroom, there was a long line of students waiting to get in—all of them girls. Nory was one of them. She stared at me. I looked up at the bathroom sign and spotted the universal girl symbol. How had I not realized this before going in? It finally made sense why there weren't any urinals.

Of course, the janitor was nowhere in sight. He wasn't going to be much of a connection.

YELLOW

THE COMMOTION OF THE CAFETERIA hit me hard. For once, I was feeling social and eager to jump in and make new friends, but then I became overwhelmed by the thought of approaching a table and asking if a parent-looking person and I could join.

"Pick a table, Harris," my mom ordered.

"I see an empty one. Let's eat there, and I'll find a group tomorrow."

"No. You can't reinvent yourself and make friends if you act like you did in San Diego. I'm right behind you. Now, go."

Working up the courage to join a table was one problem. The other problem was *getting* to a table. The aisles between them were narrow, and there was no way my wheelchair would make it through without bumping people's chairs.

I was plotting my path to the empty table when a voice rang out. "We have seats over here." A guy waved at me a little too vigorously. No one should be that excited about a stranger. Still, it beat spinning my wheels for the next forty minutes.

As expected, it was a tight squeeze. Some kids didn't move, and some scooched in to make room. All of them awkwardly smiled at me. Finally, I rolled up to the table occupied by the overly friendly student and two more male students who were playing a game with trading cards instead of eating. What I'm trying to say is that there weren't any girls.

"Thanks for letting me sit here. Kinda wild trying to find a spot," I said.

"No problem. The cafeteria is definitely tough to navigate on the first day, but I got you covered."

I looked at the two students playing cards.

"Don't worry about them. They're harmless nerds."

"What does that make you?" I asked.

"A nerd, but not like them. I like to think of this table as a refuge for the lost—an asylum from the madness that is high school."

"Oh, so this is your regular table?"

"I hope so. This is actually my first day. I'm a freshman."

I glanced at my mom, who was still unpacking my lunch. I wondered if she could sense my disappointment at sitting with a freshman.

"It's my first day too, but I'm not a freshman. I just moved here a couple of days ago."

"Where from?"

"San Diego. My dad got a new job."

"San Diego? That's so cool. Did you ever go surfing?" As soon as he finished the question, I knew he regretted it.

"Actually, yes. I crashed pretty hard once, and that's why I'm in this chair."

"Seriously?"

I laughed. "No, not seriously."

"Oh, well, it's a pretty awesome story. You should tell more people and let them believe it's true."

We both laughed. My mom smiled. If only it had been this easy to talk to people back in San Diego.

Mom raised my sandwich to my mouth, and I took a bite. My typical lunch was turkey, roast beef, ham, and pepperoni on a croissant with nothing else. No cheese or mayo or mustard, just meat.

"By the way, what's your name?" he asked.

"Harris."

"Nice to meet you, Harris. I'm Alexander Stein, but I go by Zander." He looked at my mom, clearly unsure if he should ask her name or ignore her presence.

"I'm Clare, Harris's executive assistant," she said, reaching out to shake Zander's hand.

"Sweet. I wish I had an executive assistant. Sometimes I forget what class I'm going to and bring the wrong notebook. An assistant would come in handy in those situations, and they could take notes for me in class."

"I do all those things for Harris."

"Sounds like a good deal for him. Will there be other executive assistants, or are you the only one?"

"She's just here temporarily," I interjected.

"That's too bad. Coming to school seems like a pretty easy gig. Are you going to be able to find other work after Harris?"

Mom laughed. "Don't worry: I'll keep busy and still see Harris."

I tried to change the subject before she slipped and told him she was my mom. "So, what'd you do this summer, man?"

"Not much. Just prepared for high school."

"What did that involve?"

"Not a whole lot. I mostly just watched *Mean Girls* until I had it memorized."

I almost choked on my food. "Seriously? How is that going to help you?"

"Harris, that movie provides all the answers to our adolescent questions. How do I determine the cliques? What will it take to become popular? When do I wear pink? You see, it's not just a movie, but a guide for the weak and afraid. Not to mention a great resource for devastating comebacks."

Mom gave me a sip of water and popped a chip in my mouth. I tried to ignore the fact that I had just made friends with the actual weird kid.

Then I saw her again—a green headband bouncing past our table.

Zander followed my gaze. "Do you know Nory?" he asked.

"Sort of. Her locker is next to mine. And we're in homeroom together. Wait, Nory's a sophomore. How do *you* know her?"

"I told you I spent the summer studying."

"So you seriously learned about every single person at this school?"

Zander hedged. "Well, kinda. Not really. Nory is actually my neighbor."

"Is she dating anyone?"

"Um, I'm not sure. Hey, you want to sit here again tomorrow? This is a prime table, and I want to know who should get here early to secure it."

"Definitely you. And no offense, but you talk a lot. But you also have a lot of valuable information. What's your favorite color?"

Zander didn't flinch. "Yellow."

"Me too," my mom said.

"Your favorite color is yellow?" I asked her.

I've never known any of my family members' favorite colors. I've never needed to.

Zander was unquestionably yellow, though: confident and outgoing. Only one other color separated us on the color wheel, but I didn't tell him that. Then he would have known how well suited we were for each other, and I refused to admit that I needed a bright color in my life.

BEIGE

I ALMOST MADE IT THROUGH a full first day without a teacher singling me out as the new kid and prized possession of the class. In seventh-period history class, Mr. Bavroe forced me to come to the front of the room at the end of the period so I could introduce myself. First, let me say that ending the day with Ancient World History, which was possibly the most boring class, should be illegal. Second, this was one of those classrooms where the door was in the back, and getting to the front wasn't so easy. It was one of my more embarrassing moments.

But it didn't end there. After I covered the basics of moving from California, having an older brother, et cetera, that old fuck Mr. Bavroe asked me to tell the class about my disability. Or maybe "asked" isn't the right word, since it wasn't really optional. He said something about his classroom being inclusive and how he and the other students would be honored to hear what made me so unique.

I wish I could've told him that inclusivity was not making someone feel uncomfortable for the enrichment of others.

I wish I could've told him that maybe he should teach instead of making me the subject of his show-and-tell. I wish I didn't have to look at my mom watching her son being tortured, but there was nothing she could do to intervene without blowing her cover.

I was about to provide the class with a quick rundown of my disability—at Mr. Bavroe's insistence—when the bell rang and put me out of my misery.

After that painful ending to the school day, I had my IEP meeting. The halls emptied as students bolted for the exits. Mom and I stopped at my locker to pick up my morning binder so I could complete my homework later.

Then Nory appeared again at her locker. I noticed a Dallas Cowboys sticker inside. Holy crap, she liked football. Without thinking, I asked, "You're a Cowboys fan?"

The half second it took her to recognize that it was me asking the question felt weird, and I hated myself for speaking. "What?"

My heart dropped. "You like the Cowboys?" I almost couldn't breathe. I almost drove away and pretended like I'd never said a word.

"Huh? Oh, my dad does," Nory responded.

"That's too bad. The Cowboys kind of suck."

"So then, who do you like?"

"The Giants. This means we're rivals." In my head it sounded playful, but coming out of my mouth it sounded kind of hostile.

Nory slammed her locker door shut and started walking away. "Just don't light my locker on fire or something." That *definitely* sounded hostile.

My mom's eyes were on the back of my neck. "That was hard to watch," she said.

"Well, it's difficult to flirt with a girl in front of your mom."

"Like I made a difference."

"Thanks, Mom." I drove away toward the meeting room.

. . .

A woman wearing a pantsuit was waiting for us in the guidance office. "So great to see you again, Mrs. Jacobus."

"Call me Clare. We try to keep it a secret that I'm Harris's mom."

"Of course. And let me say that we are very excited to welcome Harris to East Essex Central."

"Don't tell me. Talk to him about it."

Ms. Maszak blushed. You would think a person whose entire job was working with disabled students would know how to talk to one.

"Why are you so excited to have me as a student?" I asked. "I'm just like every other student, right?"

"Well, of course we're excited about all of our students. But we've never had a differently abled student as academically gifted as you."

"Harris hates that term, *differently abled*," my mom said. "Don't you think it sounds patronizing?"

Pantsuit had no answer. She fixed her hair and refocused her attention on me. "In the past, we've had students give presentations about their disabilities so classmates can feel comfortable asking questions. Is that something you would be interested in doing?"

"I was already forced into that unnecessary spotlight by Mr. Bavroe," I said.

"Oh, well, if you want to do something more planned and formal, I can arrange that."

"No, I don't understand why that would be something I'd want to do. When someone has a question, they should come up to me."

"Fair enough. I'm always around if you change your mind or have any problems."

"Okay," I said. I really wanted to tell her not to get all up in my business. Mr. Delty had struggled with boundaries, and it hadn't ended well for him.

Ms. Maszak led Mom and me into a meeting room where an older woman stood to greet us. "I'm Dr. Kenzing, the school principal. Fabulous to meet you both." She shook my mom's hand but didn't attempt to shake mine.

"We're just waiting for one of Harris's teachers to join us," Ms. Maszak said. "One of them has to be present at each meeting."

"I know. I've been doing this a long time," Mom told her.

"Right. Ah, there he is."

My back was to the door, so I didn't immediately see who came in, but then he sat right next to me.

"Hey, bud," Mr. Bavroe said. "Long time no see."

What a dick.

"Oh, good. You've already met." Dr. Kenzing could barely contain her smile.

"I mean, yeah. He is one of my teachers."

"Anyway, I don't think this should take long," Ms. Maszak announced. "Your mom and I already spoke on the phone, and I reviewed your plan from last year."

"There are just a few things I want to go over," my mom said. "Harris needs to be as independent as possible with his schoolwork. All his books need to be in digital format, with homework completed and submitted on the computer."

"Absolutely. I read all that in his previous IEP."

"Well, it was in there, but his previous school did nothing to accommodate him. All we did was fight with them."

Dr. Kenzing joined the conversation. "We already notified our IT department that Harris will require a laptop. One should be purchased by the end of the week."

Mom nodded, and I could tell she was impressed.

"And we'll contact the textbook publishers to see what can be done," Ms. Maszak added. "In the meantime, we'll have Harris's teachers provide an extra book so you can keep one at home. Does that work for you, Mr. Bavroe?"

"Of course. Anything to make Harris feel comfortable and help him get his schoolwork done."

"When we get the laptop, all worksheets should be scanned in so Harris can complete them electronically," Mom said.

"We'll make sure all his teachers are aware and trained to use the laptop." Ms. Maszak read the papers in front of her, then continued, "It looks like some of his other accommodations include time and a half for testing and that he'll be accompanied by a nurse."

"Right now it'll be me until we find and train someone. Harris and I are a buy-one-get-one package, and I'm always here to provide backup."

"Not a problem. Is there anything else?"

Mom began to shake her head, but I caught her eye. "The bathroom," I whispered.

"Tell them," she ordered.

Everyone was staring at me. "We had a problem finding

a bathroom to use. I need my own. I don't want to take away from the other students like I did today."

"Yes, we heard about what happened. Dr. Kenzing and I want to apologize for any embarrassment the situation may have caused. We've notified our entire janitorial staff, and they've come up with a solution. There's an unused faculty restroom on the second floor. Tomorrow they'll give you a key. It's all yours."

"You guys are definitely on the ball," my mom said.

"We're very excited to have Harris as a student and want to ensure that everything goes as smoothly as possible. Do you have any other questions?"

Ms. Maszak looked at me, which I appreciated, but I could see in her eyes that she didn't really care. I had seen that look countless times from doctors and other school administrators who would *yes* us to death but never do anything. I was pretty sure Ms. Maszak would be the same.

"What's your favorite color?" I asked.

Ms. Maszak acted like it wasn't a strange question. "Hmm, I really don't have one."

No favorite color meant no personality; I could easily walk (or roll) all over her. It also meant, like I suspected, that she wouldn't follow through on what we'd discussed.

"My favorite color is beige," Dr. Kenzing chimed in.

"Why beige?"

"It's professional and goes with everything."

I had no clue how to respond to that.

GREEN

ON THE WAY TO THE CAR, my mom started in on me. "Why were you so quiet? You didn't say a single fucking word."

"What are you talking about? I brought up the bathroom. And besides, you never gave me time to answer."

"You need to speak up. Jump into the conversation. It's called advocating for yourself, Harris."

"Stop. I'm tired from school. It was just one meeting. I promise I won't shut up next time."

Leftover pizza was waiting for Mom and me when we got home. There hadn't been any time to go grocery shopping yet.

"How'd the meeting go?" Dad asked.

Mom sighed. "Good. They seem to have their shit together, but we'll see. Every new year starts the same way."

"And how was the first day for you, bud?" he asked me.

"It sucked. I'm stuck at the loser lunch table."

"Told ya!" my brother yelled from the living room.

After taking a few bites of pizza, I told my parents that I wanted to go to my bedroom to work on my homework. Mom knew that I barely had any, but she helped me get set up at the desk in my room with the computer we'd brought from California.

"Should I sit in here with you?" my mom asked.

"No, I'll be fine. I'm not going to spontaneously combust because you're in a different room."

"All right. Text me from the computer if you need anything."

As soon as she left, I exhaled a sigh of relief. I was finally alone after surviving the worst first day in the history of high school. Nothing had changed, except now I was in New Jersey instead of California. I was still the kid with one friend who hid in his bedroom after school.

That had always been my routine. I would come home, eat dinner, maybe play some video games, and then study to distract myself from the fact that nobody was calling or knocking on the door to ask if I could hang out.

The window of my bedroom back in San Diego overlooked the street, and sometimes I could hear our neighbors running around, playing tag or basketball or whatever. One day when I was in third grade, I sat at my desk and listened to them while I read practically every single article on the internet about how people wear certain colors of clothing depending on how they're feeling or how they want to feel. My mom came into my room at some point and asked if I wanted to go play with the other kids. I said no because if I went outside they'd have to find a new game, since I wouldn't be able to tag anyone without running them over. It's hard to do anything fun when you don't feel welcome or wanted.

A message from my mom popped up on the computer asking if everything was okay. I answered quickly so she wouldn't get concerned and barge in, even though I had nothing to hide. I imagined other boys my age would've already destroyed their computers with half a dozen porn sites in the five minutes I'd been alone. Not me. I just stared at the color wheel that was set as my desktop wallpaper.

It irked me that Nory wouldn't tell me her favorite color. In ten years of asking, nobody had ever so blatantly ducked me. Sure, some people had ignored me or laughed, but no one had ever asked why it mattered.

It mattered for the same reason Nory had assumed I didn't take any honors classes.

Zander and I were two spaces away from each other on the color wheel. We could be friends; that much was true. I had no clue where Nory landed. But if she was green, the color next to blue, that would be a problem. Like I'd told my mom, green and blue are too similar. In a relationship, it's important to balance each other, and side-by-side colors can't do that.

It probably sounds like nonsense, but I've had years of practice trying to make friends with people whose favorite colors spanned the rainbow. Sure, I could get along well with someone who liked green—at least we were on the same side of the color wheel. But our relationship would end there. Case in point: my one so-called friend in San Diego liked green.

Even knowing all that, something else about Nory kept pulling on my brain. Maybe it was how she'd smiled at me or handed over her phone number. Or the fact that she'd brushed by me like I was any other person in her way.

Before really thinking about it, I sent Nory a text. If she was green, then I had to make the first move.

> **ME:** We can still be friends . . . even though you're a Cowboys fan

I clicked send and instantly regretted it. Then that glorious typing bubble popped up, and thankfully I was alone, because I couldn't stop smiling. In my head, I started playing through all the flirtatious messages we would exchange. Then I learned that Nory Fischer was a tough person to have a virtual conversation with.

> **NORY:** I'm not really a fan. Just my dad

> **ME:** Oh well then maybe I can convert you into a Giants fan. Maybe we can hang and I'll teach you about football

That was the extent of my flirting ability: an offer of useless football knowledge.

> **NORY:** Thanks but I already know about football

Shit. Why had I assumed she didn't know anything about football? I was about to give up and start reading the syllabus for my history class when another message came through.

NORY: Was that your mom with you at school today?

ME: No, my executive assistant

NORY: So . . . your mom?

ME: Yes ☺ How did you figure that out?

NORY: It was pretty obvious. But I think it's cool you get to spend so much time with her

I wondered if Nory was being sarcastic. For the most part, I enjoyed being around my mom, but I still didn't like people knowing she was my mom. A sophomore lugging around a parent was social suicide.

Another message appeared.

NORY: BTW, what's your name again? I want to save your number in my phone

We'd spoken maybe five words to each other, and she was already breaking my heart.

ME: Harris

NORY: That's right. See you tomorrow, Harris :-)

I spent way more time than was healthy staring at that smiley face and wondering what exactly she meant by it. If I knew her favorite color, I might have a clue. But instead I was left to wonder—and hope.

CONVERSATIONS ARE HARD

FOR MOST STUDENTS, THE EXCITEMENT of a new school year wears off by the second day. And everyone treats the first week like a joke . . . except for me.

Being in a wheelchair means I have to prove myself early on. If there was a pop quiz, I had to get a perfect score. Academics seemed like the only way to gain respect and achieve independence. Through hard work, I would get accepted to a good college, build a decent résumé, and land a job with a trajectory that would allow me to live without being a burden to my parents. I couldn't let the stigma of having a disability or the distraction of my classmates hold me back.

Unfortunately, after just one day, Nory was already a distraction. We shared almost every class, and it was difficult not to notice how serious she looked while taking notes and how she bulldozed through the halls. At the end of the second day, when I thought I'd finally get a breather, she showed up again.

She was standing next to me at our lockers, and her hair

was down, barely touching the tops of her shoulders. A barrette tucked the left side of her hair behind her ear, exposing a collection of earrings that started at her lobe and ended halfway up.

I hadn't expected her to have so many piercings. I was going off the assumption that her favorite color was green, which meant she should've been especially proper.

I knew a boy in second grade whose favorite color was green, and every day he wore a bow tie to school. I think it goes without saying that he hated getting dirty. Recess was practically his nemesis, so he always sat by me on a bench that overlooked the playground. We didn't talk about much, except for the occasional *SpongeBob* episode or what we wanted for Christmas.

One day, he invited me to his rock-climbing birthday party. I didn't tell my mom about the invitation, and I stopped sitting with him at recess.

Anyway, Nory caught me gawking and covered her head with a Dallas Cowboys hat.

"You gonna watch them play this weekend?" I asked.

"Aren't they playing the Giants?"

"Yup."

"Then I'll watch, because I know they'll win." Nory turned to my mom. "Mrs. Jacobus, can I ask you a favor?"

"Sure, but only if you call me Clare. What's up?"

"Would you be able to give me a ride home? My dad is stuck at work for another two hours."

"Why don't you just take the bus?" I asked before my mom could respond.

"I hate the bus. It's so loud, and I can't get any homework done."

I respected Nory's commitment to school, which I shared, although I wasn't as vocal about it. Still, she made me feel less alone in the category of teenagers who cared.

"And you want *us* to drive you home?" I asked. "You just met us. We could rob you."

"Good luck. All I have is this backpack full of unfinished trig homework. You can't even turn it in as your own."

"We can drive you home," my mom said. "You'll get to ride in Black Hawk. And we promise not to steal your homework."

"I don't," I muttered.

Did I want to spend time with Nory outside of school? Yes, but I would have rather done that via text messages, even though I was obviously terrible at them. The car ride was going to make flirting even harder.

• • •

Decades-old SUVs filled with upperclassmen filed out of the parking lot. Mom pressed a button on her keys, and the side door of our black Chrysler Town & Country slid open. A second later, a ramp folded out from the passenger side. For an accessible van, it was pretty badass; it had survived eight years in San Diego and moving my family across the country.

"Is this Black Hawk?" Nory asked.

"Yup," I said.

Mom strapped on my shoulder harness, which I only wear in the car. I wouldn't be caught dead wearing it in public, and I hated that Nory was seeing it now. I drove up the ramp and locked in between the back row and the two front seats.

"I live on the other side of town," Nory said while buckling her seat belt. "I hope that's okay."

"Harris and I have nowhere to be," my mom told her.

Except for the occasional directions, we rode in silence.

Every few seconds, I opened my mouth to speak, but I was afraid of saying something stupid or irrelevant. Honestly, the car ride would've been a lot less awkward if Nory had just told me her favorite color. I would have known what to say, how much to say, and how to say it. But people who like the color green tend to hate small talk, so I kept my mouth shut, just to be safe.

My mom glared at me in the rearview mirror. It was the third time she'd done it in two minutes. I understood that I had to talk or brace myself for another lecture on antisocial behavior. Luckily, Nory broke the silence.

"So, Harris, how do you like New Jersey?"

"It's all right, I guess. We haven't been here long enough for me to form much of an opinion."

"Yeah, it took me a few months to adjust when I moved here last year."

"I didn't know you were new, too." Zander hadn't mentioned that.

"Well, I guess I'm not. I mean, I used to live here, then we moved when I was in fourth grade, and now we're back."

My head jostled around, falling back against the headrest of my wheelchair every time Black Hawk hit a bump or my mom swerved to avoid one. I tried as hard as I could to not look like a bobblehead while Nory talked to me, but part of my disability is a lack of muscle tone, along with a slew of other fun medical conditions. Head control is a big issue, especially when my mom drove like a maniac teenager. It was fitting that she was back at high school.

"Harris, remember Mr. Lindon wanted you to send a postcard after getting settled," my mom said randomly. It took me a second to figure out who she was talking about. Mr. Lindon was the principal at my elementary school.

"I'm not doing that," I told her.

"Mr. Lindon was very nice to you when you first started school, and he's a big reason you're a mainstreamed student and not stuck in a dark classroom all day."

"You're right: he was nice. He also liked to joke about giving me speeding tickets anytime I drove in the hallway."

"Lighten up, Harris. You need to stop finding something wrong with everyone."

The problem was that everyone had something wrong with them. My something wrong was obvious and difficult to overlook, while most people's were hidden. I had no idea what Nory's was, though knowing her favorite color might've provided a clue.

"Have you always gone to public school?" Nory asked. "Also, sorry for thinking you weren't in honors."

"It's fine," I said. "And yes, I've always gone to public school. I wish I didn't, though. My brother gets to go to a fancy prep school where they serve, like, sparkling cider and finger sandwiches. What about you?"

"Pretty much. My mom homeschooled me the year before we moved for the first time. I loved spending all that time with her."

"Where's your mom now?" Something about the way she talked about her mom made me think she didn't see her much anymore. I wondered if her parents were divorced.

"Oh, she died."

"I'm sorry. Now I feel like a jerk."

"Don't. It was a long time ago."

My mom took her eyes off the road to glance at Nory. "Well, if you ever need anything, just let us know."

If I lost my mom, I'd probably be devasted forever, yet Nory mentioned it like it wasn't a big deal. Every time she spoke, I encountered a new mystery. Internally, I was screaming at myself to ask her again what her favorite color was. It would've helped me figure out if she was private about her feelings, like green, or cold and dead inside, like black.

Nory navigated my mom along a winding one-way road. To the left were houses sitting atop steep driveways tucked behind oversize pine trees. On the right, the road dropped off into a creek that zigged and zagged and split into random paths around boulders and fallen branches. Stuff like that didn't exist in San Diego. All we had were beaches covered with inaccessible sand.

Eventually we arrived at a cul-de-sac with four houses.

"Thanks for the ride, Clare," Nory said. "I'd invite you guys in for a tour, but my house has a lot of steps inside. And anyway, I should probably start dinner."

"You make your family dinner?" I asked.

"Yeah. I actually love cooking. That's what I want to do with my life."

"Do you think you'll go to culinary school after graduation?"

For a moment, Nory pondered my question. "Maybe. But what I really want to do is own a restaurant, so I'll need to get into a college that can teach me about the business side, too."

"That's very ambitious," my mom said. "What's on the menu tonight?"

"A steak for my dad and vegetable ramen for me."

"You're making two things?" I asked.

"Oh, I always do. I'm vegan, and, well, my dad is not." Nory jumped out of the van. "Thanks again."

"Anytime, hon. Whenever you need a ride, just let us know," my mom said.

"I might take you up on that," Nory answered as she closed the passenger door.

That night, while I was knee-deep in *Great Expectations*, Nory sent me a picture of her and her dad's dinners. Both dishes looked delicious—and professional. My infatuation with her shot to new heights.

WHITE

"A NURSE IS COMING for a meet-and-greet tonight," my mom said.

I looked up from my spot at the kitchen island. My wheelchair was raised to counter height. It would be an especially cool feature if I was old enough to belly up to a bar. "That was quick. Didn't you just talk to the agency a couple of days ago?"

"Yes. The case manager is supposed to visit first, but since school has already started, she wants to get a jump on sending nurses to train."

I answered a text from Zander, who was convinced his gym teacher was out to get him, then switched over to Facebook. "What's her name?"

"I don't know. The case manager didn't tell me. Why does it matter?"

"Uh, so I can stalk her on the internet. We don't know who's coming into our house." I searched for people who lived in New Jersey and listed their occupation as nurse on Facebook. I scrolled without any idea who I was looking for.

Mom walked up behind me and peered over my shoulder.

"I'm sure the nurse they're sending isn't a criminal. I know you miss your nurses from back home, but we'll find someone to go to school with you."

"Can you stop bringing up California? I've moved on. And the nurses there sucked. I'm glad we're done with them."

"What about Mitch? Did he suck when he saved your life?"

"He was just doing his job. I choked, and he got the food out of my throat. Other than that, he was loud and hopped up on caffeine."

My mom pushed my hair back from my forehead and planted a kiss on it. "Then what's bothering you, Harris? You've already made it through a few days without having Ollie at the same school. Everything is fine."

"I know that. I don't want him cramping my style anyway." The truth was that Ollie had always been much more popular and better-looking than me.

Mom sighed. She stepped around the island to face me head-on. "Harris, if you're not going to tell me what's wrong, then I'm not going to be able to help you. You already made friends with Zander. So what's the problem?"

I moaned. "Nory still won't tell me her favorite color."

"So?"

"So I have no idea how to talk to her."

Mom rolled her eyes. "You did fine when we drove her home yesterday."

The fact that my mom had found that pathetic display *fine* was depressing. "Okay, but how am I supposed to know if we can be friends?"

"I guess you'll actually have to get to know her and see what you have in common."

"How am I supposed to do that?"

"Figure it out," Mom commanded. "The new nurse is on her way."

. . .

A vomit-colored Volkswagen Beetle pulled into the driveway five minutes before the scheduled visit. Being on time was mandatory in my mom's eyes. Through the dining room window, I watched a fuzzy figure fiddle around with the glove compartment.

"Mom," I yelled, "she's here!"

I backed my wheelchair away from the window and drove into the living room to wait for the interview. All of the furniture had finally been unpacked. A set of armchairs was off to the side, and an ottoman sat in front of the couch. There was still enough room for me to navigate my wheelchair without trouble. We had minimal furniture for that reason.

Every time I interview a nurse, I get nervous, even though I'm not the one who needs to worry. There's just something extremely odd about having to explain everything that's wrong with me to a stranger within the first five minutes of meeting them. Like, just look at me. You can see what's up.

The front door opened, and I heard my mom greet the mystery woman. They exchanged pleasantries and some polite laughter. High heels clicked on the hardwood floors and grew louder with each step. It seemed like impractical footwear for a nurse, but maybe she'd just dressed up for the interview.

Why was I so nervous? I'd met hundreds of nurses.

A professional-looking woman trailed behind my mom. She was young. The agency had listened. She was also wearing a lot of makeup, which was probably what she'd been fiddling with in her car.

"Hello, I'm Shannon," she said. The nurse put out her hand for me to shake.

Even if I could've reached my hand out, I wouldn't have. I didn't want to touch a random stranger. It wasn't personal.

"Just pound him," my mom said.

Shannon laughed awkwardly. "Oh, okay."

She fist-bumped my left hand. I could tell she had never done it before. That seemed strange for someone young living in the twenty-first century.

"Nice to meet you. I'm Harris."

"Nice to meet you, too. Thanks for having me over." Shannon's face contorted into a creepy smile, like she was trying too hard or had never smiled before. Maybe both.

My mom seemed to sense the awkwardness and my dwindling patience with the meet-and-greet. "Here, have a seat, and Harris can tell you about himself."

Time for my favorite part. In all fairness, I'd told my mom that I was old enough to lead the interviews, but that day I just wasn't in the mood.

Usually, my mom asked the questions, and I observed. Within two minutes, I could tell if the nurse was going to work out. Shannon was leaning toward a no.

"I'm not sure how much the agency told you about me," I said.

"Not much, other than your name. And that I'd be going to school with you."

"Okay, yeah. Well, I have a form of muscular dystrophy. Have you ever taken care of someone with MD?"

"Babies, yes, but no one as grown up as you." Shannon attempted her smile again.

"Did they enjoy it when you talked to them like that?"

My mom interjected. "A lot of taking care of Harris is helping him with the physical stuff: putting his hand on the joystick so he can drive, getting out his books for class, feeding him, assisting in the bathroom."

"Is he on a special diet?"

"I'm a person. I eat people food."

My mom shot over a hard-core glare. "I pack him a normal school lunch. Usually a sandwich and chips. You just have to feed him slowly and make sure he chews. But Harris knows what he can and can't eat."

Mom and I spent the next ten minutes talking about the breathing treatments I do every few hours, as well as how to keep me hydrated and help me use the bathroom. The last thing required the most training, we told Shannon. We learned that she had been a nurse for two years. Most people would reject someone with so little experience, but I'd found newer nurses easier to work with since they weren't stuck in any bad habits.

"You'll train here a couple of times so you both can get comfortable with each other, then shadow me at school," my mom said. "Are your hours pretty flexible right now?"

"Yeah, absolutely. I can start whenever."

"Great. I'll let the agency know how today went, and then we'll see you soon."

I locked eyes with my mom, trying to hint that I hadn't made a decision.

She didn't get it. "You've been very quiet, sweetie."

I shook my head. "Just listening."

"Do you have any questions for Shannon?"

I shook my head again. There wasn't anything I needed to know, because I didn't plan on seeing her ever again.

"Harris will eventually want to know your favorite color," my mom said.

Shannon looked at me as if landing the job depended on her answer. Maybe it did. "Do you want to know now?"

"Not really," I said. "I already saw the color of your car."

"Oh, yeah. That's a pretty silly color, right? But it's not my favorite. It's just what the dealership had on the lot. My favorite color is actually white."

"I bet the Volkswagen dealership had white."

"Maybe. I didn't ask." Shannon was unfazed.

A few more minutes of small talk, and then Mom led Shannon out the door. As soon as she returned, I let loose.

"She's not confident," I said. "I'm not sure I want someone like that following me around a new school."

"I don't care. She's young and seems smart. Plus she's the only nurse available right now. You're going to have to give her a shot."

"Did you hear what she said? She let some salesman choose the color of her car."

My mom sighed. "Harris, I don't see how that relates to her being a good nurse or not."

"To start with, white is a very flighty color. I'll never be able to trust that she'd be ready to save my life. I'll be a nervous wreck all day."

My mom ignored me. She knew she couldn't shut down my color theories, but she never indulged them. I had to give a more concrete reason Shannon shouldn't be hired.

"You heard how she talked to me like I'm an infant, right?"

"I'm telling the agency she can come to the house to train. We'll see how it goes."

My phone buzzed, which was a very unfamiliar sensation.

A part of me hoped Nory was on the other side of the buzz, but honestly I was just excited that anyone wanted to talk to me.

> **ZANDER:** What you up to?

> **ME:** Interviewing a new nurse

> **ZANDER:** Aww. I'm going to miss Clare

My life was a mix of trying to be a typical teenager and hiring a small staff to care for me. Business decisions needed to be made, but they were put on hold as two pictures from Nory flashed up on my phone. Two separate people texting me in one night was unprecedented.

The first picture was a bowl of colorful vegetables, and the second was a piece of grilled chicken with a side of couscous.

"Wow, her food looks great," my mom said. "Like something from a magazine."

"Can you just hand me my phone, please?"

She left me alone to respond.

> **ME:** I'm having chicken tonight too

> **NORY:** Nice. I don't think my dad is enjoying the couscous

> **ME:** Lol. What are the vegetables?

NORY: Ratatouille. I'm trying some
new recipes I found online

ME: Cool. Maybe one day you can
make something for me ☺

She never responded. I checked my phone about twenty times before going to bed.

NOT MAKING THE CUT

WEEK ONE WAS ALMOST in the books. I just had to make it through Friday.

Shannon came to the house Thursday after school for training, and it didn't go well at all. She had a hard time helping me in the bathroom, and her technique for feeding me involved cutting the food into near-microscopic pieces that were almost inedible. Not to mention that talking to her was like talking to a wall.

But my parents (aka my mom) made the executive decision to have Shannon tag along at school. She said that maybe Shannon would break out of her shell once she was with the other students and felt more comfortable. I didn't think it was possible to acquire a personality so late in life, but then again, high school is a place of self-discovery. (Or is that college?)

"Why isn't Shannon driving with us?" I asked as my mom backed Black Hawk out of the driveway.

"Because she has to pass the high school on the way to our house. There's no point in her driving all the way here just to turn around."

"She's gonna be late. She won't know where to park, and she'll make me late to homeroom."

"I told her where to park, and she already texted me that she's almost there. Besides, it's fine if you're late to homeroom. That's one of your accommodations. You can even skip homeroom if your heart desires."

"You know I don't like to abuse my accommodations. If I have to be in homeroom at a certain time, I want to be there like everyone else."

"What's wrong? Why are you acting like this?"

My gaze wandered out the passenger-side window. Some of the leaves on the trees were already showing shades of red. Summer vacation had ended less than a week ago, but the crisp of that morning's air made it feel like a distant memory.

Autumn was virtually nonexistent in San Diego. Sure, the temperature dropped, but not always enough to make the leaves fall. My family liked to joke that living there was like reverse *Groundhog Day*—always the same sunny, beautiful weather.

But without seasons, it's hard to notice other changes.

"I don't know," I sighed. "Maybe because I don't want a fucking posse following me around all day."

But I knew that wasn't the sole reason for my irritability. I hadn't texted with Nory since asking her to cook for me, and we hadn't talked much in school. I'd begun to think that maybe I'd come off as too forward. I mean, I was just saying that her food looked good and I wanted to try it. It wasn't a big deal. But then why hadn't she answered?

"Well, I wasn't planning on staying," Mom told me. "I'll be there for the first couple of periods, but then I'm leaving."

"You can't leave me alone with Shannon."

"Harris, I don't know what the hell you want, but the plan is for me to stay until I feel Shannon is comfortable."

"Why am I just hearing this now?"

"Because I knew you'd freak out. Shannon can help you. She's perfectly capable. Just open your mouth and tell her what you need."

• • •

The school halls felt even more claustrophobic with two people following me.

I kept my head down out of embarrassment. My chair drew attention. The way I blocked people in the hallway drew attention. Having two adults at my back drew attention. I was a walking—technically rolling—sign that screamed LOOK AT ME.

I struggled to find a comfortable spot while Mom showed Shannon how to open my locker. "Seven, six, four," I called out. "It's not a difficult combo."

Both of them ignored me.

Nory approached and squeezed between them and me to get to her locker.

"Hey, Nory," I said. "Good morning."

"Hey," she answered without glancing in my direction. She grabbed her books and walked quickly away. I'd never felt so rejected.

"Guys, what's the holdup?" I asked.

"Stop," my mom demanded. "All right? I'm explaining all your school stuff to Shannon."

"What stuff? I literally have two binders. A morning binder and an afternoon binder. That's it."

"Fine. If you think you don't need me, then I'm going to leave. You're on your own."

"Sounds good. See you."

Mom handed Shannon the morning binder. "Have fun, you two." Then she walked away.

I motioned with my head for Shannon to pick up my backpack. "Follow me."

When I'm alone—actually, let me start over. I'm never alone. But when my mom isn't around, I have to be at the top of my game. That means making sure my nurses notice the small things, like if a chair has to be pushed in so I can get past it or if my hand has fallen off the joystick. All of this had become second nature to my family, but someone new might not realize what needs to be done. The quirks and nuances have to be carefully explained.

I was already exhausted.

We entered Wormhole's room. "What class is this?" Shannon asked.

"Homeroom. Did you go to high school?"

"I did, but I don't remember having homeroom."

"What are you talking about? All schools have homeroom. Even middle schools have homeroom."

"Maybe."

"Okay, you sit at the desk, and I stay next to it. Can you turn my wheelchair off?"

"I don't want to take a desk away from a student. I'll just stand over—"

"You're not taking a desk away from anyone. If I weren't

in this chair, I'd be sitting in that one. Now, stop making this weird. Just sit down."

Shannon obliged, but not before looking around to make sure the other students had desks. I hated myself for dismissing my mom so quickly. Smothering mom or awkward nurse? I wasn't sure which was worse.

Nory walked in behind Mr. Wormhole and from the doorway spent a few seconds just looking at her usual seat—the one next to mine. My heart pounded. Then Nory shuffled up the far aisle of the classroom instead and sat in the back.

A moment later, a student I'd never seen before entered the room. He walked up to Nory, and they hugged. Worse, it was a full-on embrace. They swayed from side to side while he towered over her—something I knew I would never be capable of.

I guess that answered my question about whether or not she had a boyfriend. Maybe it also explained why she hadn't responded to my text on Wednesday. Her boyfriend probably wouldn't approve of her cooking for another guy.

"Why are you in my homeroom?" Wormhole asked the guy who was hugging Nory.

"Oh, Mrs. Plank's room is overflowing, and guidance told me to come here."

The old man huffed and sighed. "One of you is going to have to stand."

Shannon flinched, like she was about to stand and offer her desk.

"Don't move," I told her.

• • •

On the way to second period, Shannon almost got swallowed by a sea of students, but I slowed down and heroically saved her life. In return, she remembered to give me sips of water throughout the day and make sure I was, you know, still alive. I realize those are basic nursing tasks, but you'd be surprised.

She took copious and organized notes in trig. Until the school provided a laptop for me, my nurses were my hands.

Despite the occasional weird smile, Shannon impressed me. We made it through the first half of the day without any major issues, and I was starting to feel oddly optimistic that this might actually work.

Then came the hard part—helping me use the bathroom. Shannon followed the steps perfectly. We didn't rush, thanks to the private bathroom; I no longer had to worry about opening the door and finding a mob of teenagers.

"Do you mind if I use the bathroom while you finish your treatment?" Shannon asked.

"Sure. Whatever."

She chose the farthest-away stall. A few seconds passed, and then I smelled something.

"Are you . . . taking a shit?" I asked.

"Yes. My stomach hurts. I think I ate something bad for breakfast."

"You've got to be kidding me. I can smell it. Even with oxygen blowing in my face, I can smell it. This is disgusting."

"I'm sorry, Harris. I had to go."

"And you couldn't let me wait outside? Who does something like that?"

"I didn't want to leave you unattended. Someone could kidnap you."

"We're in a school!" I yelled. "There are teachers and students everywhere. It's lunchtime. No one is going to kidnap the kid in the wheelchair!"

Finally, I heard a flush. Shannon stepped out of the stall, washed her hands, and turned off my neb. I couldn't look at her.

"Let's get out of here before I throw up," I said.

• • •

I barely remember the rest of that school day. Things were sort of a blur after being trapped in a bathroom while my nurse went number two.

During lunch, I made plans with Zander to hang out over the weekend. Seeing Nory with that other guy motivated me to work hard to keep the other friend I'd made, even if Zander was a nerdy freshman.

Finally, the last bell rang, and my mom and Black Hawk were waiting in the parking lot. "So, how'd the day go?" she asked.

"I think it went well," Shannon told her. "We didn't have any problems, although Harris does have a ton of homework this weekend."

"Can we go?" I pleaded.

"Yes, actually, we have somewhere to be. Thanks for today, Shannon. We'll see you next week."

Mom signed off on Shannon's nursing notes. I wondered if she'd documented both of our afternoon outputs.

"Bye, Harris. See you on Monday."

I didn't answer, because I wouldn't be seeing her on Monday.

"She's done," I told Mom as soon as she got in the van.

"What?"

"I don't want her to come back."

"Why? It seems like you had a great day."

"Today was not great. She took a shit in front of me."

Mom paused, probably to replay what I'd just said. "What do you mean?"

"I mean I was finishing my neb before lunch, and she asked if she could use the bathroom. I said it was okay, so she went in one of the stalls and started pooping. Right in front of me, with only a one-inch metal door in between us. Oh, but that didn't protect me. I still experienced the whole thing."

Mom laughed. Hard. "You really stayed in there?"

"What choice did I have? I couldn't leave on my own."

"Well, I'm just glad you're fine and that nothing life-threatening happened."

"That was life-threatening."

"Fine, I'll call the agency and tell them to send someone else."

"Yeah, and then we'll train them, and something else will happen that makes them leave or get fired. We went through this in San Diego. It's a never-ending cycle."

My mom didn't answer, because she didn't have an answer. We're accustomed to the onslaught of bad days and weeks, and back in California, we knew how to get through them. There was comfort even in the tough times. But being in a new place made everything seem more exhausting. My gut told me that I had many more school weeks from hell ahead of me. Comfort was not on my horizon.

I realized we'd driven past our street.

"Where are you taking me?"

"Your brother's school is having a family night for new students. Dad is meeting us there."

"His school is like an hour away. Do we really have to go?"

"Harris, this family, including your brother, does a lot for you. It's not going to kill you to go to something for someone else."

"But I'm not dressed up enough to be at his fancy prep school."

"It doesn't matter. We're going to meet his teachers and some other parents. No one will care what you're wearing."

"If I look like a slob, then I'll just be remembered as the sloppy kid in the wheelchair."

"Oh my God. Nobody is going to think that. Now, stop. I need to concentrate on the GPS so I can get us there alive."

A LITTLE TOO CONVENIENT

FAMILIES OF ALL SHAPES AND SIZES filled a swanky ball-room. That's right: Ollie's high school had a freaking *ballroom*. Not like a hotel ballroom, but one you would find in the estate of an eccentric billionaire who only uses the room for bizarre charity events that feature things like dog ice-skating.

The floor was covered with lush gold carpeting that accented the antique wallpaper and intricate moldings. On the back wall were floor-to-ceiling windows that overlooked the campus and let in an annoying amount of light.

"This is a high school?" I asked.

"It's a prep school," my mom answered.

"Why can't I go here? This is awesome. I actually feel smarter just being in this building."

Mom and I were greeted by Dad and Ollie, who seemed like they'd been waiting a while and looked mildly annoyed.

"Can we go?" Ollie asked. "This is lame."

Mom grabbed a glass of champagne floating past on a tray. I was definitely underdressed. "No. Harris and I just got here.

Besides, I want to meet some of your teachers."

"I don't think any of them are even coming. Let's just leave."

"Ollie, stop," our dad commanded. "We're here, and we're going to stay for a little and mingle. It's Friday night, and we have nowhere else to be."

"What if I do?"

"Do you?"

Ollie shrugged.

"You definitely have nowhere to be, Ollie," I said. "We just moved here. Nobody would want to be your friend that fast."

"Shut up. I'm not the one who sits at the loser table."

Mom sipped her champagne and started to guess which students were on scholarship and which families could actually afford the tuition.

"That's so mean," Ollie said.

"I'm going to hell anyway, so why not have fun? Though I do take care of your brother, so maybe it evens out."

Dad didn't participate in the shenanigans. I looked around the room, hoping to find a family with a daughter my age. I had no luck, but even if I had, I never would've had the balls to talk to her. What would my pickup line be? Something about having siblings who attended school together?

My phone burned a hole in my pocket. Nory was just a couple of taps away.

You would think that in my situation, taking out my phone would be the hardest part of the equation. But it wasn't. I could easily ask one of my parents to hand me the phone. The difficult part was figuring out what to say.

Should I apologize for coming on too strong? Because the

more I thought about it, the more convinced I was that I'd gone too far. I mean, Nory and I had just met, and I was already asking her to make me dinner. I had been in this situation before, and it was why I'd stopped putting so much energy into the beginnings of friendships; my efforts were never reciprocated.

In seventh-grade language arts, I'd sat next to a girl named Paige for the entire third quarter. Occasionally, she would lean over to rest her head on my shoulder, which was absolutely terrifying when I was twelve, but I tried not to read too much into it. We sat at long tables, and maybe she didn't have enough room to rest her head anywhere else. Paige and I would talk in class and sometimes after school, too, whenever she didn't have gymnastics.

I liked hearing about her routines, and I thought she liked telling me about them. When Valentine's Day came around, I asked my mom to take me to the store so I could buy a rose and a box of chocolates. The next day, I gripped that flower in my non-driving hand, hoped the chocolates wouldn't slide off my lap, and approached Paige at her locker.

She smiled and thanked me, but later that day, she sat at a different table in class, and she ignored me for the remainder of the school year. Her favorite color might have been green, too.

That's another thing about people whose favorite color is green—they don't like to be bothered. I decided not to message Nory.

An older man wearing a tracksuit approached our family. He slapped Ollie on the back, then they exchanged words in a manner I never would've expected from my brother. He was actually smiling.

"Irv Lemieux," he told our parents. "Head lacrosse coach here at Ridge Prep."

"Jay Jacobus. We've met," my dad said. "But I don't think you've met my wife, Clare."

The silver fox shook our mom's hand. He then knelt down to get level with me. Most of the time, I appreciated people's mindfulness, but this particular act made me feel like a child. I would've preferred breaking my neck trying to look up at him.

"You must be Harris. I've heard a lot about you. Your brother's a big fan."

"I'm a fan of his, too. Well, actually, I'm a fan and his coach."

Lemieux looked up at Ollie, who was laughing. "Is that right? I think this might work out, then. I'll coach Ollie while he's here, and when he gets home, you get on him."

"Harris does that no matter what," Dad added. "He's Ollie's biggest critic."

"Then it's a plan. We're trying to win State this year, and I think Ollie's the missing piece that'll get us there. But we need him at his best." Coach Lemieux caught the eye of a woman in the crowd, stood, and waved her over. "We have a top-notch staff, including my wife, who cooks all the team meals."

"I'm Nancy. It's a pleasure to meet you boys, and welcome to Ridge Prep."

"Harris isn't a student here, just Ollie," Mom said.

"Oh, then where are you going to school?"

"East Essex Central," I told her.

"That's wonderful. My niece went there. She's in nursing school now, but she still talks about the good times she had at EEC."

"Does she want to go back?" Mom half joked. "We're

looking for someone to attend with Harris and help him out during the day. Right now, it's just me."

I hated it when my family talked about my situation with random people. Not everyone needed to know the ins and outs of my personal care. I attempted to shut down the conversation. "I'm sure we'll find someone. We've only met one nurse so far."

"What happened to the woman who went today?" Dad whispered to Mom.

"I'll tell you later."

"To be honest, I think she'd be delighted to help your son," Nancy said.

"Oh, wow, are you serious?" Mom asked, quickly coming down from her champagne buzz. "It would be great to meet her, but we're not really in a position to pay someone privately. All of Harris's nursing is covered by insurance through an agency, and since your niece is still in school, she can't be hired by the agency we use."

"Don't worry about the money," Dad insisted. "We could make it work, if it keeps you from stressing and going to school every day."

"What a sweet husband you have," Nancy said. Coach Lemieux just watched with nothing to contribute. It seemed he was a man of few words unless lacrosse was the topic. "But I don't think you'd have to pay her very much. Miranda still lives with her parents, and I'm sure she'd love the opportunity to gain hands-on experience."

And then it was settled. Nancy gave my mom her niece's phone number, and somehow the prospect of this nurse felt different from any other. Maybe because this recommendation came from a person who'd actually seen me and not an agency that just talked to my parents over the phone. Maybe it was because Nancy's niece had gone to East Essex Central and I liked the idea of learning the ins and outs from someone who had actual experience there, not just tips from a movie (sorry, Zander). Either way, I kept repeating her name in my head: *Miranda*. I was already attached.

BLUE

SATURDAYS AND SUNDAYS WERE RESERVED for the holy sport of football. No distractions were allowed in the Jacobus household except for the occasional snack break. We cheered, we yelled, and we fought with each other over terrible calls made by terrible refs and which players sucked and which didn't suck. Even Mom got involved, and frankly, she was the loudest of all.

I'd forgotten to warn Zander, who unfortunately got stuck between my dad and Ollie on the couch and—as if I'd expected anything else—asked far too many questions.

"They slap each other's butts to get fired up," Dad answered him. "You know, like a high five."

"Okay, but that guy just did it to a referee. Also, why are you Giants fans? You're from California. Don't they have a team there?"

"Yes, they do. Three teams, actually. But I grew up in New York, and my father was a Giants fan, and his father was a Giants fan, and therefore, we are Giants fans."

"I didn't know team preferences were genetic," Zander said.

While living in California, my family had endured the torture of not always being able to watch the Giants play. Until satellite TV began offering football packages, my dad had roamed from bar to bar in search of one that could tap into the East Coast feed.

Living in New Jersey, we had no problem watching the Giants. That day, on the opening weekend of the season, they were losing to the Cowboys.

Before Zander had a chance to ask another question, my mom politely suggested that he follow her into the kitchen and help her take the pizza rolls out of the oven. By now, he was aware that Clare was my mom. That secret came out thirty minutes before the opening kickoff, when I might have said the word *Mom* on the way back from picking him up. But Zander still insisted on calling her Ms. Clare.

"Our QB better pull his head out of his ass if he wants to win this game," Dad said.

In between texts, Ollie caught glimpses of the action. "The guy is allowed to have an off game."

"Yeah, well, he's not gonna win any playing like that."

"It's not all his fault," I said. "The offensive line sucks today. They're giving him no time to throw the ball."

Zander returned, holding a plate full of pizza rolls.

"You can't eat that in here," Dad told Zander. "You'll have to take that back in the other room."

Zander looked at me for reassurance that my dad was joking. "Sorry, dude," I said. "I'll come with you. It's almost half-time anyway."

Mom shoved a pizza roll in my mouth while Zander and

I discussed the happenings at East Essex Central High. Ollie joined at halftime, devouring a handful of pizza rolls before I'd finished chewing one.

"Do you both sit at the loser table?" he asked.

Zander very pridefully answered for the both of us. "First off, it is not the *loser* table. It's a refuge. And second, I am the founder and president."

"Yikes. At least you two nerds found each other."

"Hey, you're the one at home on the weekend, watching TV with your younger brother and his weirdo friend," I said.

"Have you asked Zander what his favorite color is yet?" Ollie mocked me.

"Yes. Why?" Zander asked.

"Because it's a big deal to Harris, so he can like . . . judge you or figure out if you'll get married to each other or something. I don't know."

"Shut up," I said. "It's not that big of a deal."

"Bro, you literally ask everyone what their favorite color is, like you're Buddy the Elf."

"It didn't bother me," Zander said. "People ask weird questions all the time. Like, I was going to ask how many pizza rolls you can fit in your mouth, but I see the answer is four."

Ollie rolled his eyes and retreated back to the couch to watch highlights. Dad was in the bathroom, his last trip before the second half.

"Have you always lived in this town?" Mom asked Zander.

"Pretty much. I moved here from Pennsylvania when I was a baby, so I don't know anywhere else, but I like it here, and I think you guys will too, once you figure out where everything is. Like, there's a cool mall not too far away where I sometimes hang out."

"That sounds like fun. Harris used to love going to this mall near our house in San Diego. You guys should go next weekend. It might be a good way to meet other kids your age." She looked at me.

"Mom, I'm fifteen. You don't have to schedule playdates."

"No, dude, we should totally go," Zander said.

I sighed and caved. If I wanted a friend then I guessed that meant doing things with said friend. And New Jersey had more accessible activities than San Diego, which really only had beaches. Everybody always wanted to go to the beach.

• • •

Nory's prediction was spot-on. The Giants were losing to the Cowboys by seventeen with five minutes left in the fourth quarter. At that moment, I did something I'd thought was impossible—I decided to leave the room and stop watching. Even during the biggest blowouts, I had always stuck it out, holding on to whatever sliver of hope I had and my love for the sport I would never play. But Zander looked bored, and I wanted more Nory details.

"Zander, you wanna go hang out in my room?" I asked.

He jumped off the couch before I finished the sentence. "Finally, the torture is over."

"You can't leave," Dad said. "The game's not over."

"We're getting killed. And we've got the rest of the season to watch together. This is only week one."

"Yeah, I'm out too," Ollie said. "This game sucks."

Our dad argued. "There's only a few minutes left. You really can't wait?"

"Let them go, Jay," Mom said.

He waved us off. "Fine, but don't complain to me if the Giants come back and you miss it."

Zander and I headed to my bedroom, and I heard Ollie asking for the car keys. I guess he got them, because then I heard Mom and Dad reciting the usual requirements of "text us when you get there" and "text us when you leave."

"You really don't like football, huh?" I asked Zander, trying to refocus his attention. He was looking around my room, and I always felt self-conscious about new people seeing my stuff. Breathing machines, oxygen tanks, and medication were all in sight, but Zander didn't comment.

"I mean, I don't *hate* football, but I also like giving people a hard time. Why do you like it so much?"

"I guess it just gives me something to have in common with Ollie and my dad. Like, it's a way for me to be involved even though I can't play."

"I watch it with my stepdad, too, but that's because he makes me."

"Weird thing about my dad is that he'll only watch the Giants. After this game ends, he won't watch another second of football today."

Zander started up a random two-player game on my Xbox. Video games were a way for me to feel like I was actually doing something with my friends, since I couldn't really run around outside or toss a ball . . . not that I thought Zander would want to do either of those things.

"I'm guessing your favorite color is blue," Zander said, admiring my walls.

"I'm not some kind of weirdo like my brother said. I just like to know what colors people are into."

"Hey, man, no judgment. But there's a lot of blue in here, and your wheelchair is blue, and honestly, this week you wore a lot of blue outfits. I wonder what that says about you."

I knew what the color blue said about me: that I was dependable, intelligent, and calm. All of the English language's most boring adjectives, and each one fit the life I was living.

Dependable. Need someone to hang out with? If he's not in the hospital, you can always depend on the kid in the wheelchair to be available.

Intelligent. Every freaking person I encounter is so goddamn surprised that I'm smart, like someone with a disability can't do well in school. But it's just book smarts. I would trade all of it to see more of the real world.

Calm. I guess this one isn't so bad. A lot of people wish they could just take a chill pill, after all. But I'm not calm because I'm disinterested. I'm interested in everything; I just know that I can't do most of it, at least not without supervision. But getting worked up about that is useless. Plus, my mom has always done enough worrying for the both of us.

"Do you hang out with Nory a lot, since you're neighbors?" I asked. Zander was beating me at some skateboarding video game, but only because I was half paying attention.

"So you're not going to tell me what blue means?"

"I didn't even tell you what yellow means. But yellow and blue can be friends, so settle down."

"Fine. And no, I don't really hang with Nory."

I knew I didn't need to answer Zander's question for him to answer mine. A classic attribute of yellows is that they're people pleasers.

"I saw her hugging some really tall guy the other day. He was Asian, super muscular, looked like he could be a senior."

"Oh, you must be talking about Kelvin Zhang. He's on the basketball team. And you're right: he's very good-looking."

#FF4500

NORY WAS ABSENT ON MONDAY. That's the only aspect of the day I remember before meeting Miranda, who was already waiting for us in our driveway when Mom and I pulled in after school. Her car: a fire-red Mustang.

"Look at that," Mom said. "On time and ready to go. I like this girl already."

The next few seconds moved very slowly. Mom put the car in park and pressed a button that opened the passenger-side sliding door and dropped the ramp. There was a moment before I saw her when I heard Miranda's voice as she greeted my mom. It exploded with confidence. I still play the sound of it in my head over and over, like a favorite song. It's exactly how I want to remember her.

"Hey, dude," Miranda said as my chair finished turning to face her. She was beautiful, but not in a typical, polished way. Her hair was bleached but beginning to let in the dark undertones of her natural color, which accentuated her pale skin. She had dimples and a playful but ever-so-slightly sad smile. "Sweet ride you got there."

"I didn't say he was good-looking," I muttered. "Anyway, are he and Nory dating or what?"

"I'm not sure. I haven't heard anything about them being boyfriend-girlfriend."

I paused the game. "Dude, you said you studied up on everyone this summer. How do you not know?"

"All I really did was flip through my sister's yearbook and watch *Mean Girls*. I already told you that." Zander unpaused and completed a virtual kick flip, ending the game.

Thinking a freshman would know anything remotely helpful about an upperclassman was senseless on my part.

"So, what do you usually do on weekends?" I asked Zander.

"This," he said, pointing at the screen.

"Really? You never hang out with anyone or go to a party?"

"No. Although I do occasionally go to the mall, like I said. And sometimes I tag along with my mom when she takes my brothers to their group exercise class. That's kind of like a party."

I didn't see how a gym class or whatever could be *at all* like a party. If Zander and I were just going to sit in my bedroom and play video games, then I didn't see how he'd make my life any different. That was my normal weekend routine anyway. Now that I'd had a taste of friendship, I wanted more. I just didn't know how to get it or, more importantly, what more actually looked like.

"Thanks. His name is Black Hawk."

"Cool name. You pick up a lot of chicks with him?"

I laughed awkwardly and probably blushed like a freaking nerd. "Harris wishes," my mom said. "But he does have a chauffeur: me."

We entered an empty house—Dad wouldn't be leaving the city for another hour, and Ollie still had a long bus ride home from Ridge Prep. The fewer distractions, the better. I knew next to nothing about Miranda, but the way she talked and walked and looked at me made me believe that I'd finally found a perfect fit.

"Was it a long drive over for you?" Mom asked. "Your aunt said you live nearby."

"Yeah. My parents' house is literally down the street."

"Oh, perfect. So you'll never be late. That's my biggest pet peeve."

I didn't want Miranda to feel uncomfortable or immediately stressed about my mom's rules. "She wasn't late today, so I don't think it'll be an issue."

"I know. I'm just making sure."

The three of us sat in the usual meet-and-greet spot in the living room, but there wasn't a second of awkward silence. Miranda jumped into the conversation, admiring our home and saying how different it looked from her boyfriend's crappy apartment.

"Boyfriend? You have a boyfriend?" It was my first question.

Mom quickly changed the subject. "I think your aunt already told you, but we're looking for someone to attend school with Harris, and I'm wondering how available you are, since you're taking college classes."

"Most of my classes are in the evening or on the weekend, so my days are wide open. That's what's so cool—I'm not far away, and I've been searching for something to keep me busy besides studying."

"What year are you in your nursing program?" I asked.

"I'm in my last year, and it's been so much fun. I've always wanted to do something with medicine."

Miranda spoke directly to me without making her voice louder or slower or any other variation of baby talk. I felt like I was being seen and at the same time like it wasn't real. Like this meeting was too good to be true. In my head, Miranda was hired.

"We've never hired a nursing student to help care for Harris," Mom said. "I mean, we've had inexperienced nurses, which is okay, but none who were still in school. I guess what I'm asking is, are you ready to take on a job like this? Harris's needs aren't very complicated, but in an emergency, will you know what to do?"

"I'm CPR certified, but I don't think that answers your question." Miranda paused and thought about what to say next. Her expression turned serious. "Mrs. Jacobus, just know that if anything were to happen to Harris, I would do everything possible to help."

"That's good to know. And you can call me Clare," my mom said.

I quickly went over my school routine with Miranda. I told her she would need to take notes for me in class, and I explained my only iron-clad rule—never wear scrubs.

"I think it's so cool you go to East Essex Central," Miranda said. "I can't wait to be back there. Who are some of your teachers?"

"Mrs. Spilt, Mr. Bavroe—"

"Bavroe is still there? He has to be a hundred."

"Yeah, and he's a total jerk."

"He's always been a jerk. One time he failed me on a test because, and I quote, I 'finished too fast.' He thought I'd cheated."

"Did you?"

Miranda smiled. "That's not that point. He had no proof, and I think he was threatened by my intelligence."

Mom stood up from the couch. She was ready to start dinner and move on with the evening. "You two seem to be getting along. Miranda, what are some days you can come back to train?"

"Well, I'm free now. I don't have class until later tonight, so I can stay, if that's cool with you guys."

I nodded. And so began our adventure.

• • •

"Holy crap, that's a lot of blue," Miranda said as we arrived in my bedroom.

"It's my favorite color. I'm guessing from your car that yours is red?"

"Kinda. I think my favorite color is somewhere in between orange and red. They're both pretty similar to blue, though."

"No, they're not. Orange is on the complete opposite side of the color wheel from blue."

"Oh." She laughed. "Then it's a good thing I'm not an art major."

"Harris could go on about colors all day," my mom said.

She was right. I wanted to tell Miranda that I'd never met someone who was orange red. People are usually one or the other, but what she said rang true. She demanded attention, just like her red Mustang, but didn't feel dangerous.

My mom rummaged through the bins sitting on my bedside shelves. "Let me show you some of his meds so he can start his nebulizer and I can get dinner in the oven."

She pulled out a bottle and explained what it was and when the medicine was supposed to be administered. I'd always thought I had a pretty decent collection of pills and inhalers, which could maybe be sold for some extra cash. But none of them were antidepressants or painkillers, so that narrowed my market to the asthmatic and allergy-prone, who really aren't the black-market types.

"You run all your nebulizers off of oxygen?" Miranda asked. She held on to one of the tanks on a rolling stand.

"Yeah. I like the added boost," I said.

Miranda grabbed a vial of medication from my mom's hand, popped the cap, poured the liquid into the mask, and started the breathing treatment.

"Wow," Mom said. "Looks like you know what you're doing. Maybe you don't even need me to train you."

"I had a clinical last week where we learned all about nebs and other breathing treatments, so I'm pretty familiar. But I definitely need more training. That's probably going to be the extent of me impressing you guys today."

Anyone who didn't get overwhelmed by my mom was impressive in my eyes, and I think Mom respected it, too. The primary requirements for any nurse were confidence and the ability to take control. Miranda had confidence to spare—that was the red part—and eagerness despite her lack of experience—that was the orange part.

Mom left for the kitchen to prepare dinner and tee up the next item on the train-new-nurses list: feeding me. Miranda grabbed the remote and flicked on the TV.

"What do you like to watch?" she asked.

"Usually sports. But we don't have to watch that."

"No, it's cool. This is your room. I'm down for whatever."

In a flash, ESPN was on the screen with the latest news from the first week of action. *Monday Night Football* would kick off in a couple of hours, and I needed to be up-to-date so I could argue with my brother during the game.

"Who's your team?" Miranda asked.

"The Giants."

"Oh my God, my dad loves the Giants. My boyfriend likes the Eagles."

"He sounds like a jerk."

Miranda's laugh sounded slightly strained, like she agreed, but maybe I was imagining it. My nebulizer began to fizzle out, and she tapped the mask, moving the medicine so it could steam again.

"Hey, Harris!" Mom yelled from the kitchen.

"What?"

"Don't forget that Nory wasn't in school. You should text her the homework for tonight."

"Fine, I guess!" I yelled back.

"Who's Nory?" Miranda asked.

"My homework buddy. If one of us misses school, the other is supposed to tell them about the assignments."

"Is she cute?"

I didn't answer.

"Ooh, you're blushing."

"I guess she is, but it doesn't matter. I think she has a boyfriend."

"Why do you think that?"

I shrugged to the best of my ability. "I saw her hugging a senior in homeroom."

"And she told you that's her boyfriend?"

"No."

Miranda jumped out of her seat. "Where's your phone? Let's text her."

"No. I'll tell her about the homework tomorrow. Just turn my neb off. It's done."

"That kind of defeats the purpose of a homework buddy. I'm not taking the mask off until we message her."

I gave in, mostly because I was curious about what Miranda would say to Nory, but also because I was too nervous to text her myself. Miranda snatched my phone from my pocket with more excitement than a child unwrapping a Christmas gift.

"Okay, what should we say?" she asked.

"I don't know. You're the girl. And you're the one who wanted to do this."

"Okay, okay. How about 'What up, girl?'"

"No, please don't send that." I immediately regretted granting Miranda control of my phone.

"How about 'Are you all right? I noticed you were out today.'"

"That's kinda boring, but sure."

Miranda quickly typed and pressed send. Then she removed the mask from my face.

"She's not gonna respond," I said.

"Why not?"

"I kind of sent her a weird text the other day."

"You asked for nudes, didn't you? All guys are the same."

I appreciated Miranda's assumption that I was like every

other guy, but I quickly corrected her. "No, I'm not an idiot. I was giving her a ride home last week, and—"

"Wait, you drove her home after school? So you've already spent time with her?"

"Well, I didn't drive," I said. "My mom did. But yeah, I spent time with Nory, and she told me how she likes to cook, so then I said one day she should make dinner for me. Since then she hasn't talked to me or sat next to me in homeroom."

"Wow, that's a bold move. I like it. But obviously that guy she was hugging isn't her boyfriend. If he was, then she would've asked him for a ride."

Mom entered the room and stopped when she saw me. "I was coming in here to turn off your neb, but I see that's already done. You're on the ball, Miranda."

"It's really not that hard."

"You'd be surprised. We've had some nurses who couldn't even figure out how to put the mask over Harris's head." She nodded toward the hallway. "Time for a bathroom break."

• • •

Peeing on demand is difficult in general, but especially in front of a total stranger, and even more so when that stranger is smoking hot, like Miranda. Mom explained all the steps of helping me use the bathroom. And then my nightmare happened.

"Can I try?" Miranda asked.

I looked at my mom, screaming with my eyes for her to say no. I knew Miranda was ready, but I wasn't.

"Usually I show the nurses on the first day so they can see what to do and then try it themselves next time," Mom said.

"I'm a tactile learner. I'd like to try, if that's all right."

"Are you okay with Miranda trying?" Mom asked me.

Miranda looked at me, and I couldn't avoid her eyes. One moment they were blue, then green, then almost translucent, like I could see into her mind and read what she was thinking. God, I couldn't say no.

I gave my approval, and Mom handed over the urinal to Miranda. I kept telling myself to think about football.

The mission was successfully completed. No bodily fluids came out of me except pee, and more importantly, nothing spilled.

"That was pretty easy," Miranda said. "You guys made me think this was going to be a big deal."

"Harris is a pretty easy gig. A lot of helping him is just common sense."

As predicted, dinner was a breeze. Miranda had no problem feeding me and gave me appropriately sized bites in between perfectly timed sips of water. She even quickly picked up on my eyebrow and head directionals.

Everything seemed too perfect. My family had moved to a new place and in the first two weeks found the ideal nurse to take care of me, all because of being in the right place at the right time and saying the right words to the right people? If I hadn't experienced all of it myself, I wouldn't have believed it. But Miranda was real.

"The Broncos are gonna beat the Raiders tonight," I told Ollie.

"What are you talking about? The Broncos are the worst."

"I have their running back on my fantasy team, so I'm hoping for a big game."

"Yeah, well, your fantasy team sucks. That's why I'm in first and you're in last."

I was about to accuse Ollie of cheating, since he was the commissioner of our league, but then my phone buzzed, and I forgot about football and fantasy football and that there was even a game that night.

Miranda pulled out my phone before I could ask. Her face lit up.

"It's from Nory," she sang.

"What'd she say?" I felt like I'd asked for Nory's hand in marriage or something, when in reality I was waiting for her to ask for tonight's homework.

"She said, 'I'm fine, thanks. Just wasn't feeling well. Did I miss anything?' I knew she would answer."

"Okay, you were right. Tell her she missed my cuteness." This time, I felt my cheeks turn red.

"God, you're such a nerd," Ollie said. Surprisingly, Mom stayed silent.

"No, it's a good line," Miranda said, "but maybe you're coming on too strong again. Let's say, 'Got a lot of homework, and there's a trig test on Thursday. We can meet after school tomorrow, and I can catch you up.'"

"But we don't have a test on Thursday."

"It's just an excuse for you to hang out with Nory."

"Got it."

Miranda typed the message, but not before my mom reminded us that we needed to send Nory the actual homework, which involved getting my backpack, finding my agenda, and snapping a few photos.

Dad had just gotten home and went through the usual back-and-forth with Miranda before retreating to his and Mom's bedroom to change out of his suit. His new job kept him in the office later than his job in San Diego had, not to mention the time he spent commuting back to New Jersey from the city. We all knew he tried his hardest not to miss dinner—he'd promised the move wouldn't change anything— but it was hard not to notice that he wasn't around as much.

"You know, *you* still have to do your homework," Mom told me.

"I know. I'll do it after Miranda leaves."

Unfortunately, Miranda seemed to take that as her cue to go. "It's getting late. I have to head out soon for class," she said.

"Okay, well, it was cool meeting you."

"Same. Hopefully I can come back."

"For sure. You're awesome."

Before Ollie and I left the table to do our homework, Mom made me swap phone numbers with Miranda. Once I got my first cell phone, I started doing this with all my nurses so we could stay in touch in case they had to cancel or I was sick. At the beginning, I'd enjoyed the idea of collecting contacts . . . but before long, my phone was full of numbers for people I would never talk to again.

"Miranda seems cool," Ollie said.

"Yeah, I think so."

"Do you like her? I mean, you think she'll work out?"

"She seems smart. She did a lot today, and Mom barely had to teach her."

"Cool. So you like her?" My brother was a big fan of that, asking the same question twice in a row.

"Yes."

I ended the conversation because I heard our parents talking to Miranda and knew it had to be about paying her.

I wanted to listen, but at the same time, I didn't. Burying my face in my physics textbook seemed like the best choice. I would never know anything about Miranda's compensation. I liked it that way.

. . .

I was alone in my room, watching TV, when my phone buzzed again. It was another text from Nory agreeing to meet after school the next day and admitting she needed help with trig. I was getting more action in one night than I'd had in my entire life.

I sent a text to Miranda.

> **ME:** She said she'll meet after school tomorrow

> **MIRANDA:** 👍 Did you answer her?

> **ME:** I said cool

> **MIRANDA:** Ok but you don't always need to have the last word. That's why you have me tho. I'll teach you something and you teach me something

> **ME:** What does that mean? What can I teach you?

MIRANDA: I'll teach you about girls and you teach me how to be a nurse

ME: Deal

I immediately deleted the text thread.

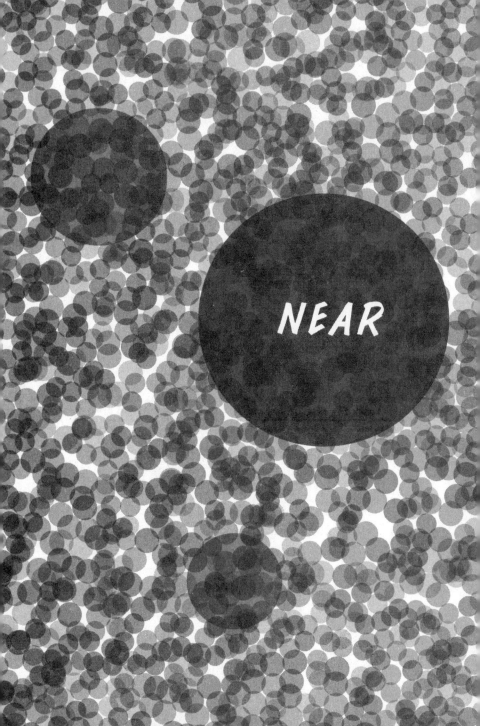

NOW THEY SAW ME

MOM AND I WAITED in Black Hawk for Miranda to arrive so we could drive to school. The mornings run more smoothly when my mom doesn't have to attend with me, and we were ready to go fifteen minutes earlier than usual while Miranda was running a couple minutes late.

"She was early yesterday," Mom said. "Where is she now?"

"She'll be here. We have a ton of time. By the way, I'm staying late today to meet with Nory and go over the work she missed."

"That's fine. Did Miranda say she can stay?"

"Yes. We were talking about it at dinner last night. Remember?"

Mom ignored me and watched in the rearview mirror as Miranda pulled her Mustang into the driveway. Homeroom didn't start for another half hour, and we lived only a few blocks from school, but Mom looked annoyed.

"What are you wearing?" I asked Miranda as she climbed into the van.

"Just a little school spirit. It took me forever to find this in my parents' attic. The first home football game is this Friday. Everyone will be wearing East Essex Central swag. "

"I didn't notice anything yesterday."

"Oh, they will be today." Mom turned off our street, and Miranda flipped up the hood of her navy-and-gold sweatshirt. "Go, Wombats."

• • •

"Do you need me to come in and show you what to do?" Mom asked.

"No, we'll be fine," I said.

"I mean, no offense, but I probably know this building better than both of you," Miranda added. Almost every kid entering school was wearing EEC colors; clearly Miranda knew what she was talking about.

"All right. Just text me later when you want to get picked up. And let me know if you see Ms. Maszak. It's been a week, and you still don't have your laptop."

I recognized some of the students as we walked into the building, and they were looking at me differently, too. It had to be Miranda. It was a nice break from what people usually noticed about me.

Miranda navigated the halls with ease. I told her my locker number, and she showed me a faster and less crowded route to it. Along the way, she pointed out some of her old lockers and a few hideaways if lunch table options ever became limited.

"Who do you have for homeroom?" she asked. She spun the combination lock like she was a jewel thief. I actually felt cool with her next to me. I felt like I wanted to be seen.

"Mr. Wormhole."

"Never heard of him."

"Really? Looks like he's been here forever . . . kind of a salty old man. I think he hates Dr. Kenzing, or maybe the whole school. I don't know why, but they keep adding students to his homeroom, and each time he totally loses it."

"That's funny. Wait until he sees me walk in."

"Well, he already knows I bring someone with me."

"That's not what I mean." She waved her hand up and down her body.

Luckily, I had to explain very little to Miranda. She knew to carry my backpack and which books to grab from my locker and that she should sit at the desk next to me. She entered homeroom confidently, without wavering or worrying that she was stealing anyone's seat.

"I *do* know him," Miranda said, gesturing to Mr. Wormhole. "My senior year, some kids poured baby oil all over one of the staircases, and he fell down the entire flight. Poor guy was out for the rest of the year."

"Jesus Christ. Why the hell would he come back?"

"Guess he needs the money."

"What happened to the students who pulled the prank?"

Miranda shrugged. "I think they got expelled. One of them lost his football scholarship to college. People do really dumb shit when they're in high school, trust me. But I don't think you're the type of person who has to worry about that."

I blushed and was going to play it cool and tell Miranda she didn't really know me yet, but Nory entered before I could say anything. I got distracted by watching her walk arm in arm with Kelvin, which looked pretty great. And goddammit, why did Kelvin Zhang have to be so freaking tall?

At least I had Miranda.

Contrary to popular belief, I don't envy people who can walk. My parents raised me not to pity myself, not to wish for my body to be different, and honestly, I never have. It's no fun being ordinary, anyway. But I'm also not naive. Sometimes it felt like being able-bodied was the only way to live a full teenage life.

"Is that her?" Miranda caught my eye.

"Yes."

"Oh, she's really cute in, like, a nerdy kind of way."

"That's my type, I guess. She's a little awkward. Honestly, it's always kinda weird when we talk. Maybe you should help me get a different girl. Nory has that guy, anyway."

"No. We're not giving up on her that fast. And if she really *is* as weird and awkward as you say, then that's good. You can help break her out of her shell."

"I have my own shell."

"Yeah, well, we're working on that. Do you know who she's with?"

"Kelvin Zhang. He's on the basketball team."

Miranda pondered. "Honestly, that's not very impressive. Basketball players are just freaks who never stopped growing and can put a ball in a hoop. You have your wheelchair. Now, that's interesting."

I wanted to believe Miranda. But either way, Nory and Kelvin clearly had *some* kind of relationship. The kind where you walk into homeroom arm in arm. How was I supposed to compete with that?

. . .

Apparently, we *were* going to have some sort of quiz in trig even though we were barely into the second week of school, and Mrs. Spilt wouldn't shut up about cosine and hypotenuses. I didn't mind, though, since it meant that technically speaking, I hadn't lied to Nory.

Miranda struggled to keep up with Mrs. Spilt, who barely finished writing down equations before erasing and replacing them. Nory was furiously scribbling in her notebook, too. I pictured myself studying with her after school, casually breaking down the ways to solve for angles in a triangle. I'd be confident but not arrogant, knowing that Nory was probably just as smart as me and wouldn't need much help. Of course, I would offer to help if she asked, and we'd smile at each other, because . . . well, that's just how I imagined it.

"You don't have to go overboard with the notes," I told Miranda. "I already know this stuff."

"Are you sure?" Her eyes flickered between me, my notebook, and Mrs. Spilt at the whiteboard.

"Yeah. It's all review, and you probably noticed the problems are all the same but with different numbers."

Miranda put down the pencil and whispered, "I didn't notice. What the hell class is this, anyway?"

"Honors trigonometry."

"You're taking honors trig? As a sophomore? I think I had algebra."

"It's the only honors math course the school offers to sophomores. And trig isn't *that* hard. I'm sure you take tougher classes in nursing school."

"Yes, but at least those teach me how to save a person's life. When are you ever going to use this?"

"I don't know. Maybe if I'm an engineer?"

"Do you want to be an engineer?"

"No."

Miranda and I laughed, not because learning trigonometry was pointless but because Mrs. Spilt spotted us talking and gave us the death stare. It was seriously a killer look. She definitely had children. Probably teenagers. Maybe they were EEC students, too.

I've never felt embarrassed when I get caught talking to my nurses in class. We could be discussing health issues, like how triangles give me a headache. The teachers never know for sure, and it's none of their business.

"Your homework for tonight is problems twenty-three through thirty-five in the back of your textbook," Mrs. Spilt said to the class. "And don't forget to start studying for Thursday."

Miranda jotted it down in my agenda. "That's a lot for one night."

"You act like you didn't just graduate from high school. It's all busywork, busywork, and more busywork."

"I guess I just never did my homework, then."

• • •

When lunchtime rolled around, it seemed like it was more of a relief for Miranda than it was for me. I think she was trying too hard with the note taking.

"Is this the abandoned teachers' bathroom?" Miranda asked. She helped me pee and started my breathing treatment in record time.

"I guess. Is there more than one?"

"I don't think so. My friends and I used to sneak in here to smoke."

"Cigarettes?"

"Yeah, or weed. Depended on which friends I was with."
Miranda looked at me sideways. She could probably tell that
the revelation was harsh on my virgin ears. "Don't judge me."

"I'm not judging."

"Yes, you are. I can see it on your face."

Maybe I was judging a little, or maybe I was just surprised,
because it was the first thing she'd told me that changed the
way I looked at her, even though it shouldn't have. Doing
erratic things was a typical red attribute.

So she wasn't perfect. Who is? High school's about getting
in trouble and making memories with people you'll probably
never see after graduation. I wanted more of that in my life.

• • •

We met up with Zander at the usual lunch table. I was almost
embarrassed for Miranda to see just how much of a loser I was.
I wanted to maintain whatever glimmer of wonder she might
have about my social life . . . but then again, she already knew
I could barely talk to girls.

"Is this the new girl?" Zander asked.

"Yup, that's me. Also known as Miranda."

"Zander. Pleasure to meet you." He reached out his hand
like he was greeting the queen. "Welcome to my lunch table,
also known as the Refuge for the Lost."

"You really need to stop saying that," I told him. "No one
will ever want to sit with guys who name their lunch table,
especially if it's a name that celebrates having no friends."

"Maybe it needs rebranding, but I'm just trying to claim
this spot as our own."

"Well, it's not yours," Miranda said. "Check under the
table."

Zander ducked his head, searching for I didn't know

what. A moment later, he popped back up. "There's just some random initials engraved."

"*M* and *K*, right?"

"How did you know that? Are you some kind of wizard?"

"No. I put them there. *M* is for *Miranda*, and *K* is for *Kaylin*. She was my best friend."

"This was your table?" I asked.

"You went here?" Zander added.

"Yes and yes. I sat here until my senior year. It's the perfect location. Close enough to the food without having to smell the gross frying oil, and only a few feet from the door in case an emergency exit is required."

"Where'd you sit for your last year?" I asked.

"I'll tell you when you're older."

"Oh, I like this girl," Zander exclaimed. "She has secrets. So you know the inside scoop, like which teachers suck and who's a creep and who you can pay off to get good grades and the best times to ditch?"

"Yup. But you'll have to earn all that."

"Shouldn't you already know that stuff?" I asked Zander. "I thought *Mean Girls* taught you."

"It varies from school to school."

"Mean girls?" Miranda asked. "What does that mean?"

"Zander watched *Mean Girls* all summer because he thought it would give him an advantage in high school."

"Oh. Well, it is a great movie." Miranda gave me another bite of my sandwich, which I'd barely eaten because of all the talking. She stood up from the table. "I'm gonna get a Snapple from the machine. You want anything?"

I shook my head. Chewing and swallowing demanded my full attention.

A couple of upperclassman-looking guys wearing varsity jackets walked past our table just as Miranda left. They were laughing, and one of them bent down behind me and said, "Dude, your aide is hot." A round of slaps on my back followed.

"Who the hell was that?" I asked Zander.

"Lex Brockman. He's a senior and the captain of the football team. And a total jerk, as you can tell." Zander snorted with disgust.

A random person complimenting my nurse sent a wave of conflicting emotions through me. I felt flattered by the attention, then confused, then enraged that someone had the arrogance to think I cared whether they found Miranda attractive.

Miranda returned holding out the Snapple bottle cap for us to read. "Look, it says that the first penny had the motto 'Mind your own business.'"

"That's fitting."

Miranda frowned. "Did I miss something?"

"Nope."

The three of us ate our lunches. Miranda had a peanut butter and jelly sandwich. She said she'd eaten one every day during high school.

I told Zander I'd be studying with Nory later, and he said I should bring her flowers, which I immediately shot down. He then began to complain about how during gym class, he was "forced" to stand and hold a stick while someone threw a ball at him. Supposedly, this was more evidence that his gym teacher was out to get him. I casually mentioned that perhaps he was playing baseball, but he seemed convinced that it was personal.

• • •

"Ms. Gilsip, what are you doing in my class?" Mr. Bavroe asked Miranda. "I thought I was done with you years ago."

"You were, but now I'm back to haunt you for all the times you bored me to death."

Mr. Bavroe dropped his stack of textbooks on the wooden desk at the front of the room. Students were still entering in dribs and drabs. The school day was less than an hour from ending, and no one wanted to spend the remaining minutes learning about Han Dynasty Chinese agriculture. Apparently, that had been true even when Miranda was a student.

"History may not be the most exciting subject, but it's important," he said. "Learning about our past mistakes means we can make better decisions today. You of all people should know that."

I had no clue what that meant, and when I looked at Miranda to ask, she appeared to be lost in her own thoughts. She was staring at the desk in front of hers, not blinking, not moving. Just thinking.

Mr. Bavroe opened up a closet and pulled out another textbook. He walked toward Miranda and me in the last row, and without saying anything, he delivered the half-destroyed book. I assumed that it was my copy to keep at home.

"Seriously, Ms. Gilsip, why are you in my classroom?" he asked Miranda.

She awoke from her trance. "I'm helping Harris. I'm his new nurse."

"That's fantastic. I'm always happy to see my old students doing something with their lives." Mr. Bavroe sounded like he actually gave a shit about Miranda.

The room was finally full of exhausted students. Mr. Bavroe returned to his perch at the front of the room, which was a stool he sat on while lecturing (or rambling). But this time, he just assigned work so he wouldn't have to teach.

"Read pages fifteen through twenty-eight and answer the five questions at the end of the section," he told us. "Hand in your responses before leaving."

Apparently, that day even he couldn't muster much interest in history.

RAINBOW

I CHOSE A TABLE at the center of the library in a cluster of students who were staying late to study or just chat quietly with their friends. I couldn't really tell the difference, but I was happy to be a part of the crowd.

A few feet in front of me was a small counter with teen magazines, computers, and the checkout desks. Most of the square footage of the library was occupied by biographies and academic books. There were only two measly stacks of novels tucked far in the back.

Schools like to complain that kids rarely read for pleasure, but they don't provide enough material to choose from. Come in, pick up the new edition of *Penguin Mating Habits*, and get out.

It also didn't help that the librarian sat with her arms folded tightly and scowled at every person who entered. After-school hours were obviously not her favorite time.

I remember all of this very clearly. I think sensory details get embedded in long-term memory when you're waiting for someone. And I waited for what seemed like a lifetime for Nory to show. I was facing the door, and students came and went, but none of them was my homework buddy.

Miranda was my only companion, and I turned to her to distract myself from worrying that Nory might not show. "What was Mr. Bavroe talking about before? He said something like, 'You of all people should know' about learning from past mistakes."

She waved me off. "I might not have been the most well-behaved student."

"You got in trouble a lot?"

"Don't judge."

"I'm not judging. I think it's cool."

"Yeah, so did I."

Then Nory burst through the door. Her backpack was strapped over both of her shoulders but hung low, almost below her butt, bouncing up and down with every quick and awkwardly shuffling step she took. She didn't make eye contact with anyone or look around. I'd never seen someone walk the way Nory Fischer did and look cute doing it.

But then I saw *him* a few paces behind her.

"Sorry I'm late," Nory said, sitting down across from Miranda and me. "I forgot to tell my dad I was staying, and he was waiting for me outside."

"Oh, we can meet up another time if you have somewhere to be."

"No. It's all good. I sent him away. He'll get over it, but I'll probably have to help mow the lawn or something this weekend."

Kelvin caught up and sat down next to Nory.

"I hope you don't mind that I invited Kelvin," Nory said,

sort of apologetically. "He has Mrs. Spilt last period, and we could both use some help before Thursday's quiz."

Miranda stared at me. I don't think I need to say that I was disappointed. "It's cool. The more people, the better." That was a lie. "I'm having trouble, too." That was another lie, and I instantly regretted making myself appear less smart in front of Kelvin.

"Should we try to answer some of the homework questions?" Nory asked. She flung her backpack onto the table and took out her textbook.

"Have you guys met Miranda?" I asked. How could they have? It was her first day. But I didn't know what else to say, and I felt rude for not introducing her sooner.

"Oh, yeah, I saw you in homeroom this morning," Nory said. "Will you be here now instead of Harris's mom?"

Miranda nodded.

Nory announcing in front of Kelvin that my mom had been attending school with me was a real punch to the gut. She said it like it wasn't at all surprising that the kid in a wheelchair needed an aide and that the aide was his mother. At that point, I wanted to pretend I'd forgotten I had somewhere to be and leave, but making a dramatic exit in a wheelchair isn't all that easy. I would've had to ask Miranda to put my hand on the joystick and turn my chair on, and the whole thing would have become a bigger mess than it already was. I decided to sit there and get the hour over with.

But none of it made sense to me. One moment, Nory and I had seemed to be turning into friends, and then the next, Nory was hanging on to Kelvin and inviting him to secret study sessions and telling everyone within earshot that my mom came to high school with me.

"Okay, this one is asking us to calculate the hypotenuse," Nory said. She tapped her pen a few times on her notebook, looked at me, and then looked at Kelvin, who was playing on his phone.

"That's just the Pythagorean theorem. Pretty easy," I said.

"Man, there are too many theorems and formulas," Kelvin complained. "How do they expect us to remember them?"

"SOH-CAH-TOA," I said.

"What?"

"SOH-CAH-TOA. It's a way to remember the formulas. Sine equals opposite over hypotenuse. Cosine equals adjacent over hypotenuse. Tangent equals opposite over adjacent."

Nory laughed. "Dang, a white boy just schooled you in math. Your mom would be so upset."

"Don't hit me with that stereotype crap. I'm a Chinese basketball player."

Nory laughed again. I was the third wheel, making sure the other two didn't fall off the straight-A bike.

We made it through about half the homework problems before Nory and Kelvin got texts from their parents saying it was time to come home. Miranda hadn't said much. She was distracted by her phone, typing what looked like some angry messages. It brought down the mood of what had turned out to be a pretty decent study session.

Kelvin was the first one out of the library when his mom swung by to pick him up. Knowing that he was an upperclassman without a car provided relief; somehow, it seemed to level the playing field.

Nory took her time packing up her stuff while Miranda texted my mom that we were done. The library had been empty for a while, so it was just us and Scrunch-Face-Folded-Arms.

"Thanks for sending me the homework yesterday and for offering to help me study today," Nory said.

"No problem. That's what homework buddies are for."

Nory nodded. "Let me know if you're having trouble in any of our other classes, and I can try to return the favor."

In the cheesy teen-movie version of my life, "return the favor" would've been an innuendo. In reality, though . . . not so much. "Yeah, maybe physics," I told her. "I hate that class."

We made our way together through the desolate hallways. Miranda trailed behind to give us some space. School was actually quite nice with no one around.

"Where did you move from again?" Nory asked.

"San Diego."

"Nice. I hear it's gorgeous out there. I have some family in Phoenix, but that's a totally different state and nothing like San Diego, so I'm not sure why I brought it up."

"I mean, they're both boiling, but at least California has beaches. I can't imagine living in the desert."

A comfortable silence settled over us on our way to the entrance. Just being with Nory, even if nobody saw us, was enough.

Nory stopped before opening the front door. "So why are you in a wheelchair?" A second passed, maybe less, before she cut me off from answering: "Sorry, that was rude. You don't have to tell me."

"It's fine. I don't mind. I have a form of muscular dystrophy called spinal muscular atrophy. It pretty much means I have weak muscles."

"Are you going to die?"

"I guess eventually, like everybody else. I've already lived past my life expectancy, so who knows. Now you have to tell me your favorite color. I tell you if I'm going to die, and you tell me your favorite color."

Nory smiled. "I don't think that's how it works."

"So you get to know about my rare genetic disease, but I can't know your favorite color?"

"Yup." A car pulled up in front of the building. "That's my ride. I need to get home and finish making dinner. Have you ever used a slow cooker?"

"My mom has."

"Well, today's my first time, and I'm making a bean soup with spinach. I think my dad will make a funny face at it and have a leftover burger he grilled the other night." Nory seemed to think about the menu for a second and then headed out the door. "Anyway, see you tomorrow."

"Not even a hint?" I called after her. "About your favorite color, I mean."

She glanced at me over her shoulder. "It's in the rainbow."

"That doesn't narrow it down enough!" I yelled.

Through the window, I watched Nory get in the car and drive away. I didn't go outside with Miranda until the car had left the parking lot.

The air was cold and damp and smelled like rotting leaves, but the setting sun felt warm on my exposed arms. By the time I got home it would already be dark. Shorter days meant less of everything. But somehow, longer days never meant more.

"Dude, I think she likes you," Miranda said.

"What are you talking about? She has Kelvin."

"I'm not sure about that. I was watching her the whole time. I saw the way she looked at you . . . and at him."

"How did she look at me? We were doing homework."

"Every time she asked a question or didn't know the answer, she looked at you. Not Kelvin. You."

"Duh. The point of me being there was to help them."

"Okay, but she also said she wants to meet up again, right?"

"She was just being nice."

"Mmm," she replied noncommittally. "Plus, she felt comfortable asking about your disability. That's cool."

"She only did that because she's weird and obviously too nosy."

Miranda jumped in front of my wheelchair and pressed the off button. "Stop doing that, Harris. It's all right for people to take an interest in you without them being weird or just polite or having a motive. I've only known you for two days, but you're a pretty cool guy. You're witty and smart and really chill."

"Thanks, I guess. Blue is a chill color."

"Huh?"

"Nothing. What was going on with your phone before?"

It took her a second to catch up with the shift in topic. "My boyfriend. I told him I was staying late, but he forgot and was mad that I wasn't already at his place."

"Don't you live with your parents?"

"Yeah, but I promised I'd spend the week at his apartment. He wants me to move in, but I want to try it out first."

The next car to pull up was Black Hawk. "Did you have a good day? How was everything?" Mom asked.

"All good," Miranda answered. "No problems whatsoever. But I think Harris might have a love interest."

Mom didn't flinch. "Harris, did you see Ms. Maszak?"

"No."

"All right. I'll call her tomorrow. I knew they were just bullshitting us about getting a laptop so fast."

• • •

Miranda put her sweatshirt back on before getting out of the van. "Thanks for an awesome day, dude. I'll see you tomorrow."

"Did you thank Miranda for staying late?" Mom said to me.

I rolled my eyes. "Thanks, Miranda."

"No problem."

She got into her Mustang and drove away. I thought about what she'd said about the way Nory looked at me. I wondered if she was just telling me what I wanted to hear or if I wasn't analyzing our study session enough.

RED ALWAYS WINS

SINCE THE SCHOOL HADN'T PROVIDED a laptop yet, I was allowed to leave class during my trig quiz so I could tell Miranda what answers to write. We found a table in the back corner of the library so there'd be fewer distractions from other students who were there for study hall.

Miranda placed the one-sided quiz in front of me. I felt confident since there were only four questions, but a knot still tightened in my stomach. The quiz required that I show my work, and I was sure that Miranda hadn't spent enough time in Spilt's class yet for me to shout out equations and trigonometry jargon.

The first problem was, thankfully, very easy. It gave the degrees of two angles in a triangle, and I had to solve for the third.

"Okay, Miranda, write down one-hundred-eighty minus seventy-two minus thirty-six," I said.

She did, then plugged the numbers into the calculator we were allowed to use. The number seventy-two flashed on the screen, and Miranda circled option B on the paper. So far so good, but the next two questions were a little harder and would require a lot more scribing from Miranda.

"For the next one, I need to use the law of sines to solve for the length of the other two sides of the triangle," I told her.

"So what do you want me to do?"

"First write sine thirty and then draw a line underneath like you're making a fraction, and put the number two as the denominator. Then set that equal to—" I noticed that Miranda was looking at something on her phone. "What are you doing?"

"Reading about the law of sines so I know what we're doing."

"You don't need to know what we're doing. I'm telling you what to write."

"But how do I know what to write if I don't understand what you're telling me?"

I convinced myself that since I knew how to solve the problem, it wasn't cheating if Miranda looked up the formula. There wasn't another choice if I wanted full credit for showing my work.

Miranda spent a minute or so scrolling through a Wikipedia article, and then I finished solving questions two and three. I really hoped the librarian couldn't see Miranda holding her phone under the table.

The last question had me stumped, and I read it probably ten times without a clue as to what it was asking. I was fine with numbers and solving equations, but I struggled with theoretical questions, especially if they were true-or-false.

"What's up?" Miranda asked. "You've been staring at that one for a while now."

"Because I don't know the answer. I don't remember Mrs. Spilt teaching us about radians."

Miranda leaned over to read the question and then typed something on her phone.

"Don't look up the answer," I said. "That's cheating."

"Okay, well, then you can randomly choose an answer, and you'll have a fifty-fifty chance of getting it right. But if you don't, you'll get a seventy-five on the quiz, which is a C. Or I can look up the answer because I'm curious and it's not cheating since I'm not a student, and then I'll *accidentally* circle the correct answer."

I thought about what Miranda had said. My entire conscience was screaming *no*. I had never cheated on anything, and I hadn't planned on starting . . . but it wasn't my fault that Mrs. Spilt had forgotten to mention radians in the study guide.

Miranda smiled innocently enough. "It's pretty ridiculous to get a bad grade because your teacher didn't tell you how to solve the problem." She slowly tapped her pencil on *true*.

Blue and red were both confident colors. I was pretty sure that eventually I could've answered the question without cheating but Miranda's confidence that we would never get caught won out.

I closed my eyes and nodded. I listened to the sound of pencil on paper.

THE DOWNSIDE OF OUTSIDE

FRIDAY WAS THE FIRST home football game. Cheerleaders paraded down the halls wearing their short skirts and waving pompoms in the faces of students who dared to exhibit zero school spirit. Guys on the football team wore their home uniforms, waiting for the grass stains of victory. For all I knew, the East Essex Central Wombats sucked, but they sure seemed to believe their own hype.

Mom had bugged me the entire week about going to the game because it would be "good to get out of the house and socialize." I'd played the whole thing off like I really didn't care about it or have any interest in attending a high school football game, which she didn't buy for a second.

Zander and I had already made plans to go for at least a little while, just to show our faces. I marketed it differently from my mom and told Zander that not going would solidify our reputation as outcast losers. I thought talking to other students at the game could be avoided, but Zander disagreed.

Since the study session on Tuesday, Nory and I had spoken only through pictures of her dinners and a few slow-cooker recipes my mom made me send. Most of my in-school free time was consumed by being the messenger between my mom and Ms. Maszak.

According to Ms. Maszak, there had been a "miscommunication" about how long it would take to get me a laptop. The company they'd ordered it from had a "backlog," but my mom and I knew that meant the school had never placed the order to begin with and they were just trying to dig themselves out of a hole. My mom then told me to tell Ms. Maszak that in the meantime, she should come over to our house and help me fill out the tedious worksheets we got for homework, because my mom was done being my hands. Of course, my mom didn't say this in such nice words, but I toned them down before I relayed the message to Ms. Maszak.

Fighting with the school and making them feel bad is fun for my mom. The administrators in charge of disability accommodations always seem to assume parents are lazy and will forget what's in their kids' IEPs, but not Clare Jacobus. She is their worst nightmare. I'm lucky to have her as my mom.

High school Friday nights, I learned, have an electricity to them. Most kids in the crowd that night didn't seem to care whether their team won or lost; it seemed like football games were just an excuse to hang out after a long week. The marching band rattled off fight songs and drum cadences to the semiorganized movements of the cheerleaders. The smell of hot dogs, popcorn, and Astroturf overwhelmed the senses and made each step closer to the field exciting and terrifying.

This was what high school was all about.

"I'm just going to hang out here in case you boys need anything," Mom told Zander and me.

"Thanks, Ms. Clare," he answered. "I'll make sure Harris doesn't die."

"What a friend," I said, but I was looking at my mom. I must've seemed nervous.

"You'll be fine," she mouthed.

Zander and I headed away from the entrance, where all the parents huddled, and toward the student-filled bleachers. We had no destination and hadn't planned anything past arriving.

"What do you want to do? I hear everyone hangs out by the concession stand," Zander said. We'd stopped halfway down the line of bleachers and were staring at the field through a chain-link fence.

"The game is about to start. Let's watch the kickoff."

"Fine. But then we're getting a pack of sour gummy worms."

"I don't want gummy worms."

"Good, because I wasn't planning on sharing."

The visiting team placed the ball on the kickoff tee and lined up. Their players were undersize and ran slowly down the field. I imagined the first home game was always scheduled against a weak opponent to ensure a win.

"Are we any good?" I asked.

"I think so. This is my first game, but I heard the team won some kind of championship last year."

"Seriously?"

"Yeah, but Lex is the quarterback, so whatever. You wanna get some food?"

"No, dude. I want to watch the game."

"Well, I'm hungry. You stay here and watch guys tackle each other, and I'll be right back."

I didn't answer him. Our offense was quickly marching toward the end zone. First, there was a fifteen-yard pass by

Lex, and then twelve yards picked up by the running back, who was short and fast and hid behind the offensive line well. I think he was one of the kids who'd patted me on the back after seeing Miranda.

My view of the field was terrible and mostly obstructed by the fence and the players standing on the sideline. I'd never understood why most bleachers didn't have ramps so people in wheelchairs could actually see what was happening and sit with everyone else. I had only encountered a handful of bleachers like that in California, when we had traveled for Ollie's lacrosse games, but they were all at affluent private schools. No doubt Ridge Prep had them, which meant I would have an unobstructed view of him kicking the other teams' asses.

I guess I could've raised my wheelchair to be taller than the fence, but I couldn't reach the button myself, so I would have had to go ask my mom for help, and anyway, I didn't like the way my chair looked when it was elevated.

"Hey, Harris. You having a good time?"

I rotated my wheelchair to the right and saw Nory leaning on the fence. "Yeah. So far." The team had just scored, and the crowd was cheering so loudly I could barely hear myself talk.

Nory nodded a couple of times like people do when they're trying to think of something to say. "How do you think you did on the trig quiz yesterday?"

"Pretty good. I thought it was easy."

"I thought the same until that question about radians. I had no idea what the answer was."

"It was true," I said, as if I'd actually known and hadn't cheated, but I wanted Nory to keep asking for help, and she wasn't going to do that if I didn't prove myself worthy.

"Damn. I put false. Oh, well. A seventy-five isn't bad for the first quiz. I probably would have failed if we hadn't met."

"No problem." We were still yelling at each other over the cheering and the band. Well, Nory was yelling. I tried, but, you know, having a restrictive lung disease made that almost impossible.

We were silent for a moment, but I didn't mind. Nory fiddled with the ends of her hair, and I remembered reading that girls play with their hair when they're talking to someone they find attractive. It also could've been a nervous tic, but I preferred the idea of Nory being into me.

"Do you like the school's colors?" I asked. "Navy and gold?"

"They're okay, I guess. A little too masculine, though."

"Yeah, I mean, I guess navy is, but gold is perfect for sports. It's a very successful color."

"So you're saying the team would never win if the colors were blue and pink?"

I fumbled for an answer. Nory saw my panic and giggled.

"Don't worry: I'm just joking," she said. "I think it's cool that you know so much about colors."

"Really? Nobody ever says that."

"Absolutely. You're passionate about something. Ninety-eight percent of the kids at this school just want to Snapchat and watch Netflix."

"Well, you're passionate about cooking. I think that's cool. And you can make a career out of it. I can't really do that with color psychology."

Nory leaned away from the fence and closer to me. It was just the two of us. I forgot there was a football game being played thirty feet away.

Zander returned holding a bag of gummy worms and a paper bowl of nachos, which was literally six tortilla chips covered in fake cheese sauce. He shoved a fistful of worms in his mouth and washed it down with the nachos. He offered me a chip, but I declined.

"Are you going to tell me your favorite color?" I asked Nory.

"I was thinking about it, but now Zander's here, and I don't want him knowing my secret."

"Hey, don't let me ruin the fun," Zander said. "Harris will have a heart attack if you don't tell him, and I'm pretty sure he doesn't want me to give him mouth-to-mouth with nacho lips."

"That's not true," I told Nory. "I mean, I won't have a heart attack."

"I'm gonna go get a snack," Nory said. "It's too loud over here. I can barely hear what you're saying. See you guys."

Nory walked away, and Zander, who had a mouthful of food, waved goodbye for both of us. Sometimes I wanted to invent a headrest for my wheelchair with speakers that would project my voice. My mom thought there wasn't an issue and that everyone could hear me just fine, but every time I'm in a loud place, people have to lean down and stick their ears in my face just to understand what I'm saying. According to my mom, that's their problem. But right then, it sure felt like my problem.

"You said you didn't judge my color questions," I told Zander.

"I don't. But I know that Nory hasn't told you her favorite color yet, so I'm just helping you out. I got your back, man."

I wasn't sure he was actually helping all that much, but I

didn't bother saying so, especially since just then the defense ran onto the field and the band started playing again.

"Did we get it in?" Zander shouted.

"Get what in?" I shouted back.

"The football? Into the rectangle at the end of the field?"

"Yeah. We scored a touchdown."

Zander finished his nachos. "So, how long are we staying for? I'd say our presence has been felt."

I'd had a similar thought. Part of me wanted to stay, because live football was in front of me, but I also wanted to run away as soon as possible. I hated that my conversation with Nory had ended because she couldn't hear me, which just validated my reasons for never going anywhere or surrounding myself with more than five people. There's nothing worse than having the courage to speak and the desire to talk to another human being and then having your words fall dead before they're finished leaving your mouth.

I watched Nory disappear behind the bleachers and join a large group of students. She bounced from one person to the next, laughing and talking and doing all the things a social person does.

"Dude, we just got here," I said. "Let's at least stay until halftime."

Zander didn't look happy, but he stayed next to me, watching EEC's opponent fail three times to run the ball more than one yard. Eventually, he held a gummy worm in front of my mouth. I leaned my head forward and grabbed it between my front teeth, even though his fingers smelled like cheese. You only live once, I guess.

GAINING ATTENTION

HALFTIME ROLLED AROUND, which meant it was time to give my mom a visit and maybe eat something. The Wombats were up by twenty, and the other school was losing steam. One of their so-called star players had left the game with a possible concussion.

As soon as Zander and I reached my mom, she shoved her hand under the cuffs of my pants to feel the bottoms of my legs. "Your legs are frozen. Let me get the blanket from the car."

"No. I'm not putting a blanket over my legs."

"Can you even get cold?" Zander asked. "You can't feel anything."

"Dude, I'm not paralyzed. I have feeling."

My mom took a knit hat from her sweatshirt pocket and pulled it over my head. "Well, you're wearing this. And I'm going to the concession stand to get you some hot chocolate."

"Whatever."

"Can you grab me one too, please, Ms. Clare?" Zander said. "Thanks."

If I'm being honest, it was cold outside. September in New Jersey didn't mess around. I'd never felt crisp air in my lungs in San Diego, and each breath made everything feel . . . possible.

"You want to head closer to the bleachers?" I asked Zander. "The cheerleaders are performing, and we'll get a better view down there."

"Nah." Zander jumped up and down, his hands fully tucked into the pockets of his sweatshirt and the hood covering his face. "Your mom's right: it's freezing. I'm not moving until I've chugged a cup of hot chocolate."

From our vantage point close to one of the end zones, I tried to catch a glimpse of the dance routine, but all I could make out were the backs of the trumpet players.

My mom shoved a straw protruding from a Styrofoam cup into my mouth, and I took a sip. The liquid tasted nothing like hot chocolate—more like burnt water. Could water even get burnt?

"What have you been doing during the game, Ms. Clare?" Zander asked.

"I talked with a few parents. Checked in on Harris's dad at home. Watched the game. The team is excellent."

I took another swig of the tasteless hot water. Zander had already finished his cup and returned to the half-eaten bag of gummy worms in the pocket of his sweatshirt.

"Are you sure you don't want the blanket?" Mom asked again.

"I'm fine. I'll look stupid wearing it."

"I want the blanket," Zander said.

"No. It's really not that cold out. Let's head back toward the bleachers. The second half is starting."

"I saw a bunch of kids hanging out behind the bleachers," Mom said. "You and Zander should go mingle."

Zander began walking in that direction. "Yeah, dude, let's go. We can catch some heat from the concession stand."

"Maybe later. I wanna watch more of the game."

I drove down the sidewalk to the middle of the field. Zander followed, because we both knew he wasn't brave enough to socialize with a bunch of rowdy high schoolers by himself. He was all talk and no action.

The team was back on the sideline, talking out the game plan before kickoff. Lex Brockman paced back and forth in front of the bench while taking sips of Gatorade. He saw me watching and gave one of those *what's up* nods. Then he crossed the track that circled the field and came up to the fence where Zander and I were stationed.

"'Sup, bro?" he asked.

I acted real cool. "Just chilling. You guys are kicking ass."

"Yup. So where's your new friend?"

I knew he was asking about Miranda. "She couldn't come tonight."

"Huh. Can you even see anything through this fence?"

"Sort of. It's not too bad."

Lex walked over to the gate and swung it open. "Come on the sideline with the team so you can actually see what's going on."

I looked at Zander, who shrugged and nervously ate his final gummy worm. We accepted the offer, though Lex seemed annoyed that Zander was joining us.

The head coach immediately noticed us and waved at Zander. "I'm surprised to see you here," he said.

"I'm just here with Harris," Zander told him.

"Well, either way, I'm glad you finally came to a game."

I figured the coach must've been his gym teacher, the same one who'd traumatized him by making him play baseball. No wonder he was surprised to see Zander at a game.

The excitement of being on the field quickly drew my attention. I was able to hear the crunch of every tackle and the thumping of feet on the artificial grass. I easily could've told the coach that the opponent's safeties were playing low and that calling a few play-actions would force them away from the line of scrimmage.

Any closer and I would've needed to put on a helmet. And I knew that if I'd been able to play, I would've been on the field, not on the bench. No doubt.

"Dude, isn't this awesome?" I asked Zander.

"I guess so. The fat offensive linemen are blocking the wind."

I spun around in my chair to face the stands and the cheerleaders behind us, braving the cold weather in their short skirts. I saw Nory under the bleachers. She was still laughing and talking and bouncing from one person to the next, and I hated that I wasn't one of those people—the people she was talking to and the people who were fearlessly social.

But maybe there was hope for me. The jocks had welcomed me into their world, and I didn't want it to be a one-time experience. I wanted to be one of them.

East Essex Central won by thirty-four. Lex threw three touchdowns.

VICTORIA'S SECRET IS FOR ADULTS

ON THE LAST DAY of the summer before I started seventh grade, my mom and I went window shopping at our favorite mall in San Diego. This wasn't a typical mall full of cheap outlets and bored thirteen-year-olds hanging out in the food court. No, sir. Our mall was high end and practically had a dress code—everyone always dressed up to walk through the designer stores.

I don't remember where Ollie and my dad were. If I had to guess, Ollie was at camp and Dad was at work. Mom woke me up early, which I didn't mind, given the occasion, and I put on a pair of khakis and a button-down shirt. She wore her favorite sundress.

Through the sunroof of Black Hawk, I watched the bluest, clearest California skies surf over my head during the forty-minute drive to the mall. Here's the thing I forgot to mention—my mom hates shopping. Honestly, I believe she would rather endure the pain of childbirth again than search for a pair of shoes. So I was a little surprised she chose such a beautiful day to be stuck inside a windowless building.

We probably spent a good six hours at the mall. Mom tried on a two-thousand-dollar cashmere dress, and I asked a very snotty sales associate to hold a pair of Italian leather shoes because I wasn't sure if I was totally in love with them. The funny part was, we'd left the house with only twenty dollars, which could hardly buy a hat . . . but it was definitely enough to split an appetizer and grab a slice of cheesecake from the Cheesecake Factory before we left.

That night, we didn't talk about the shopping trip with Ollie or my dad. There was no point. Mom and I had gone to the mall and barely spent any money. It wasn't really newsworthy.

But for some reason, I couldn't sleep after our rich person impostor day. I probably called my mom and dad every hour to turn me over or take off some of my blankets.

The more I think about it, I guess I was stuck imagining every other kid my age at the beach, taking advantage of the perfect San Diego weather. For a few hours, my mom had distracted me from the fact that I couldn't join them. Not because I wasn't allowed, but because sand and wheelchair tires just don't go together. Going to the beach meant sitting in a folding chair, getting a sunburn, and watching everyone else have fun.

I didn't fit in with the outdoorsy California lifestyle. I was much better off in New Jersey, where the cold weather forced people into more accessible places.

When Zander invited me to spend Sunday at *his* mall, I warned him that I had high expectations. From the outside, it was pretty generic looking, and as expected, the parking lot was overcrowded with obnoxious New Jersey drivers and families from New York City who'd decided to come out to the suburbs. Better sales tax? I don't know, but it took us nearly fifteen minutes to find a parking space. The handicap parking on all sides of the mall was filled, as if they were giving away free wheelchairs. We eventually settled for a regular parking spot that had an empty space next to it so we had room to drop the ramp.

Did I tell you the mall in San Diego played jazz over the loudspeakers? I think I forgot to say that.

The first store we stopped at was Lucky Brand Jeans. My dad was hell-bent on finding a new pair. It was practically the only reason he came with us.

He stepped up to the register, where a girl was folding jeans for restocking. Dad kind of just stood there, posing, right leg stuck out, hands on his hips. He held the position for what seemed like an unnecessarily awkward eternity.

My dad does this same routine every time we shop. He'll walk into a store, say nothing, and expect the employees to know exactly what he wants. He's a salesman, so he wants to be sold.

"Can I help you find something?" the girl asked.

Dad stood still for another moment. "Well, I'm looking for a new pair of jeans," he finally said. "I recently lost a little weight, and I want to try something sporty. Hip."

"No problem." The salesgirl walked around from behind the counter. Zander watched with amazement. Mom picked through a rack of denim jackets. "Do you know what size you wear?" the salesgirl asked.

"I don't know. Why don't you tell me?"

The girl walked away, probably to find a tape measure or quit.

"Dad, you know the size of your pants," I said. "Give the girl a break."

"Hey, you know me. I gotta make them work for the sale. These are expensive jeans, and I should get some service."

"The people who work here make, like, ten dollars an hour folding clothes. I'm pretty sure they're not interested in being your personal stylist." I turned toward my mom. "Do Zander and I really have to stick around for this?"

"Your dad should be done here soon."

"Soon? It just took Dad two minutes to tell that girl he wants to buy a pair of jeans in an all-jeans store."

"I thought that was funny," Zander said.

"Please let us walk around by ourselves," I begged. "Nothing will happen."

"Fine. But answer me if I text you to check in," Mom said.

Zander and I left the store before anyone returned to measure my dad. Waves of people moving in both directions met us at the door, making it almost impossible to move. I felt like I had to put on my turn signal just to merge with them. It was nothing like the mall in San Diego.

"Which way?" I asked Zander.

"Um, right. Go right."

The mall noise was deafening, and everything reeked of Auntie Anne's, even though the kiosk was on a different floor. Zander couldn't even walk next to me—that's how many people there were. We crept single file past the Apple Store and Spencer's Gifts and the guy trying to rub lotion on innocent shoppers. Like, how was that legal?

Finally, we caught a break by one of the department stores.

"Is this place always so crowded?" I asked.

"Usually. I think that's what makes coming here so fun.

It's like a huge party during the day, but you don't have to listen to terrible music."

"No, just hundreds of people sneezing and coughing. So, where do you want to go?"

Zander shrugged. "I just like walking around. It helps clear my head."

My phone buzzed in my pocket, and I knew it was my mom checking in. Zander answered with a confident *We're fine.*

Off we went.

Zander and I covered all three floors of the mall. He stopped to buy a bracelet and a cheap pair of sunglasses and, of course, a hot dog inside a pretzel. I only stopped to admire an older gentleman playing the piano.

Mom texted me eight times. We answered each message the same way.

We were waiting to get in an elevator with a bunch of strollers when I heard someone call my name. I turned around to see Miranda walking toward us with some guy. She was holding a Victoria's Secret bag. I didn't know why that bothered me.

"Hey, guys," Miranda said. She had a massive smile on her face. "Funny seeing you here."

"I mean, we all live in the same area," I said.

"You two aren't here alone, are you? I know your mom has to be around somewhere."

"She's downstairs with my dad, trying to buy jeans."

"Who's this guy?" Zander asked. I liked his style. He didn't pussyfoot around.

Miranda wrapped her arm around the guy, who was wearing a pastel polo. "Oh, this is my boyfriend, Brad."

I kid you not: his name was Brad. He was short and looked like he frequented the gym but occasionally missed leg day to work on styling his hair. All the typical Brad attributes.

He failed miserably when he attempted to shake my hand, then floundered, trying to figure out what to do with his hand when I didn't shake back. Miranda laughed.

"You're the kid Miranda goes to school with?" Brad asked. I don't know why he posed it as a question, like Miranda hung out with a lot of disabled kids and he was trying to figure out which one I was.

I nodded.

"You need to keep a close eye on her while she's back at that school."

What the hell did that mean? Miranda looked kind of pissed, so I said, "I think she'll be fine."

Miranda rolled her eyes and focused on me. "How was the game on Friday? I heard we won big-time."

"Yup," Zander said, "and Harris and I got to watch from the sideline." He said it like he was actually proud.

"That's cool. And you're doing a little shopping today?"

"Mostly just wasting time," I admitted. "The Giants are playing Monday night, so I was free."

"Well, have fun." Then Miranda did the strangest thing. She leaned over to adjust my shirt, which I guess was wrinkled. She whispered, "Your mom would freak if she saw you driving around like that."

"Thanks?"

She walked away, holding Brad's hand and the Victoria's Secret bag. We'd missed four opportunities to get in the elevator.

I turned my wheelchair to face Zander, whose expression

hadn't changed for an alarming amount of time. "Hey, can I ask you something?"

"Is it about Miranda?"

"Yes."

"Okay, but first let me remind you that she's, like, six years older than us."

"So?"

"So I see the way you look at her. Just now and at school. You can't fall in love with her."

"Dude, what the hell? Can I just ask my question?"

"Sure."

"Why do you think she asked where my mom was?"

"I don't know. Probably because we're kids and your mom is always around."

"We're not kids. Are we?"

"Compared to her and mini-Hulk, yeah."

I didn't like being reminded of our age gap. At school, she felt like one of us. But seeing her out in the real world with Brad, holding a Victoria's Secret bag, made me feel the distance. She was living a grown-up life that I wasn't sure I'd ever live, being in a wheelchair.

"Was it weird that she adjusted my clothes?" I asked.

"Yeah, dude, that was weird."

My cell phone buzzed again, and it was my mom asking for our current location. Zander's mall also has a Cheesecake Factory, so we told her we'd meet them there. I needed a slice of cheesecake.

• • •

After we got home from the mall, Dad modeled all four of his new pairs of jeans. Some of them were a little too acid-washed for my taste, but Dad was acting really goofy, so shopping at

Lucky Brand must have been a refreshing experience. Ollie didn't make any comments except for the occasional eye roll or embarrassed laugh.

I texted with Nory in between each outfit.

> **ME:** Have you been to the mall on your side of town?

Nory didn't immediately answer, so I sent another text.

> **ME:** Never mind. That was a dumb question. I'm sure you've been there

> **NORY:** Oh hey. Yeah, I go there a lot. They have a pretty decent food court

> **ME:** I didn't see it. Zander and I ate with my parents at the Cheesecake Factory

> **NORY:** Nice! Next time you're there let me know and I'll come by if I'm free

I didn't know how to continue the conversation or if I had anything else to say. When Dad returned wearing the third pair of jeans, he asked if we liked them, and in unison, we answered, "They're fine."

NOT HER BOSS

MIRANDA WAS A FEW MINUTES LATE AGAIN, and it didn't sit well with my mom. I knew the reason: Miranda was staying with her boyfriend this week—and probably modeling for him whatever was in that Victoria's Secret bag she'd been holding.

Even so, that wasn't an excuse for being late. Miranda knew what time she needed to be at my house regardless of where she'd slept the night before.

"Zander and I saw Miranda at the mall the other day. She was with her boyfriend." I guess that was my way of hinting at where Miranda could have been.

"And did she say why she's always late?"

"No, that didn't come up in the conversation."

"You need to talk to her about this, Harris. If she keeps showing up late, we'll have to find someone else. I can't deal with the stress."

Of course, I made it to homeroom with plenty of time to spare. My mom just likes to worry.

* * *

Nory and I had honors physics together second period. Overall, it was a mind-numbing yet diabolically difficult class.

But that day, Mrs. Ivavych, an older Russian woman who wobbles when she walks, announced that we'd be starting a group project.

Now, I know you're probably thinking that Nory and I got paired up and fell madly in love. Well, you're wrong. Sort of.

When Mrs. Ivavych told us to use the last five minutes of class to find a partner, every student leaped off their lab stool to grab a friend. This was one of the classrooms where I had to sit in the front row, but I heard all the commotion happening behind me.

Miranda and I hadn't said much to each other the entire morning. Besides thinking about her and Brad and that pink bag, I was also annoyed that she'd been late again that morning. I really wasn't a fan of hearing my mom complain to me about it like it was something I could control. In my head, I told Miranda that she needed to start arriving on time, that I was done making excuses for her and she needed to start taking this job more seriously. But I said nothing. I looked at her and couldn't stand the thought of reprimanding her like I was her boss. We were friends. I didn't want her to see me as a job.

What really bothered me was her incessant texting. "Can you put your phone away? We're in class," I said.

"Jeez, what's your deal? You've been pissy all morning."

"I'm fine."

Except I wasn't, because I knew she was texting Brad, which shouldn't have bothered me as much as it did. He was her boyfriend. Miranda was a twenty-something-year-old woman with a boyfriend, and I was a fifteen-year-old boy, sitting at the front of my physics class and hoping someone would approach and ask to be my partner, but no one did.

Then, like every heroic teacher rescuing the wheelchair kid, Mrs. Ivavych did something miraculous.

"Nory," she called, "you worked with Olivia all last year." Mrs. Ivavych also taught freshman earth science. "You work with Harris, and Olivia, go with Ashley."

I heard the rapid shuffling of Nory's feet. She flopped her backpack onto the lab table.

"Hey," I said.

"Hey."

That was all—just a simple hey. No smile or any other acknowledgment. I don't think she even looked at me. All of this from the same girl who sent me pictures of her dinner every night and told me I was different from everyone else at EEC.

"All right, class. Discuss with your partner what you want to research for your project," Mrs. Ivavych said. "It has to be a topic that's not on the syllabus."

"Do you have anything in mind?" I asked Nory.

The bell rang. Nory grabbed her stuff. "I'll text you," she said, and raced out of the room, leaving me in her dust. Somehow, we could text about food or the mall, talk at football games or in an empty hallway, but it seemed like Nory couldn't stand to be seen with me at school. The duality of Nory Fischer was exhausting.

MORE PEOPLE + LESS LONELY = YOU'LL NOTICE

"ARE YOU OKAY?" MIRANDA ASKED ME. Zander was in line, buying lunch.

"I don't know. I keep thinking about Nory. I don't understand why she acts one way when we text and another way in person."

"I wouldn't really worry about it. She seems a little socially awkward. Maybe it's easier for her to text, like it is for you."

"I mean, yeah, it's easier for everyone to text, but I'm not a different person in real life. And you should have seen her at the football game. She wasn't socially awkward there. Or after our study session—you saw her then."

Miranda didn't answer; she was back on her phone. She rolled her eyes and shoved it in her jeans pocket.

"Brad?" I asked.

"Yup, checking up on me for the thousandth time today."

"Why?"

Miranda shrugged. "He just worries."

I wanted to ask her what about, but the fact that she didn't volunteer this made me feel like she didn't want to tell me.

Which made me feel like shit. "Oh. Well, you know, you were kinda late this morning. My mom was pissed."

"I know. I slept at Brad's, and I didn't realize how much traffic I'd hit."

"No problem. Just leave earlier next time." I hated the words as they came out of my mouth. Like, obviously she needed to leave earlier.

Zander sat down holding a plate with a slice of pizza. "Lunch today sucks. This pizza looks like rubber." He took a bite. "Tastes like it, too."

"Why don't you just bring lunch?" I asked.

"Yeah, like my mom's making me lunch."

"Make it yourself."

"Dude, I'm just trying to get out of the house as quickly as possible in the morning."

"Okay. Make it the night before?"

Nory walked by our table, and I didn't hear what Zander said. She didn't look over at me. I had stopped assuming she would.

Then I glanced at the tables where the football team sat. They were a big, rambunctious group, laughing and stealing food off each other's trays. It looked less lonely over there.

"I think I'm going to sit at another table tomorrow," I said.

"Which one? You don't like this location?"

"I do, but I mean with Lex. And the guys from the football team."

Miranda stopped feeding me. Zander nearly choked on his pizza.

"You were invited to sit with them?" Zander asked.

"No."

"So you're just gonna demand that they let you sit there?"

"No. I'll ask. You should come, too."

"Harris, allow me to inform you about the dynamics of high school." Zander started pointing to random tables. "Over there are the jocks—who you want to sit with—then there are the band geeks, and next to them are the theater nerds, and behind them are the emo kids. If you turn your attention to the left, you'll see the popular students, followed by the rich assholes. Then there's us."

"And what are we?"

"I don't know, but we don't sit with the jocks."

"This isn't *Mean Girls*. I can sit wherever I want."

He looked at Miranda for backup. "Don't look at me," she said. "I go wherever Harris goes."

For a while, we were silent. I did feel bad, but moving to a new table was all about reinventing myself. Despite my first encounter with Lex, he didn't seem too horrible, and the only thing Zander actually seemed to know about him was that he was a jock. At every school in every town, people are terrified of jocks or assume they're babbling jerks. But my brother's a jock, and he's pretty decent, for the most part.

I broke the silence. "Dude, it's not a big deal. We can still hang on the weekends, and I'll see you in the halls. And you can still come with me tomorrow to the new table."

"No. I'll stay here with Yu-Gi-Oh! and Pokémon," he said, referring to the other two guys at the table, who were still playing with trading cards. They didn't look up. I wasn't even sure they knew we were there.

"Okay, well, let me know if you change your mind."

"I won't," Zander said, his eyes on his rubber pizza.

WHEEL OF FORTUNE
HAS THE ANSWER

AFTER I DECIDED TO MAKE THE SWITCH, I fought with the idea for the rest of the day and through the night. Trust me, I really did. It wasn't just some brash choice I made while chewing on my lunch. The jocks offered things that Zander couldn't, like proximity to girls and the chance to talk about sports. Mostly I wanted to make the change so I would be near people who could help with my fantasy football team. At least that was what I told myself.

"What's wrong, honey?" Mom asked. "You seem pretty out of it."

"Nothing. I'm fine." We were watching *Wheel of Fortune*, our nightly routine before the sitcoms aired.

"You know you can tell us anything."

"Yeah, nerd. What's your deal?" Ollie added.

"I'm just thinking about switching lunch tables."

"Wow. That's serious," my brother joked.

"You don't want to sit with Zander anymore?" Mom asked. "What happened?"

"Nothing happened. There's a table with some guys from

the football team who look pretty cool, and I thought I'd join them."

"Have you ever talked to any of them?"

"Yeah, this one kid, Lex. He opened the gate during the game so I could watch from the sideline."

Mom muted the TV. We hated when she did that. "Zander is a sweet kid. It'd be a shame to lose him as a friend. I think you're pushing him away too quickly. You did that to some nice kids in San Diego."

"Oh my God. I'm still going to be his friend. I just want to make more friends. Isn't that what you've been telling me to do?"

Dad decided to chime in. "I think it will be good for Harris to branch out. It can't hurt. I'm proud of him for putting himself out there."

I appreciated the sentiment, though "putting myself out there" sounded like I was going to advertise myself as the lonely disabled kid.

"Can you hand me my phone?" I asked.

Mom stood up from the couch and placed the cell phone in my lap. I made a few adjustments, and then I had a firm grip. I typed a message with my left thumb as fast as I could.

> **ME:** Am I an asshole for wanting to sit at a different table?

I didn't expect her to respond, but I needed a second opinion. *Wheel of Fortune* put up the final puzzle, and my mom and dad yelled random words at the TV. Did other parents watch evening television with their teenage sons? I think it was their way of making sure we didn't do drugs.

> **MIRANDA:** No way, dude. If you want to hang out with the jocks, then we'll fucking hang out with the jocks

> **ME:** But what if they say no?

> **MIRANDA:** That's not going to happen but if it does I'll just flash my boobs or something

> **MIRANDA:** I'm joking

A woman from Idaho won ten thousand dollars and a trip to Barbados. She missed the final puzzle for an extra hundred thousand. It was actually pretty easy, and she had most of the letters on the board already. The category was WHAT ARE YOU DOING? and the answer: FINDING MY WAY AROUND. The *R* was visible, and so were the *F*, *I*s, *N*s, and *D*s.

• • •

Even with all the noises in my room, I heard my cell phone vibrate on the cabinet next to my bed. Mom had just finished my nightly medical routine of a nebulizer treatment and cough assist.

"Can you check my phone?" I asked. Mom reached for it, the screen still lit. "Let me see it."

When you rely on other people the way I do, there's no such thing as privacy (which is why I usually deleted texts from Miranda, especially the one about her boobs). My mom unlocked the phone and read the message. "It's from Nory. She says, 'Sorry I forgot to text you. I was swamped after school. What did you have in mind for the project?'" Mom reread the message to herself like something didn't make sense. "What project?"

"A group physics project."

"Who else is in your group?"

"No one. Just us."

"You asked her?" She sounded surprised.

"No. We were paired."

"That's fun, honey."

"Can you just answer her, please?"

Mom readied her fingers. Or I should say, readied a single pointer finger. She was not a proficient texter.

"Tell her that I haven't really thought about it yet but we can talk in class tomorrow."

I waited while she typed the message. It was hard for me to understand how Nory could've been so busy. We barely had any homework. Did she participate in after-school activities? She didn't seem like the type . . . but I didn't really know her. Then I remembered she cooked dinner for her dad, but she hadn't sent me any pictures in a few days.

"Can I see what you sent?" Mom held the phone in front of my face. "You wrote *grass* instead of *class*."

"Oh. Autocorrect must've changed it."

"Mom, you gotta be careful. I need to sound somewhat smart."

"Sorry."

"It's fine. Did she answer?"

"No, not yet."

My teeth were brushed and my face was washed. Every

few minutes, Ollie stumbled into my room, half-awake yet unwilling to go to sleep. In less than a year, he would be in college, bothering the people in the dorm room next to his who were trying to get ready for bed. I wondered how long it would take them to realize that they needed to close their doors. That wasn't an option for me. My mom liked my door open in case I had an emergency, which meant anyone was free to come and go or walk past and see me naked.

The phone buzzed again.

"Ollie, can you help your brother answer that?" Mom asked. "I want to get cleaned up and throw on my pajamas."

Like I said, I got zero privacy. It was honestly a relief nobody sent me nudes.

"Someone named Nory says, 'Okay. We'll talk more in class tomorrow.' You wanna answer?"

"No."

LOCKERS HAVE MEMORIES

MIRANDA SPENT THE MAJORITY OF the next morning telling me about the wonderful date she'd gone on with her boyfriend. They were both sushi lovers. I couldn't have cared less about the whole thing, but I was happy she'd had a fun night, although I doubted that Brad had really found the only sushi restaurant in New Jersey that served authentic Japanese sushi.

She even showed me a nauseating number of photos of her and Brad with mouthfuls of eel rolls.

"It wasn't even that expensive," she said.

"Is that why he chose this place?"

She laughed like she thought I was just joking. I wasn't. "We split it. We always do."

"I thought you said he makes a lot of money. Shouldn't he always pay, then?"

"Maybe. But, you know, feminism and all that."

I decided not to touch that one. "Do you ever hang out with anyone else? You're always with me or Brad."

Miranda waved a hand. "Of course I have other friends,

but Brad likes it when I'm around, and I spend most days with you, so there's really no time to see anyone else."

I felt grateful, but also a little guilty. Did Miranda *want* to hang out with people other than Brad and me?

Mr. Wormhole stopped us at the door to homeroom. "Ms. Maszak wants to see you in her office before first period starts," he said.

I didn't argue. An excused absence from homeroom was fine with me.

"Empty hallways are so cool," I said to Miranda as we made our way to the office. "It makes me want to speed all the way to the end."

"Go for it," she dared.

I made sure nobody was walking in either direction, and then I took off full throttle. Miranda's footsteps pounded behind me on the linoleum floor, but I rounded a corner and there was no looking back.

"Wait for me, Evel Knievel!" she yelled.

I slowed to a stop and waited for her to catch up. Not a single person had seen us, but I was sure every homeroom we'd passed had heard the electric hum of my wheelchair. I hoped the students had thought it was a UFO attack.

"You really went for it," she said. We were both laughing, mostly at how slow Miranda was.

"I'm trying to get us in trouble. It feels like we're breaking some kind of rule being out here."

"Maybe the speed limit."

Miranda slowed down almost to a full stop and fixed her eyes on a row of lockers. All of our chaotic energy was suddenly gone.

"What's going on?" I asked.

Miranda extended her arm and touched the lock on one of the locker doors. "This used to be Kaylin's locker."

"Right. Your friend. Do you still talk to her?"

"No. She died."

"Oh. I'm sorry. I didn't know. Were you guys close?"

She nodded. "We were almost like sisters. She used to say we were partners in crime, and she was right. We did some stupid shit."

I wanted to ask how she had died, but I also wasn't sure Miranda was in the right headspace to tell me.

"Come on," I said. "Let's go see what the office wants."

We moved slowly and silently through the hallway until we reached the office. Miranda rejected my offer of another race, and she didn't want to guess what Ms. Maszak wanted. She'd totally shut down, never lifting her eyes from the worn floor.

For the first time, I wondered if Brad was right. Maybe Miranda shouldn't have been back at East Essex Central.

• • •

It turned out my laptop had finally arrived. We both noticed it sitting on the secretary's desk when we walked in, though after seeing it, I wished it wasn't for me.

"Ms. Maszak left this for you," the secretary said.

"Seriously? *This* is the laptop she ordered? It's archaic." The secretary had been around for a while, too; maybe that's why she didn't seem to realize the laptop was a relic.

Miranda attempted to pick it up. "And it's heavy. They couldn't find something lighter for me to carry around?"

"What am I supposed to do with this? Does it even work?"

Our endless questions annoyed the secretary enough for

her to put down her crossword puzzle. "Hon, you'll have to
ask Ms. Maszak. I'm not the one who bought the computer."

"Well, where is she?"

"She's in a meeting."

"What about Dr. Kenzing? She knows about the laptop."

"You need an appointment to speak with Dr. Kenzing."

The bell rang, and Miranda and I left with the cinder block
and the awful impending doom of telling my mom about this
later.

WHEN SHE SMILES AT YOU

NORY ABRUPTLY DROPPED ONTO HER lab stool. I tell you, that girl moved in the strangest ways. "I grabbed a copy of the rubric on my way to homeroom," she said. "We have the rest of the school year to work on the project."

"Oh, that's a relief. So we have some time to choose a topic?"

Nory smiled coyly. "Well, actually, I already thought of one."

"What?"

"Colors." She couldn't hold back her excitement.

I was a little more reluctant. "Colors?"

"Yeah. You already know a lot about them, so it should be pretty easy. All we have to do is make a video explaining the topic and create a mini textbook about it."

Embarrassingly enough, I actually had no clue about the physics behind colors. It all seemed too clinical. But I felt pressure to act like I knew what I was talking about. "I'm sure the physics of colors is in the syllabus," I said. "It's pretty basic."

Nory smiled. "It's not. I already checked."

So much for that. "Okay, then let's do it."

"Awesome. And who knows? Maybe along the way, you'll figure out my favorite color."

"You should just tell me now," I said, as casually as possible, "so we'll know if we'll make a good team."

Nory scrunched her eyebrows. "I don't see how my favorite color would affect the way we work together."

"Let's say you're green, or blue, like me—then we'll have a similar work ethic. But if you're on the other end of the color wheel, we might butt heads."

"And how did you form this theory?"

"Years of observation. And research."

"I think not knowing makes it more exciting. Who knows how this thing will turn out?"

Mrs. Ivavych came over to our table. "What did you decide on?"

"Colors," Nory cheerfully announced.

"No, that's not enough. Combine it with light. The physics of color and light go together."

We had no choice, so we smiled and nodded. Then Mrs. Ivavych left us alone.

"You guys should make a schedule of when you'll meet to work on the project," Miranda said.

I glared at her. She went right back to playing on her phone, or more likely texting Brad.

"Good idea." Nory beamed.

Her enthusiasm flustered me. Was she excited about hanging out or just about planning the meetups? She did have a datebook, for crying out loud.

"I'm usually free on Tuesdays and Thursdays and Sundays," she said.

"On Sundays I watch football."

"Oh, well, um . . ." Nory flipped through the pages of her datebook.

Miranda whispered in my ear, "A girl is trying to spend time with you."

"Never mind," I said. "We can watch the games while we work, if you want."

"Sure. That sounds good."

Then Nory smiled at me. Sweet dear Lord, for the first time, she really smiled at me.

"So we'll meet after school if we need to, but definitely every Sunday at my house." Nory scribbled in her datebook. "My dad loves football."

"I can't get into your house."

She looked at my wheelchair. "Sorry, I forgot. Your house?"

"Cool."

Mrs. Ivavych started lecturing, and for the next fifty minutes, I sat between two girls. One was my coach, and the other had smiled at me.

CHANGE STARTS WITH LUNCH

ZANDER WAS ALREADY SITTING at the usual table, watching me drive deliberately toward the back of the cafeteria. The jocks had pushed together two tables to make room for almost the entire starting lineup of the football team.

The lunch period had just started, but their party was already in full swing. Girls were on guys' laps, and food was being thrown as much as it was being eaten.

"Can I sit here?" I asked Lex. "With you guys?"

It was noisy—people were coming and going, and Lex was pulling over extra chairs—but I thought he'd heard me, though he didn't respond right away. Then he looked at Miranda. "Yeah, man. Absolutely."

He pushed a chair away so I could pull in with my wheelchair. So far, everything was okay. Nobody stopped to figure out why the disabled kid and his nurse were sitting next to them. There were only a couple of awkward smiles as other students shifted over to make more space.

"I don't think we've met." Lex extended his hand to Miranda. "I'm Lex."

"Miranda." She briefly returned the handshake.

"So you help out with my buddy here?"

"Yup."

"Lucky him. And now us. I guess you two will be joining our table . . . or is this a special visit?"

"No," I said as Miranda began to unpack my lunch. "I thought we'd sit with you guys, if that's cool. I'm a big football fan." I know. I sounded like a loser.

"No problem. Stay as long as you want. The more the merrier. Right?"

I knew Lex would be chill. Jocks are not the stereotypical assholes we see in movies. Sure, they can be cocky, but I'm used to handling their testosterone-filled baggage. I live with Ollie, and in my head, I'm an athlete, too. My body just didn't get the memo.

"Bro, Coach is such a dick." A new guy claimed the seat between Lex and me. Everything was so fast and exciting. I felt zero regret about changing tables. "He said I can't miss practice to go on the field trip."

"Field trip?" I asked. It seemed like an unusual thing for an upperclassman to worry about. "Aren't you a senior?"

"Yeah. So?"

"Nothing. Field trips are awesome."

"Where are you going again?" Lex asked.

"To a museum with my history class."

"You should talk to Coach again, Jameer," Lex said. "He's usually pretty understanding."

"Not this time. He's made up his mind. Like, bro, I'm trying to become an archaeologist."

One of the other guys chimed in. "Jameer, can you even spell *archaeologist*?"

"Man, screw you. I'm gonna get some food."

In between all the commotion, Miranda gave me bites of my sandwich while she nibbled on her PB&J. I liked that both of us always had the same lunch. A deli sandwich every day might have been monotonous, but at least I knew what to expect.

The more I thought about it, though, I didn't *want* to know what to expect anymore. Knowing what came next was starting to feel stale, and being around Miranda had gotten me used to the unexpected. I wanted to change, and that started with switching lunch tables and not eating the same sandwich every day.

"Harris, you just moved here?" Lex asked. He was eating from a plastic grocery bag containing a bagel with cream cheese, Gatorade, chips, a ton of carrots, an orange, and a few Oreos. It was like the clown car of lunch bags.

"Yup. From San Diego." I wanted to ask how he knew my name.

"Sick. I hear there are some hot girls out there."

"I guess—"

"Speaking of hot girls . . ." Lex turned toward Miranda. "Did you move here with Harris?"

"Easy there, Lex," Miranda said. "I have a boyfriend. And no. I'm from here. I graduated from East Essex a few years ago, actually."

"No way. I'd love to hear more about that sometime." Lex awkwardly winked at Miranda, then got distracted by some of his friends arguing over who knows what, which gave me some time to eat. I'm not particularly gifted at eating and talking. I'd be horrible at business dinners.

"We don't have to sit here if you're uncomfortable," I whispered to Miranda.

"Dude, I don't care. These football players are just like the guys I graduated with. Besides, they seem to like you."

"Maybe. Do you see Zander?"

She turned around in her chair to scan the room. "It doesn't look like he's at the table anymore. But guess who's looking right at you?"

"Who?"

"Nory. She's just staring, not even eating. It's kinda weird."

"Well, don't stare back."

Miranda turned to face me. "Jeez. Chill. You should be happy. Your plan to get her attention is working."

"That's not why I'm sitting here."

"You're lucky, dude," a guy next to Lex said to me. "I wish I had someone to feed me."

"Jet, you don't need that," Lex said. "Have you looked in a mirror? You have no problem putting food in your mouth."

"Your name is Jet?" I asked.

"It's a nickname."

"An ironic one," Jameer said, sitting back down again. "He's the slowest guy on the team—that's why I've gotta work so hard during games."

"What are you talking about?" Jet asked. "I saved your ass twice on Friday."

"Jet's right," I said. "He might not be the quickest left tackle, but Jameer, you have no idea how to cut inside."

"Oh, shit," the table said in unison.

"What the hell do you know about football?" Jameer asked.

"I know that if the defensive end contains, you panic and try to dance around in the backfield but end up losing six yards."

Everyone laughed. Jameer, not so much. He was having
a rough day, so maybe I should have laid off, but I was show-
casing my worth to the table.

"Don't laugh, Jet," I said. "Did you know the offense runs
a zone-blocking scheme? Because it doesn't seem like you do."

Jameer was amazed by my scouting report. "You can tell
all this from watching one game?"

"Yup."

"You ever play?"

"No. I just watch."

The guys shifted closer. "What else did you notice?"

And I told them.

SPEAK UP

"HARRIS, YOU KILLED IT AT LUNCH TODAY," Miranda said. She was practically sitting backward in the car so she could see me. It seemed she'd forgotten about passing Kaylin's locker earlier in the day. "You were cool and confident. I'm proud of you, dude."

"Thanks. I tried. I'm not sure where any of it came from."

"It was all you. I had no doubt the football team would think you were a cool guy, because you are. I knew it the second I met you."

"Oh, right. Today you sat at a new table," Mom said. "Sounds like it went well."

"Yup. Lex had no problem with me being there, and he introduced me to some of the other players. A guy named Jameer, who's the running back, and Jet, who plays offensive line. Also Kendall and Vin, who are on defense. There were a bunch of other players, too, and their girlfriends, but I didn't really talk to them."

"And they seem like nice guys?"

"I think so. What do you think, Miranda?"

"I mean, they didn't make fun of Harris, if that's what you're asking. But I'll kick their asses if they do."

Mom laughed. "All right. As long as you're on top of it."

I knew I'd be capable of handling myself around the football team. Sports was my middle name . . . sort of. The point is that my parents had raised me to stick up for myself.

"Is Dad going to be home for dinner?" I asked. "Vin's parents have season tickets for the Giants. I want to ask Dad if we could go to a game sometime."

"Dad has to work late again today."

"That's the third time this week."

"His new boss has him meeting clients tonight."

"He never missed dinner in San Diego."

"I know, but this is different. We all talked about it before the move, and everyone was on board because it was a great opportunity for Dad's career, Ollie's lacrosse, and a better school for you."

"Yeah, but I only agreed because Dad said nothing would change."

Mom ignored me, because she knew the truth was that everything had changed. Ollie and my dad were barely home, which meant she was alone for most of the day. Some families say they need breaks from each other, but not mine. We're at our best when everyone is together.

"Clare, if you're interested in getting a part-time job during the day to stay busy," Miranda said, "there are some cute stores in town that are always hiring."

"Thanks, but I need to be on call in case Harris needs something or you need a day off."

I understood that my mom sacrificed a lot because she

loved me, but I still felt guilty. Like, because of me, she wasn't able to live her own life. She always told me that's just what you do for your kids. Luckily, we didn't need the extra money. Some people weren't as fortunate.

"Anyway, would you like to have dinner with us, Miranda?" my mom asked. "I have chicken breasts in the slow cooker."

Miranda looked at me. "What do you think? Should I stay?"

I never wanted Miranda to leave, honestly, but I was beginning to worry that she had no life outside of Brad and me. Still, if she wanted to hang around, who was I to argue with her?

"If you want," I said.

"Great, I'll stay."

. . .

Mom finished preparing dinner while Miranda and I handled my after-school routine of using the bathroom and doing a breathing treatment. For the first time in a long time, all the pieces of my life felt like they were fitting into place. I had a nurse who was actually cool and normal and didn't treat me like I was contagious or an infant. My circle of friends was growing to the point that I could use the plural "friends."

"I like you," I said to Miranda.

"Is it because I'm holding your penis?" She was helping me in the bathroom.

"Um, no. I just think you're cool, and I like hanging out with you."

"Aww. I like hanging with you, too. Being with you doesn't feel like work. I feel like I'm with one of my friends."

"Same. It feels like we've known each other for longer than two weeks."

"Maybe we have. Maybe we were lovers in another life."

I recognized that it was a joke, but her choice of words almost made for a super embarrassing situation. Luckily, we finished up in the bathroom without incident.

Mom barged into my room halfway through my nebulizer. She was holding the school laptop.

"They gave this to you today?" she asked.

"Yeah. I was gonna tell you at dinner. It looks really crappy."

"No shit. I just tried to turn it on, and nothing happened. I plugged it in, thinking it was dead, and it still didn't turn on. Did Ms. Maszak give it to you?"

"She called me down to the office before homeroom, and the computer was sitting on the secretary's desk. I tried asking the secretary about it, but she had zero information."

I looked to Miranda for backup, but she stayed quiet. Sweat prickled my fingertips as I braced for my mom's explosion.

"And where was Ms. Maszak?" Mom asked. "Why wasn't she there?"

"I don't know. The secretary said she was in a meeting."

"Then you fucking sit there and wait, Harris."

"Why are you yelling at me? I'm not the one who bought a broken laptop. And I couldn't wait around for Ms. Maszak. The bell rang, and I had to get to first period!" I tried to yell back, but the oxygen mask covering my face made that kind of difficult.

"You should've known better than to accept this. Anyone can see it's not going to work. Okay? And before you left school, you should've found Ms. Maszak and asked her what the hell she was thinking."

"I'm sorry," I said. "I'll talk to her tomorrow."

Mom started to cool down, but she was still pissed. "This is your education being affected. Remember that."

"I can still do my homework. It's not like I need the laptop right now."

"I know that, but Miranda or me or your dad or whoever has to sit with you and do it. You're almost a month into the school year and still can't do homework independently. It's frustrating."

Mom left the room, and it was a good thing she did, because I was all out of excuses for being an idiot. I also wasn't in the mood to be further humiliated in front of Miranda.

• • •

Once Ollie got home, my mom called us into the kitchen for dinner. It seemed like we'd moved on from the fight, and Ollie didn't have a clue, as usual. Not like it was a big deal. Mom freaks out daily. I think that's just what moms do.

Miranda ended up leaving before any food was served. She said Brad wanted her to come over before her night class. I wanted to remind her that she said she'd stay, but I also didn't want her around in case Mom blew up again. Sometimes my mom is a hard person to be around, and I was afraid a double dose would push even Miranda over the edge. I needed her long-term more than I needed her to feed me chicken that night.

After dinner, I thought about texting Lex or Jameer, but I was afraid. Of what, I didn't know. Instead, I sent a message to Zander asking if he wanted to come over on Saturday.

Before he responded, a text came from Nory.

> **NORY:** Why were you sitting with the football team?

ME: I just thought I'd meet some more new people

NORY: Oh. What about Zander?

ME: I invited him but he didn't want to come

ME: What did you have for dinner tonight? My mom made chicken . . . again

In a flash, a picture came through of a tortilla topped with zucchini, little tomatoes, corn, avocado, and something white on top that looked like cheese. I saved the image with all the others Nory had sent. At first I had saved the pictures just because the food looked tasty and I wanted to show my mom so she could attempt the recipes. But then it became an album all about Nory. I liked the idea of having a collection of her dishes. Maybe I would save enough to make a cookbook.

NORY: This is a vegetarian tostada my mom used to make. My dad loves it so I only had to cook one thing tonight

ME: Does it annoy you when you have to make two different things?

NORY: Not really. It's good practice and it makes my dad happy to have a steak every now and then

ME: You're a good daughter ☺ I don't think I'd be as considerate

ME: So are you free to come over Sunday and work on the project?

NORY: Yup :-)

I was going to answer, but then I remembered Miranda telling me I didn't always need to have the last word. And then Zander texted to accept my invite for Saturday. My weekend was booked for the first time in, well, ever.

PINK

THE VACUUM CLEANER was at full volume. Mom had already mopped the floors and dusted the assorted tchotchkes throughout the house. Once my mom got started, there was no stopping her.

"Mom, you don't have to clean," I said. "I'm just having a classmate over. It's not a big deal."

"Nory isn't a random classmate. And we haven't hosted her before, so I want to make a good impression."

"Oh my God. Shouldn't I be the one worrying about that? And you didn't bleach the whole house when Zander first came over."

"That was different."

"How?"

"Because Zander isn't a girl. You should want the place to look nice."

Ollie walked into the kitchen wearing his Virginia lacrosse sweatshirt. I swear he never took that thing off.

"Dude, do you own any other clothes?"

"Shut up. I'm going out."

Mom turned off the vacuum. "Where?"

"One of the guys on the team is having a barbecue. He lives around here, so I thought I'd check it out."

"You don't want to stay and meet Harris's friend?"

"No, I don't want to see another one of his nerd friends."

"Use Dad's car," Mom said. "Should you bring something to the barbecue?"

"No. Mom, stop. Nobody does that."

Ollie hurried out the door before she asked any more questions. Our mom could start a full-on investigation if she had the time, but she needed to shower and get dressed before Nory arrived. Ollie made a perfectly timed escape.

As soon as Mom stepped out of her bedroom, Nory rang the doorbell. No matter how long we lived in that house, I would never personally enter through the front door. It was the same way in San Diego. Both houses had three or four steps leading to the front door, so I always had to use a ramp in the garage. I thought it was weird not knowing how a guest experienced my own house. I would never see the same view.

Nory stood awkwardly at the door. A car drove away as soon as she was inside, and my mom was overly enthusiastic about the whole situation. She offered Nory a snack and a drink, both of which she declined, then gave her a tour of the house.

I really didn't know what to say. Having Nory inside my house was like seeing a teacher eating at a restaurant. You know them, but the person is out of context, and everything seems different, as if they live two separate lives.

Eventually, I said, "Did it take you a long time to get here?"

"Not really. My dad has to work today, and it was on his way."

She was tightly clenching the straps of her backpack. She could have been nervous, or maybe she was just anxious to finish working on our project so she could leave.

"Cool. So we can go in my room to work on the project, if you want, or—"

"No way," Mom said. "You guys can work at the kitchen table so Dad and I can keep an eye on you."

"Mom. Come on."

"The fact that you're in a wheelchair doesn't mean you're not capable of hooking up with Nory."

"Oh my God. Are you serious?"

Nory was laughing. "It's fine. We can work out here. I don't mind hanging with your parents."

She set up her laptop on the table. I pulled up next to her, but not too close.

"What kind of video do you think we should make?" Nory asked.

"You should make a music video," my mom answered for me. "That would be fun. Right?"

"A music video?" Nory sounded confused.

"Yeah. Harris writes songs all the time, and you could put in some cool light and color effects."

Nory looked at me. Her mouth twisted into a playful smirk. Sitting this close to her, I could see that she had green flecks in her eyes.

"I mean, I used to when I was a kid," I said. "I had a nurse who was convinced I could be the next Eminem. But I don't write songs anymore."

"Still, that might not be a bad idea. I'll be surprised if another group thinks to make a music video. Thanks for the suggestion, Clare."

"No problem. I'll be in the living room if you guys need anything."

Nory and I had been alone at the football game, but this was different, obviously. We could actually hear each other speak, for one thing, and it magnified the intimacy of every moment.

"I really like your mom," Nory said.

"Yeah, she's pretty cool. But I wish she would stay out of the project."

"Why? She had a great idea."

"I know, but after you leave, she'll obsess over the video and try to plan the whole thing."

"I loved doing school projects with my mom."

"Oh, I didn't mean it like that. I do like spending time with my mom." I was always saying the wrong thing to Nory. She didn't even have a mom; I should have been more sensitive.

"You're fine." Nory smiled. "It's okay if you're sometimes annoyed by your mom."

"Do you have a favorite memory of your mom?"

"I don't know if I have a favorite, but the year she got sick, we moved to New York to be closer to my grandparents so they could help out. I was supposed to start third grade, but I was terrified to leave my mom, so she homeschooled me. I loved every second of it."

"I'm sure she loved it, too. And you probably distracted her if she was in pain."

Nory's eyes glowed. "I like to think that. I was definitely the most well-behaved third grader in the universe. She would lie in bed, and I would listen to her read to me for hours."

"I know what you mean. When I was younger, I got sick

all the time, and my mom would never leave me alone in the hospital. She would read to me and bring math worksheets so I could stay on top of my schoolwork. I didn't mind, though. She was a great teacher."

"It sounds like both of our moms were pretty awesome."

Nory focused on her computer, and it looked like she was trying not to cry. Honest conversations are unpredictable. One minute you're talking about music videos and the next it's hospitals and dead moms. And in between those moments you see who a person really is. I liked the real Nory. A lot.

I attempted to lighten the mood. "So, what's your favorite color?"

Nory rested her chin in her hand. "You tell me."

"When I met you, I thought it was green, but my guess has changed a few times."

"So what is it now?"

"Maybe yellow? I always see you talking with people, and yellow is a social color."

Nory laughed. "Will any of your expertise be useful for this project?"

"Probably not. It's a different kind of science."

"How is it science that yellow is a social color?"

Nory was an enigma, but eventually, a color would fit. She was cheerful and outgoing, but also reserved. Perhaps yellow wasn't quite right. I made up my mind that Nory was pink: friendly but a bit secretive.

"It's called color psychology," I said, "and it can explain someone's personality based on their favorite color, or what color they wear the most, or how they feel when they look at certain colors. Stuff like that."

"Oh, so it's like astrology?"

"No, it's not like astrology at all." It wasn't the first time my obsession had been compared to that zodiac witchcraft.

"How is it different? They're both ways of guessing someone's personality."

"Yeah, but astrology pretends to know your future because of what month you were born. It's ridiculous."

"I really don't see the difference."

"Okay, tell me how you feel when you see something red," I said.

"I don't know." Nory shrugged. "I guess kind of energetic. A little worked up."

"Exactly, and you can't help it. Every color has associated emotions that can accentuate our personalities."

"Then what's your favorite color?"

"You want to know mine, but I'm not allowed to know yours?"

"Yes."

I had Nory's undivided attention, so I played along. I was sure any other girl wouldn't care, but Nory wasn't like any other girl I knew. The volume on the living room TV had been lowered to a murmur. My parents were listening to our conversation, or at least my mom was.

"Blue," I told her.

"So, what, that means you're a really chill dude or something?"

"Sort of. It means I'm trustworthy."

"Your astrological sign would probably say the same thing," Nory said with a smile. "Anyway, we better get started on this project, since it seems like we'll be starting from scratch."

She was still smiling, and the green flecks in her eyes seemed brighter. I didn't need to be an expert in color psychology to predict the effect that had on me.

. . .

I wanted to watch the Giants game, but I couldn't make myself drive away from Nory, not even for a minute. Every time my dad clapped or shouted, I thought about taking a quick peek at the score, but then Nory started talking, and I felt perfectly comfortable sitting in the kitchen and listening.

We (by which I mean Nory) took notes on the different ways light interacts with an object: reflecting, refracting— sciencey stuff like that. In my head, I started writing a rap for the music video. Not that *refracting* has any good rhymes.

Nory's phone lit up. "My dad is on his way to get me."

"What's the background image on your phone?"

She flipped it around so I could see. "It's a famous cathedral in the city my mom was from."

I examined the two bell towers on either side of the cathedral. The building had sort of a pink hue. I wondered if that was why she'd chosen this particular shot. "Pretty cool. Where is it?"

"Mexico, in a city called Morelia."

"Oh, I didn't know you were Mexican."

"Yeah. I mean, my mom didn't really talk much about her childhood, so it never really seemed like a big deal. But it wasn't, like, a secret that she was from Mexico. She cooked a lot of Mexican dishes when I was little, and sometimes she spoke Spanish to me before bed, but I never really thought much about it until she was gone and it was too late to ask her my questions."

It seemed kind of sad to me, but Nory smiled as she said

it, letting me know she enjoyed talking about her mom, even if it *was* kind of sad. I realized that Nory and I were both trying to find ourselves. I mean, obviously, she had an entire heritage to unravel while I was just trying to figure out how to survive high school, so the stakes were pretty different. Still, it felt like a connection.

"Anyway, once she died, I started to be more curious about her, and my dad told me she was from Morelia. Unfortunately, he doesn't know much more than that—he said she didn't like to talk about her childhood, except to say that her parents died when she was young and that it was hard for her to assimilate here at first. But I've been trying to learn more about where she came from and the cuisine she might've grown up with."

"That's really cool. I'm sure your mom would love that you're taking an interest."

"I think so, too. But it's not just her. It feels like I'm also learning about myself."

After Nory left, I spent the rest of the day watching football and researching the city of Morelia. I also tried to brush up on my remedial Spanish in case there was ever an opportunity to impress her with a few lines. Apparently, the Giants beat the Dolphins 35–17. I barely paid attention to the game.

I LIKED IT WHEN
HER HAIR WAS DOWN

THE COLD WEATHER FORCED ME to start wearing a jacket, and being in a wheelchair makes putting on and taking off a coat a minor pain in the ass. I tried to fight it as long as I could, but my California body still hadn't adjusted to the frigid East Coast.

On the bright side, my jacket was actually pretty cool. My mom had bought me one of those North Face fleece zip-ups. Everyone at school seemed to have one.

Nory seemed to be the only girl who didn't take part in the trend. Miranda blended in with the rest of the cold teenagers, while Nory continued wearing jeans with nice blouses or sometimes sweaters. Occasionally she let her hair down, but mostly it was on top of her head in a messy bun or pulled back in a braid or ponytail.

Today her hair was down. "Hey, Nory." She was at her locker, putting away her books before lunch. "Are you going to the football game tonight?"

"Maybe. I have to ask if my dad can drive me. I'm not sure if he's working tonight."

"Well, if you need a ride, I can drive you."

"Really? Okay. I'll text you if I can go."

Jameer and Lex snuck up behind me. "Tell her she looks cute," Lex whispered.

"By the way, I think you look nice today."

Nory tucked a few strands of hair behind her ear. "Thanks." She rushed off into the mob of hungry students.

"You coming to lunch?" Jameer asked.

"Yeah. I have to do something first though. I'll be there in fifteen."

"All right. And you better be at the game tonight. You're our good luck charm, bro."

I tried to hide my smile. Every day I felt more and more like I was on the team. The guys asked for my advice and actually listened to my suggestions. They were never patronizing, so I knew Jameer really meant it. The team was on its longest winning streak in a decade, and I wasn't complaining if they believed I had some influence. It felt good to be a part of something.

. . .

Miranda and I were already running late to the bathroom. Thank God the school had an hour-long lunch. On certain days, my last morning class was on a different floor and on the opposite side of the building from the bathroom. It probably took five minutes to fight through the students and then another ten to actually use the bathroom. Then I had to take the elevator to the first floor. Add in the time I spent talking with the guys, and I only had maybe ten minutes of actual eating time.

We passed Ms. Maszak's office on the way to the cafeteria,

which reminded me that she supposedly had another laptop to give me.

"Let's stop by and pick it up now," I told Miranda.

She nodded and followed me into the office. "I just hope this one works. Clare Bear was pissed last time."

"Clare Bear?"

"Your mom. I gave her a cute nickname. It kinda fits."

This time, Ms. Maszak wasn't in a meeting. She hand-delivered the new laptop, and judging by the look on her face, my mom had finally gotten through to her.

"We put a rush on the order," Ms. Maszak said.

It had been three weeks since they'd given me the first laptop. "I don't think it was much of a rush," I mumbled.

"Please apologize to your mom and tell her we're investigating why the wrong computer was delivered."

Ms. Maszak was full of shit. The wrong computer was delivered because they had ordered the wrong computer.

"And what about training?" I asked. "My mom wants to make sure there will be training for my teachers and me."

"Absolutely. I'll schedule all of that for next week."

We were about to leave with the considerably lighter computer when Dr. Kenzing stepped out of her office. "Miranda?"

"Dr. Kenzing. Hey." Miranda took a step back.

"It is so fantastic to see you. I had no idea you were the former student who's helping Harris." Dr. Kenzing took in Miranda as if she couldn't believe she was standing in front of her. "You look great."

"Thanks. You look exactly the same."

Dr. Kenzing's smile turned wobbly, and then she burst into tears, which was pretty surprising—I'd been assuming she had no emotions since she told me her favorite color was beige.

With obvious reluctance, Miranda walked up to Dr. Kenzing and gave her a hug. Dr. Kenzing said Kaylin's name a few times—Miranda's best friend. That was all I could hear. The rest was inaudible, and Miranda never said a word.

"What was that about?" I asked Miranda after we'd walked away.

"Nothing. It's just . . . we hadn't seen each other since Kaylin—that's all."

But something told me that wasn't all—not by a long shot.

CLASSIC HIGH SCHOOL THINGS

ZANDER CAME HOME WITH ME after school so I could give him a ride to the game, and he'd agreed to stand on the sideline with me. The catch was that I had to promise we would hang near the concession stand during halftime so he could warm up.

We were finishing the chicken nuggets my mom had made when my phone buzzed. It was a text from Nory asking if I could still give her a ride.

"Nory wants to go to the game, but she needs a ride. Can we drive her?" I asked my mom.

"No. The game starts in half an hour. I'm not driving to the other side of town and back. She should've asked an hour ago."

"We were talking about it all day, Mom. And it doesn't matter if we're late. Nobody's taking attendance."

"Harris, it's dark out, and I'm still learning my way around here. We're not picking her up. I'm sorry."

"Nory's my neighbor," Zander said. "I can navigate us there."

Sometimes I doubted Zander, but I really appreciated his can-do attitude. Unfortunately, the effort got us nowhere. Mom just ignored him, which was something she often did when faced with a reasonable option.

"What if I ask Miranda to drive us? She could probably get us there with her eyes closed."

"Nobody drives the van except for me and Dad. You know that. Because if anything were to happen—"

"Mom, please," I begged. "You want me to make friends, right? Well, this is how I can make friends."

I was desperate. A girl wanted to hang out with me in the dark. I wasn't going to miss out on that because my mom was too nervous about driving down the street.

I sent a quick text to Miranda.

> **ME:** Hey. Can you give me a ride to the football game? Clare Bear is being Clare BEAR

> **MIRANDA:** On my way

• • •

Amazingly, Mom actually agreed to let Miranda drive Black Hawk. I tried not to be offended that she seemed more worried about something happening to the van than something happening to her second-born child, but mostly I was glad when she handed over the keys.

Contrary to my mom's belief, we were able to pick up Nory and arrive at the game before kickoff. This was mostly due to Miranda's aggressive driving. With her behind the wheel, I felt free, but also terrified and like I wished my mom was there. But most importantly, I felt like a teenager.

The night was slightly warmer than expected for October. The sky was cloudless and full of stars.

"Where do you guys want to sit?" Nory asked.

"Last time, we were able to go onto the track and watch from the sideline," I said.

"Oh, that's cool. Can you do it again?"

"Not sure. Lex Brockman let us in before, but I don't see him on the field yet."

Both teams were still coming out of the locker rooms. The three of us headed toward the bleachers with Miranda trailing behind.

Jameer spotted us and jogged over to open the gate. It was like the entire team knew that Harris Jacobus (plus guests) got VIP seating.

"Do you want me to stand with you?" Miranda asked.

"If you want. I think I'll be fine."

"Okay. I'll sit up in the bleachers so I can see if you need anything."

She understood that she should give me space, which I appreciated. But I thought about how eager she'd been to drop everything and drive us, even though she wasn't actually spending that much time with us. I hoped she didn't feel like every time I called she had to come running.

The Wombats took an early lead against some high school whose name was so long that their cheerleaders could barely fit it into a chant. Jameer was running like a madman, and Jet held steady at the line.

"The guys are killing it tonight," I said. "I think Lex already has over a hundred yards."

"Did you know Harris abandoned me to sit with him at lunch?" Zander asked Nory.

"I didn't abandon you," I said. "I just wanted to meet some more people. If I'd really abandoned you, then you wouldn't be standing next to me right now."

"Well, in that case, thanks for allowing me to be graced by your presence."

"I *am* from California, so you're welcome."

"Sorry, but the West Coast is the worst coast," Nory said.

"All right, what's so great about New Jersey?"

"Pizza, bagels, access to New York, annoying jughandles," Zander answered. "What does California offer?"

"Nice weather and hot girls—and guys," I added, with a nod toward Nory.

"Is that all?" Zander asked.

"Dude, that's all you need."

We all laughed, even Nory.

. . .

I held up my end of the bargain and went with Zander to the concession stand so he could defrost during halftime. The grass behind the bleachers was muddy from a rainstorm the night before, and my wheelchair jolted over every bump. Miranda had to put her hand behind my head just so it would stay up. My hand fell off the joystick a few times, too, but she always put it back quickly.

"See, Zander? We're still friends," I said. "I'm falling out of my wheelchair for you."

"Your chivalry is noted. Now, excuse me while I see a man about a bag of gummy worms."

"And I'm gonna use the bathroom," Nory said.

They left Miranda and me sinking into the mud behind the bleachers, where kids were taking sips out of suspicious-looking water bottles and throwing noisemakers at each other.

I realized I hadn't thought about colors all evening or whether I was blending with Zander and Nory and everyone else at the game. Our conversation flowed, and I felt as close to them as new friends can feel. I'd spent the rest of my attention trying not to think about how dirty my wheels were and the wrath I would surely face from my mom.

"Kaylin and I used to hang out behind these bleachers," Miranda said.

"Yeah, it's the place to be at games."

"Oh, I'm not talking about just football games. We would come back here to ditch class or a boring assembly." Her face lit up. "We should do that sometime!"

"Miranda, I'm not gonna skip class to sit under the bleachers in the freezing cold for no reason."

"I mean, we can do it when it gets warmer out." Then she tugged at my knit hat so it fully covered my ears. "It's a classic high school thing."

I didn't know how to answer. I chalked her suggestion up to the red side of her personality.

"You didn't have class tonight?"

"Nope."

"And you didn't want to spend Friday night with your boyfriend?"

"He's working on an important project and doesn't want me to distract him."

"Oh. Well, thanks again for taking us."

"No problem. This is a hell of a lot better than watching movies with my parents."

On cue, Zander returned, half the bag of gummy worms already eaten. "Hey, I heard some guys talking about a party after the game. Should we go?"

"A party? Where?"

"Don't know."

"How are we supposed to go if we don't know where it is?"

Nory walked back into our circle. "What are you guys talking about?"

"Zander said there's a party tonight, but he doesn't know where."

"Oh, it's probably at Tess Santoro's house. She has one every Friday."

"Do you ever go?" I asked.

"Not really. My dad likes me home before eleven."

The three of us decided that going to the party would be a waste of time and that the football game was a sufficient social outing for the weekend. We finished watching the game— well, listening to it—from behind the bleachers. It *was* warmer back there.

THERE HAD TO BE MORE

BY THE TIME EVERYONE WAS dropped off, it was almost ten o'clock, officially making it the latest night I'd ever spent without my parents. The previous record was probably no later than seven or eight, when my parents left to get a pizza on a Saturday night and I was home with Ollie . . . so I didn't think that counted.

But this time I was alone, driving on empty roads with Miranda and singing along to the radio. My mom had texted half a dozen times, and after the third "Are you okay?" I had given Miranda my phone.

"Something reeks," Miranda said.

"I know. It's my tires. They're all muddy from driving through the grass. My mom is going to kill me."

"No, she won't. We'll stop at my house, and I'll clean them off. My dad keeps a hose out front."

"I don't know. My wheelchair can't get wet."

"Dude, I'm not gonna soak your chair. I'll just spray the wheels and get the mud off."

It felt like we were doing something illegal. Maybe it was because of how dark it was outside or because everyone else was sleeping, but washing my tires in Miranda's driveway was the most exhilarating part of the night.

The water wasn't doing much. Chunks of mud were stuck in the treads, and eventually Miranda rummaged through her parents' garage and found a brush to scrape away the remaining pieces.

"Thanks, but you don't have to do this. It's not really a part of your job."

"Yes, it is. My job is to take care of you, and I think that involves returning you home not smelling like crap."

Miranda rinsed off her hands and the brush with the hose. We weren't saying anything, but neither of us rushed to get back in the car. Instead, our eyes locked on the clear sky. For a while, we just stared and tried to memorize the way it looked. At least, I did. I wanted to make sure I didn't forget a single detail.

"Why do you want to be a nurse, anyway?" I asked.

Miranda didn't answer immediately. She also didn't move at all. "I told you about my friend Kaylin?"

"Sort of. You mentioned her."

"I told you she died, right?"

I nodded.

"Kaylin and I started getting into trouble at school and going to parties," Miranda said.

"Okay . . ." I felt like I was missing something. Every teenager goes to parties.

"I don't mean local parties thrown by kids whose parents were out of town. I mean we went to parties at colleges or in sketchy neighborhoods near the city, almost every night. Kaylin's home life was kinda fucked up, and she liked to blow off steam."

"What do you mean?"

Miranda sighed. "Her mom had just married some guy, and he liked to go into Kaylin's bedroom while she was sleeping. Anyway, we would get drunk at parties and sometimes do drugs. Nothing serious, just weed. But one night, Kaylin tried heroin, and she overdosed."

"Oh, shit," I said. I don't know what I'd assumed happened to Kaylin—a car accident, maybe, although to be honest, I hadn't really thought about it. But a drug overdose was definitely not what I was expecting. "Were you at that party?"

Miranda paused. "No, I wasn't." Her voice sounded thick with guilt, and I wondered if she blamed herself for what had happened.

"After Kaylin died, the rest of the school year was a blur," Miranda said. "I graduated and left home. I started drinking and using drugs: pills, cocaine, whatever was available. I think I just wanted to be with her again. Eventually, I hit rock bottom, and I realized Kaylin would've wanted me to do something with my life. I got clean and decided I wanted to be a nurse. Maybe I can save someone else's life."

For a while, the only sound was the water dripping off my tires. "I'm sorry I made you tell that story," I said at last. "I didn't mean to upset you."

"It's fine." She snapped back to reality, quickly unlocked Black Hawk, and dropped the ramp. "Let's get you home. It's getting late."

I wanted to look at Miranda the same way as before, but

I couldn't. I kept picturing her hanging with God-knows-who and snorting God-knows-what so she could get closer to Kaylin.

Maybe she was a completely different person back then, scared and rebellious. But I couldn't stop thinking about how she'd pressured me to cheat and wanted to ditch class to hang out under the bleachers.

How much *had* she changed?

TELL THEM WHAT THEY WANT TO HEAR

"WHAT'S UP, PLAYA?" JAMEER SAID. He slapped me on the back and started eating from his bag lunch.

I told him I was chilling. That seemed like a cool response.

"Yo, I went to the museum yesterday," he told me. "Coach finally caved and let me miss practice."

"Nice. How was it?"

"Pretty cool, actually. You ever hear of a guy named Louis Leakey?"

"Yeah, he was an archaeologist, right?"

Jameer nodded. "There was a huge exhibit about him and the origins of the human species. I think I'm going to dress up as him for Halloween."

Who would've thought that I'd be sitting at the jock table and talking about the origins of humans? It kind of blew my mind.

"Can this Louis Leakey guy also bring up your yards per game?" Vin asked.

"Shut up. I had almost two hundred the last two games."

Vin flipped back his blond ponytail so it would be out

of his way while eating. He said it made him look tough on the field. I disagreed, but I didn't tell him. The dude could've eaten me *and* my wheelchair.

"Harris, why don't you ever come to our away games?" Vin asked.

"They're usually pretty far from here, and I can't drive."

"You should travel on the team bus with us."

"How would he get on?" Lex asked. "It doesn't have a lift."

"Oh, right. That's messed up."

"I could drive you," Miranda said. "If your mom gives us the van and I don't have class, I really wouldn't mind taking you. I think it'd be fun."

"I think that's a great idea." Lex practically spit his food across the table. "You should definitely come and watch us, Miranda. We could always use more cheerleaders."

"How many cheerleaders do you think it'll take to stop you from throwing two interceptions?" Miranda asked him.

The table lost it. "Damn, you want some gravy with that roast?" Jameer asked Lex.

"Whatever." Lex brushed off his teammates. "Harris, are you gonna come to an away game or what?"

"I don't know," I said nervously.

"I've already driven Black Hawk, and we did fine," Miranda told me.

"I don't think you're invited anymore," Lex half joked, although his face said he was still pretty mad.

Miranda rolled her eyes and kept her attention on me. "I wouldn't let anything bad happen to you or Black Hawk."

"You've only driven the van around town. There's no way my mom will let you drive it any farther, and she's not going to drive more than an hour to some random high school for a football game."

"That sucks," Vin said.

"Yeah, man, we'd love to have you on the sideline for every game," Jameer added. "We should ask Coach to get a bus with a lift for next season."

Everyone at the table nodded, which was great, except all of them were seniors and would have no say in what happened after graduation.

"Why are you in a wheelchair, anyway?" Lex asked.

For some reason, I was caught off guard by the question. Even though they had *just* been talking about my wheelchair, it felt weird to explain my disability to the jocks.

Before the silence grew too awkward, Miranda leaned forward. "Harris was in a huge dirt bike accident in California when he was a kid."

The way Miranda said it, I almost believed her myself. I gave her a side-eye, but then I realized maybe it didn't matter if they knew my real disability. They could all see I was in a wheelchair. Who cared about the details?

"Damn. How old were you?" Jameer asked.

"Eight or nine, I guess," I said. And it was a guess, because I honestly didn't know how old I was in this fictional world Miranda had created.

Everyone shifted their eyes to Miranda, as if they required her confirmation.

"Harris could've gone pro if it wasn't for the accident," she said.

"You poor thing," one of the girls said from the far end of the table.

As impressed as I was by Miranda's improv, I already

hated myself for lying. I didn't want to get any more tangled in it.

"I probably wouldn't have gone pro," I said.

"Harris is just being humble. I heard he was the youngest ever to win a race on the junior circuit."

Luckily, the bell rang, and everyone quickly lost interest. Like ants, they scattered out through the exits.

"What the hell was that?" I asked Miranda.

"I was just giving them what they want. Something cool and interesting. You're welcome."

I thought I was already cool and interesting—at least, that's what Miranda had been telling me. But maybe it wasn't actually true.

By the time last period rolled around, the story had already spread through the entire student body. Random girls and guys came up to me and offered varying degrees of awkward sympathy, all of which was happily accepted by Miranda.

One of my classmates retold the story to me as if I hadn't been there. Okay, technically I hadn't, but in his version, it was a BMX accident. I was shocked by the velocity of a good rumor.

RELATIONSHIPS ARE HARD

THE NEXT DAY, MRS. SPILT let us out of trigonometry fifteen minutes early. Most of the other students wandered the halls or escaped outside to vape or head off-campus for lunch. I preferred my private bathroom. It was like a secluded hideaway that no one except Miranda and me knew about.

My mom would've freaked if she'd found out that I liked to hang out in a bathroom, but honestly, it was pretty clean. I was the only daily occupant, and it wasn't like I hung out there a lot; on a typical day, I was in and out in ten minutes.

With time to spare before lunch, Miranda left me lying back in my chair. My wheelchair didn't tip just so I could pee; the thing was practically a La-Z-Boy recliner, minus the built-in cup holders and faux leather.

"You look like a king on his throne," Miranda said.

"I just need some hot girls to fan me and feed me grapes," I said.

"We're going to lunch. A hot girl will feed you then."

"Who? Am I training a new nurse?"

Miranda's cell phone buzzed three times in a row. She'd been getting texts all morning.

"Is that Brad?" I asked.

"Yeah. He's pissed today."

"Why?"

"He missed the deadline for his project, and apparently that's my fault."

"How? You stayed away like he asked." She had talked about that the night of the football game.

"I know, but he said he was worrying about me the whole time and couldn't focus."

Hearing about Miranda's relationship exhausted me. I could respect that having a boyfriend or girlfriend takes work, but this guy seemed flat-out needy and weird. You can't blame someone else because you didn't do your job. Like, what kind of asshole does that?

"How'd you guys meet? You and Brad?" I asked.

"A dating app."

"Really? I mean, I would think you'd be able to find a decent guy without the internet."

"You'd think that, but unfortunately, all guys suck." She grinned. "Well, maybe not *all* guys."

Miranda faced me. She ran her fingers through my hair. My body tingled as her nails scratched my head.

"Dude, your hair is so long," she said. "You need a haircut."

"I know. Usually my mom does it, but we haven't had much time. Our weekends have been packed."

"Oh, can I cut it? Please? I'm free Sunday morning."

"Sure, weirdo."

Noise began to echo through the hallway outside the

bathroom door. That was our cue to go to lunch, so Miranda sat me up and put on my backpack.

"Can I come over for dinner tonight?" Miranda asked as we walked to lunch. "Brad doesn't want me around so he can finish his project, and my parents aren't home."

"And you'd rather hang out with me than your friends?"

"You are one of my friends."

I blushed. "Okay, then I guess you can come over for dinner. I don't know what my mom is making, though."

Miranda cheered and pecked my cheek. "I have no doubt that Clare Bear has something good up her sleeve."

My phone buzzed, and Miranda grabbed it to see who was texting me. My cheek still tingled from her kiss.

"It's a text from Nory," Miranda said. "She asked if you wanna meet after school today to work on the physics project. Do you want me to tell her you're busy?"

Part of me wanted to hang with Nory. But Miranda had nowhere to be, and spending time with her required much less effort.

"Yeah," I said. "Just tell her we're meeting on Sunday anyway, so we should be good."

BE SPONTANEOUS

LATER THAT NIGHT, AFTER MIRANDA left to spend the night with her boyfriend, I hid in my bedroom to finish my homework . . . and to text Nory. I guess Miranda's extrovert skills were rubbing off on me.

I wanted Nory to be my girlfriend. I didn't know if that was just because she was the first girl I'd met at EEC or if we actually had a connection. I also didn't know what a relationship would look like for me, but having one before I graduated felt like a requirement. Like, in order to have a normal high school experience, I had to get a girlfriend, kiss her, and then eventually lose my virginity after prom.

ME: Should I start writing the chapter for light reflection and we can review this weekend?

NORY: Sure. I was actually just reading about infrared, so I'll start on that. Thought I'd get a little done since we couldn't meet

ME: Yeah, sorry. I was busy

NORY: No worries 😊 It gave me time to try a new recipe

ME: What'd you make?

NORY: Vegetarian meatballs made out of black beans and quinoa

ME: Did your dad eat them?

NORY: Yup! He had no idea they weren't meat

ME: Every time I think about meatballs it reminds me of when I had them in the hospital and they were crunchy 😟😕

NORY: That's so gross. Terrible hospital food is why I started cooking. I hated watching my mom eat that stuff

ME: You must have been the sweetest eight-year-old in the history of eight-year-olds

> **NORY:** Thanks ☺ Did your mom cook for you when you were sick?

> **ME:** Not when I was in the hospital. She didn't leave

> **NORY:** Well, next time you're sick I'll make you someing really delicious

> **ME:** Now I wish I was sick haha

> **NORY:** lol I didn't mean it like that

My mom barged into my room. "Is Nory still coming over on Sunday to work on your project?"

"Yeah, why?"

"Your dad has to attend a charity event for work. Families are invited."

"Is Ollie going?"

"No, he has some mandatory thing for the lacrosse team."

"Well, can't I just stay home? Nory and I really need to work on our project, and I don't want to miss the Giants game."

"I'm not leaving you home alone. Unless Miranda is available, you're coming with us."

I moaned; imagine how it feels to be fifteen and unable to hang out with a friend unless there's supervision. My mom was about to leave, then turned back around. "Ask Nory if she wants to come. Girls like a little spontaneity."

"Where is it?"

"An art gallery." Finally, she left my room.

I tried to come up with a smart way to tell Nory we'd be getting in the minivan to go stare at art with a bunch of investment bankers. It almost felt easier to ask Miranda to come over so my parents could go without us. But I didn't love the thought of Miranda hovering in the background of my study session with Nory.

> **ME:** So my dad's company is having an event at an art gallery on Sunday. I know we planned to work on the project, but it might be fun to go

> **NORY:** Ok! That sounds like fun. I'm down

I wanted to reply with something flirty, but my conscience told me I would just sound creepy. Another voice, which I recognized as Miranda's, told me to go for it.

> **ME:** Awesome! BTW I liked the sundress you were wearing today

> **NORY:** Thanks :)

PURPLE

MY MOM AGREED WITH MIRANDA—I needed a haircut. They woke me up early Sunday morning with the same smug look on their faces, which I really didn't appreciate. It was like they'd been planning this torture for weeks.

As it turned out, Miranda wouldn't have been available to hang out while Nory and I worked on our project anyway. Brad had already planned an afternoon date for the two of them. I told myself I wasn't bothered by this, and I mostly believed myself.

When we were growing up, my mom just gave Ollie and me buzz cuts in the garage. Ollie had to get his head shaved because he played sports and it was easier to put on a helmet that way. I followed along because I wanted to be exactly like him.

But after a few years, I began to hate the monthly haircut routine. It always happened on the weekend, when I just wanted to sleep in and play video games. On an average day, I could get dressed and into my chair in under an hour. Haircuts added another forty minutes, plus I was never allowed to choose the cut—my mom lacked the skills to do anything other than scrape my scalp with the clippers.

I groggily eyed Miranda. "You haven't seen my morning routine," I said.

She shook her head. "By the time I get here, you're already waiting for me in the car."

"Well, you're about to see me fully naked, so prepare yourself."

"I help you in the bathroom. What else is there to see?"

"My atrophied little body."

Mom huffed. "You don't have a little body. I can't even lift you anymore."

In the bathroom, Mom and Miranda transferred me onto a plastic chair they'd set up. We'd tried cutting my hair in my wheelchair, but it created a catastrophic mess, and sitting on the plastic chair wasn't so bad, apart from it hurting my butt.

Because of SMA, I lack enough muscle control to balance or hold myself up. My body is very floppy, and in my wheelchair, there are various well-hidden support pads to stop me from falling over. While I got my hair cut, keeping me upright was going to be Miranda's job.

"Place a hand in the front so I don't fall forward," I told Miranda. Her grip on my shoulders didn't feel secure enough.

"I've got you. You're not gonna fall."

"Okay, I just don't want to crack my head on the floor."

Mom covered me with a towel and a barber's smock and started the electric clippers.

"Actually," Miranda interrupted before the first cut, "do you mind if I do it? Harris and I were talking the other day, and I think I can style something he'll like."

The two switched places. Miranda changed the blade on the clippers to a less drastic number, and I breathed a sigh of relief.

Miranda started on the sides of my head. She buzzed off a little, then swapped the blade and buzzed a little more. It was like she was sculpting me. My back was facing the mirror, so I couldn't see the progress, but Miranda's look of intense concentration made for a certain amount of trust.

Besides, if I hated it, I could always ask my mom for the usual.

• • •

When Nory arrived, the first thing I noticed was that she was wearing the sundress I'd said I liked. Her hair was down, and the white spaghetti straps on her dress showed off her shoulders. I swore I smelled coconut.

"Nice haircut." Nory smiled. "I like it."

"Thanks. You look very nice, too."

Then we were just two teenagers awkwardly staring at each other while my parents and Miranda watched.

"Harris, why don't you go use the bathroom, and then we can leave," my mom said.

I would've argued that she didn't need to treat me like a child, but she asked Nory, too. I followed Miranda into the bathroom.

"Dude, I'm freaking out right now," I said.

"Why? You're gonna have a great time."

"Okay, but we'll be in the car together, which means she'll see my shoulder harness, and my head always flops around on drives."

"She already saw you in the car when we picked her up for the football game and when you drove her home from school."

"True, but the first time she mostly concentrated on giving my mom directions, and the second time it was dark outside, so she couldn't really see me. Also, is this a date?"

"What makes you think it's a date?"

"I don't know. You saw how she's dressed. Also, she smells like coconuts."

"Just because she put on a nice outfit and perfume doesn't make it a date." Miranda thought about it some more. "Or maybe it does." She laughed.

I couldn't pee. Besides being nervous, my bladder was empty, and I was too busy asking questions to concentrate on expelling anything from my body.

"What if we're alone and she wants me to kiss her?"

"Then do it."

"It's not like I can lean in and kiss her. And I've never kissed a girl, so I wouldn't even know what to do."

"Oh my God, Harris."

She grabbed my face and planted her lips hard on mine. It almost sent my head flying back, but Miranda held on, and her lips lingered. I imagined my eyes looked like they were popping out of their sockets. Hers were closed. She stepped away and wiped her lip gloss off the corner of my mouth with her thumb.

"There, you've kissed a girl," she said. "Not so hard, right? Just don't fall in love with me."

• • •

The gallery was about forty minutes south of where we lived. Earlier in the day, I'd asked my parents to behave and remember that we'd be with a non–family member. On trips to new places, including local destinations, they tended to argue about how to get there while the GPS was giving them step-by-step directions. Thankfully, they honored my request and kept the road rage and back seat driving to a minimum.

My mom and dad took the time they would've used to complain and used it to drill Nory with questions about her dream of owning a restaurant. Of course, Nory had it all planned out. She recently decided she would attend culinary school and help manage a restaurant after graduation. She would learn from the chef there and take some business classes.

I had no clue what I wanted to study in college or what career path to follow. Asking people about their favorite colors and then explaining what they meant probably wouldn't be very lucrative. I liked football, but breaking into sports was tough even for an able-bodied person.

Could I even go to college? Who would take care of me? Would my mom live in the dorm?

I should've been having these conversations with my parents, but small discussions always became a big deal in my family. My mom would do endless research about accessible colleges and nursing agencies, and she would definitely nag me to call advisers at those colleges even though I still had two and a half years of high school. Everything she'd do would be in my best interest, but sometimes I just wanted to stop overpreparing and be a teenager.

Outside the gallery were lines of mostly men in suits, many of them standing next to their wives, who were either holding a baby on one hip or chasing after toddlers. It was a sight to see, and all the kids made me even more nervous. Don't get me wrong: I have nothing against children, but they like to stare and ask questions about my wheelchair, and the parents always make the encounters awkward by pulling their children away or apologizing and flashing cringeworthy smiles of sympathy.

Kids are just curious, and I'm always happy to answer their questions. I think adults are curious, too, but society teaches us that it's wrong to ask those sorts of questions.

"Great to see you, Denis." My dad shook the hand of an older gentleman. "You finally get to meet my wife and son."

"Where's that lacrosse star of yours?" Denis asked.

Dad waved off the question. "He's out with some teammates. But this is my younger son, Harris, and his friend Nory. And this is my wife, Clare."

I've never understood why my dad works in finance. He doesn't have the look, that's for sure. He's a bigger bald guy with a biker-looking beard. Everyone else in his field is usually tall and skinny with slicked-back hair and oozing an overwhelming vibe of douchebaggery. That was the case that day as well.

Five minutes later, I was getting bored with the chitchat. "Can Nory and I head inside?"

Mom nodded without turning away from the conversation with my dad's boss.

We followed a group up a twisting ramp that led to a patio and the front door of the gallery. Everyone in front of us was moving so slowly that my hand got tired from holding the joystick up. There was a tight left turn and then a quick right, and I didn't have enough strength in my arm to keep driving.

The options were to stop and rest halfway, acting like I'd spotted something interesting, or ask Nory for help. I did a couple of quick calculations in my head. Mostly, I heard my mom's voice telling me that people are willing to help and I should just ask, blah blah blah.

"Hey, Nory," I called. She was almost at the top. "Can you help me the rest of the way? My hand is kind of tired."

Nory rushed back down the ramp. Her eyebrows were scrunched together like she was concerned but also confident that she knew what to do. I didn't need to say anything else.

She grabbed my right hand and pushed so my wheelchair turned. I made it the rest of the way myself.

On the first level of the gallery, there was a small room that spotlighted local artists. Some of the work was pretty good, and some of it was flat-out weird. Everyone ogled a sculpture of an ear of corn. Nory and I had no idea what it meant, and I was sure no one else did, either, but they all acted like it represented the way we treat farmers. *Or maybe the corn sculptor left a barbecue and felt inspired*, I wanted to say. It would be a lot easier if artists openly said what was running through their heads, but then there'd be no mystery or debate, and that would be bad for business.

"Is that a painting of SpongeBob?" I asked Nory.

We went over to the far end of the room to look at the framed cartoon. It wasn't very big, and honestly, it didn't do SpongeBob justice. He looked like he was on drugs, or maybe the artist was on drugs while painting it. Somebody was on drugs.

"I think it's saying how brainwashed we are by television," Nory said.

"I see. Or maybe SpongeBob had enough of working at the Krusty Krab and decided to fight the man by going on a hunger strike."

She laughed, and I smiled like I'd won the lottery.

The second floor had only a few pieces. I had once watched this movie where a dating coach told his client to take the lead in an art gallery. If your date lingers on a painting, don't stand next to them. Look at the art for a few seconds, then move on. I guess it makes them chase after you or tells them you're capable of enjoying the art on your own. Something like that.

I tried to keep that in mind, but it was tricky driving my wheelchair with so many people packed into the building. At one point, though, Nory did linger on a painting for a pretty long time. I had already made a full sweep around the room before she moved.

When I came back to her, she was just staring, head tipped back, barely blinking. I looked with her.

"This is a portrait of José María Morelos," she told me. "The city my mom was from is named after him."

"Do you ever wish your mom was around so you could ask her questions?" I caught myself. "Sorry, that was a dumb question."

"No, it's fine. I mean, yeah, I'd obviously love to hear her stories, but it's also like this mysterious scavenger hunt. Every time I discover something new, it's exciting and makes me think of my mom."

We shared a smile and then moved on to the other artwork in the room, which I had already seen. But I was mostly paying attention to Nory, who talked about José María Morelos and how he was a revolutionary leader during the Mexican War of Independence and then executed for treason. I liked the way her hands and eyes told the story.

Eventually, we found my parents on the third floor, talking by the cocktail table. Barely anyone was looking at the art, and I thought the show was a charity event, but I didn't see anyone collecting money, either.

"Do you want to go walk around the town?" Nory asked.

A simple thing like going for a walk isn't so simple when you're in a wheelchair. I'd never been to that town before. It looked cool enough, with plenty of shops and restaurants, but I didn't know the curb cut situation or if the sidewalks were in good shape or if other buildings we might want to go in were accessible. There were a lot of variables to consider.

My mom saw my face. "You'll be fine. Just text me if you need anything." She handed Nory a credit card.

We explored the small downtown with surprisingly little trouble. A few times, my hand fell off the joystick, but Nory never flinched and quickly picked it up. There were stores I couldn't get into, so we skipped those, and I think Nory might have flipped her middle finger at one of them.

Then she asked a question that scared the hell out of me. We were circling back toward the art gallery when she said, "I'm kind of hungry. Do you want to get something to eat?"

Only a handful of people had fed me: my mom, my dad, nurses, and Ollie. I wasn't sure if Nory knew what she was getting herself into, and I didn't want to remind her.

"Yeah, sure," I said as casually as I could manage, trying to pretend that nothing was wrong with me and I was just a guy about to have lunch with a beautiful girl.

Since we were dressed up (and since we had Mom and Dad's credit card), we chose a nicer-looking restaurant near the center of the downtown. The hostess sat us near the window, which was kind of romantic. As soon as we were seated, Nory took the cloth napkin off the table and placed it in my lap without me even asking.

I started to feel a little more comfortable. Nory didn't seem to mind the prospect of feeding me. I was probably making everything a bigger deal in my head. I scanned the menu to find something easy to eat.

"Are you having fun?" I asked.

Nory gave me a playful smile. "I am now."

I felt my cheeks get hot and my brain turn to putty. I tried to think of something cool to say, but I had nothing. Luckily, a waiter came by our table to pour water and provided a distraction from my failed attempt at flirting. Nory lifted my glass to my mouth so I could take a sip from the straw.

"Do you have glitter on your eyes?" I asked after she set my water back down.

"Oh, yeah." She laughed. "It makes me feel like a fairy."

"I like it. You look cute."

The waiter came back just then. I wondered who was blushing more, me or Nory. I ordered crab cakes, and Nory chose pasta.

"Aren't you vegan?" I asked. "The pasta has cheese on it."

"Oh, not anymore. I couldn't live without dairy, so I guess I'm just vegetarian now. Actually, I started eating some fish, too, so maybe I'm pescatarian?"

"When you become a chef, do you think it'll be hard to cook meat if you never eat it?"

"Not really. I mean, I used to eat meat, so I think I'll be fine as long as I understand the flavors. Recently, I've been cooking some of my mom's recipes, like her pork enchiladas. My dad said mine are close, so I'm pretty sure I can get it right eventually, even if I don't ever eat it myself."

"Do you put red or green sauce on your enchiladas?" I asked. "Green is my favorite when I order them at restaurants."

Nory giggled. "It's called verde. And that's my favorite,

too. It's made with tomatillos. That's what makes it green."

I was trying to be present in the conversation, but I was so nervous about Nory feeding me that I could barely pay attention, and I knew it was making things awkward. My palms were sweating. I'd never had to actually *ask* someone to feed me. I didn't know if there was a correct way to phrase the question without sounding helpless.

"By the way, my dad bought a small camera we can use for our music video," Nory said.

"He didn't have to do that. We can use our phones."

"It's no problem, and I think it'll come out better with a real cam—"

"You know you have to feed me, right?"

Nory grinned. "Duh."

And with just that one word, all my anxiety disappeared. I let out the breath I'd been holding and, for the first time that day, really enjoyed being with Nory. I even forgot there was a Giants game I was missing.

A few minutes later, our lunch arrived. Nory grabbed my fork and scooped up a bite of crab cake.

"I feel like I'm going to get our utensils mixed up," she said.

"That's fine, as long as you don't have cooties."

"Can I make the choo-choo train noise when I feed you?"

"Usually I'd say no, but for you, sure."

I chewed slowly to make sure I didn't choke, and I asked for extra sips of water. Nory was a natural. She didn't rush and gave me perfect-size bites. Only once did she accidentally stab her pasta with my fork, but we just laughed.

We had the best table along a row of windows that looked out over the quiet downtown and the museum in the distance. Occasionally, the clouds would part and a sliver of sunlight would show up on Nory's shoulders. I forced myself to remember all the small details; maybe one day I'd need to tell the story of our first date. Really, though, I just wanted to remember the feeling of being alone with her.

In that restaurant, we weren't a kid in a wheelchair and his friend. We were simply a boy and a girl, together.

"How's your lunch?" I asked Nory.

"It's actually really good. I wasn't sure if the zucchini would ruin the pesto, but it adds a nice texture."

"I love listening to you talk about food. I feel like you already know so much."

"I think you learn the most when you're passionate about something."

"Is that why you continued to cook after your mom died?"

"Sort of. I mean, yeah, cooking with my mom definitely got me passionate about food. After she died, cooking made me feel like she was still with me. Then my dad found her book of Mexican recipes tucked away in a kitchen drawer. I didn't even know she had a recipe book. I never saw her refer to it. She always just seemed to know how to make everything." Nory tried to force a smile, but her mind was somewhere else. "Even though I really don't know much about my mom's childhood or the Mexican side of my family, I do know that all of those recipes come with so much love and history. Cooking keeps me connected to that."

"I think that's awesome."

She smiled—genuinely this time—then nodded at my plate. "Mind if I try your crab cake?"

The thought of her sharing my food made me happier than it probably should have. "Help yourself."

Nory took a bite, and I waited for her assessment. An elderly couple sitting next to us smiled. I liked that people were seeing me out with a girl who wasn't my mom or my nurse. I imagined Nory and I driving to this small town every year, sitting at the same table and eating the same lunch.

"This is a really good crab cake," Nory said. "It's not dry, they seasoned it just right, and the aioli is perfectly smooth."

I laughed.

"What?"

"Nothing. It's just that you make the funniest face when you're tasting food."

"Really? That's embarrassing."

"No, it's adorable. Your nose gets all scrunched, and your eyes turn bright green."

"If you say so." She smiled. "Nobody's ever told me that before."

The waiter snuck up on us. "Can I offer you dessert?" he asked.

"I saw the table over there order a slice of chocolate cake," I said to Nory. "Want to split one of those?"

"Sure."

The waiter rushed away, and Nory smiled again. "I love cake," she said. "No other dessert will ever beat it."

"Agreed. In San Diego, we lived near a bakery that made a ridiculously good chocolate cake. We'll see if this one holds up."

"Tell me more about San Diego. Did you like it there?"

"Honestly, I don't really know—I didn't experience much of it. I spent most of my time in hospitals or recovering at home. The main attraction is the beach, but the beach isn't the easiest place to drive a wheelchair, and I couldn't ride a bike on the boardwalk, so I don't miss much about it."

"I'm sorry. Did you at least have friends to visit you?"

"Sort of. I only had one friend, but we almost never hung out outside of school."

"Why?"

"I'm not sure. I guess that was just our relationship—we needed each other at school."

"You know, our childhoods were very similar. Hospitals. Few friends. Dedicated to school."

"I guess we're two lonely nerds sharing our sad stories over lunch."

The waiter placed a huge slice of the three-layer chocolate cake on the table. A dollop of whipped cream and a mint leaf garnished the plate.

Nory immediately took a bite. "A little dry. But my cooties will probably make it taste better."

She fed me a piece off the same spoon. To me, it tasted really good, if not on the same level as the cake from San Diego.

I could feel my heart beating faster. "Is your favorite color purple?"

Nory rolled her eyes, but she still smiled. "Today, my favorite color is whatever you want it to be." She attempted to wink, but she wasn't very good at it. It was the cutest thing I'd ever seen.

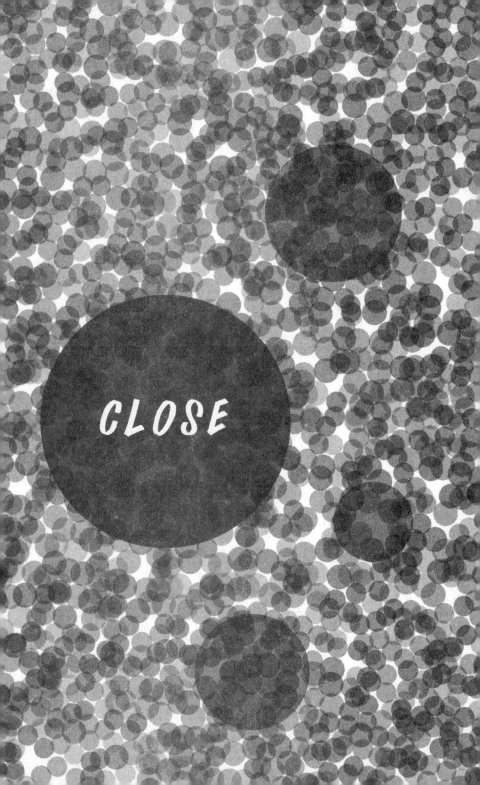

CLOSE

HOW TO KNOW IF IT'S A DATE

AT OUR LOCKERS THE NEXT MORNING, Nory snuck up from the side, gave me a quick hug, and then disappeared after getting her notebooks.

As soon as I'd woken up that morning, I couldn't wait to get to school and see her. I thought for sure she would start acting different in person after our day together. And I guess a hug was progress, but why was she always so rushed? We were going to the same homeroom. Was it ridiculous for me to think we could at least walk together in the hallway now? Compared to feeding me, that didn't seem like too big of a deal.

Zander saw the entire brief encounter. He raced over with a goofy grin. "Did Nory just hug you?"

"Yeah." I didn't want to give him much if there really wasn't much to give.

"And? I mean, how did that happen?"

"We hung out together yesterday. At an art museum. And then we went out to a restaurant."

"You went on a *date* with Nory?" Eyes wide with excitement, Zander looked at Miranda for confirmation.

"It's true," she said. "She wore a dress and perfume—the whole nine yards."

"Hold up." Zander took a breath. "Let me get this straight. You and Nory went on a date, and I'm the last to hear about it? I don't know if I should be proud or offended."

"Well, I don't know if it even *was* a date," I said.

"What do you mean, you don't know if it was a date? I thought you said you went to an art gallery and then out to eat."

"We did, but my parents were there, so I don't think it really counts."

"Your parents weren't at the restaurant," Miranda chimed in. "You told me you and Nory went out to eat alone."

For some reason I blushed. "We did. But that doesn't mean it was a date."

"You shared a dessert," Miranda prompted. I was starting to regret telling her anything.

Zander's eyes got even bigger. "That sounds like a date to me."

"How would you know?"

"*Mean Girls* isn't the only film I've seen."

The three of us headed toward my homeroom. Zander's was in the opposite direction, but I don't think he cared if he was late. Not if I kept spilling details of my weekend to him, which I didn't mind doing. I liked the idea of someone passing by and overhearing my romantic adventure.

"Did you kiss?" Zander asked.

I just kept driving. Even if I had kissed Nory, it was none of his business.

Zander jumped in front of my wheelchair and pressed the off button, sending a wave of students crashing into the back of me. "Go around," he told them. He got really serious. "Harris, this is critical: Did you or did you not kiss Nory Fischer?"

I sighed. "No. I didn't."

Again, Zander looked at Miranda, who shrugged. "Oof," Zander said. "Then I'm sorry to say, it wasn't a date."

Even though I'd just been arguing that it probably wasn't a date, hearing Zander say it wasn't made me realize how much I wanted it to be one. "What are you talking about? You said it had all the other date variables."

"Right. But it didn't have *the* date variable, which is a kiss. Every successful rom-com date ends with a kiss. And it doesn't have to be lip action. A simple peck on the cheek will do."

"What do you think, Miranda?" I asked.

"Don't ask me. I haven't been on a lot of dates, but most of them ended with sex."

I was sort of shocked that she said that, though I wasn't sure if it was because I judged her for having sex on first dates or because I thought it was weird that she was telling a couple of teenagers about her sex life.

Zander side-eyed me. "We didn't have sex, either," I told him.

As much as I hated to admit it, Zander might have been on to something. Nory and I might have had a great time, but there was no clarity. Maybe that was why she was still acting distant—maybe she also didn't know what the day had meant or where we should go from there.

I needed to figure out a way to tell Nory that I thought it was a date. And if she said she thought it was, too, I needed to make it official and kiss her.

COMEBACK KING

"FLORIDA STATE?" LEX ASKED.

"The Seminoles. That's too easy," Jameer answered. "Arizona?"

"Wildcats," I said.

The lunch period was moving pretty slowly. The team's winning streak hadn't ended, so there wasn't any fighting or roasting of whoever'd dropped a pass or missed a tackle. Since we had nothing to discuss and this wasn't the sort of group that talked about tests or homework, we resorted to playing a game: naming a college and then trying to remember its mascot. Useless trivia made time move faster, and as a bonus, it distracted me from obsessing over not having kissed Nory.

"Oh, I've got one," Miranda said. "Rutgers."

"Rutgers is the only college you could think of?" Jet asked.

"Be nice, man," Lex ordered. "Miranda wants to play, too. The answer is the Scarlet Knights. Now it's my turn."

"You want a hard one?" Miranda asked the table. "What was the original nickname for Stanford?"

"They're the Cardinal," Vin announced confidently. "But for some reason, their mascot is a tree. I don't know why."

"I asked what their *original* name was."

None of us knew the answer, not even me, and I had some heavy hitters up my sleeve. A bunch of the guys tried to guess without success; if anyone tried to take out their phone to cheat, they would've been verbally torn apart.

Miranda beamed. "Stanford's team was originally called the Indians. They changed it to Cardinal in the seventies." She looked at Vin. "And the tree is a redwood, which is commonly found in Northern California."

Lex laughed. "Damn, girl, you keep making me fall in love with you."

"Well, you're too late. I already have my man." Miranda wrapped her arm around my neck. I knew she was talking about Brad, but I liked that it made the guys jealous.

I heard Nory's goofy laugh echoing from the lunch line. I tried to turn my head to get a glimpse of her, but my head doesn't really turn, and I could only see her out of the corner of my eye. The classes we had together were starting to feel like not enough. I wanted to see her more, and texting just didn't cut it.

"You tap that yet?" Lex asked.

"Bro, we got a lady here," Jameer said. "You can't speak like that."

"I'm not a lady," Miranda informed them. "I know what guys think about."

Lex looked at me. "So?"

"We went on a date over the weekend," I said, not bothering to add that I wasn't entirely sure it really was a date. "But nothing happened."

"Are you coming to my Halloween party?"

"I guess. I didn't know about it until now. Why?"

"There will be tons of girls to talk to. Test out your moves."

"I don't need to test out my moves. I like Nory."

The truth was, I was deathly afraid of both drinking and drug use, thanks to dire warnings from my parents and doctors. And hearing about Miranda's past certainly didn't help, either. But Zander and I had agreed to experience a high school party just once. Maybe this could be it.

"Is your house accessible?" I asked Lex.

"Yeah, it's a one-story. Come."

Jameer randomly pointed to the backpack on my wheelchair. "What do you keep in there?"

"Stuff I need." I wasn't about to fill him in on the various medical devices I have on me at all times in case of an emergency. And I was sure he wouldn't want to know about the bottle I used to pee.

"Stuff like a parachute?"

"Why would there be a parachute in my backpack?"

"I don't know. In case you accidentally drive your wheelchair off a cliff."

I laughed because it was funny that Jameer could actually think I carried around a parachute wherever I went. But it was clear the guys didn't understand my disability or really even want to understand it. They just wanted a cool story, like Miranda said. She'd been right to lie to them.

"By the way, Harris, I keep forgetting to ask you something," Lex announced.

"What?"

"How do you take a shit?"

Miranda looked at me, and I knew she was wondering if I

wanted her to beat him up, but I had the perfect answer. "Well, I sit on the toilet, I take a shit, and then your sister comes over and wipes my ass."

I drove away while Miranda tried to keep up, but she was laughing hysterically, which slowed her down. I'm not embarrassed to say I told my family all about it at dinner. I had a feeling it would live forever as one of my greatest comebacks.

I DON'T KNOW
WHAT I DON'T KNOW

MIRANDA SUGGESTED THAT I CONVINCE my mom to let Nory and me work on our physics project in my bedroom based on the argument that she wasn't with me when we left the gallery and I didn't die. She agreed only if I left the door open. Such a typical parent request.

When Nory arrived, she gave me another hug, except this one lingered longer than the one at school, and I so badly wished I could raise my arms to hug her back, to feel her. I hoped she knew I was a great hugger in my mind.

I introduced her to Ollie, who only half cared and half kept watching the Giants game with my dad. Yup, I was missing another Giants game. I mean, I was going to have a girl in my bedroom. Any other hormone-fueled teenage boy would've done the same.

So then, there I was, in my bedroom, alone with Nory. Younger Harris would've been freaking out. And by younger Harris, I mean me from a month ago.

"You can put your laptop on my desk if you want," I told Nory.

She was admiring my blue walls and the random family photos I had on my shelves. "Do you mind if I sit on your bed? It looks super comfy."

I stuttered, "I—I guess not."

And before I could comprehend the fact that I had a girl in my room, I now had a girl on my bed. I silently thanked Miranda for the genius suggestion of working in here.

Nory flopped back on the bed. "Why is it moving?"

"It has air bubbles that inflate and deflate."

"That's awesome." She sat up and pulled her computer out of her backpack. "What part do you want to work on today?"

"Well, I had some free time this week, so I wrote the chapters on primary color interactions and light dispersion. I emailed them to you."

She tapped a few times on her laptop. "Oh, I see them now. Thanks so much."

"No worries. I just felt bad that we got nothing done last weekend."

"No, I think this looks great." Nory flipped through her notebook. "So, this puts us way ahead of schedule, then. All we have left is to write two more chapters and do the music video."

I wanted to be up on my bed with Nory, accidentally letting our feet touch, but I had to settle for just being near her. Any closer and I might have passed out. Not to mention that I was still trying to come up with a tactic to ask if last week was a date.

"Anyway, did you have fun last weekend?" I asked.

"Oh my gosh, yes. I was telling my dad all about it and how the art was all so weird. Thanks again for inviting me."

"I'm glad you came and had fun. I would've been so bored by myself."

Nory and I sat silently for what seemed like an eternity, but I'm positive it was less than a minute. I feverishly tried to think of something to say to restart the conversation. Then I remembered that Nory's favorite color was possibly green, which in my experience meant she'd like when people got to the point. And even if she wasn't green, I no longer wanted to pussyfoot around. I needed to know.

"Maybe we can do it again sometime," I said. "Go on another date, I mean."

And just like that, it was out there. Subtle, but out there.

Nory slowly looked up from her laptop. She smirked. "Was that a date?"

"Well, I mean, I guess. I sort of thought so. But then I was talking with Zander, and he said it wasn't a date because we didn't kiss, but everything he knows about life he learned from watching movies, so . . . Did . . . did *you* think it was a date?" I knew I was rambling. Her smile got to me, and maybe I was dizzy from her coconut perfume.

Nory slid off my bed and walked toward me. She was sort of laughing, but not in, like, a sexy, playful way. She was laughing because I was such a nerd, but so was she, which I liked.

But then there was a single knock on my open door, and my mom entered. I swear parents have a sixth sense of knowing when to interrupt their children. "Everything okay?"

"Yes," I said quickly, dismissing her.

"All right. Let me know if you need anything."

"Thanks, Clare," Nory said.

My mom had kind of ruined the mood, and Nory climbed up on my bed again as if nothing had been about to happen. I wanted to act as cool as her, but my mind wouldn't let me. I still had so many questions.

"Why don't you like being seen with me at school?" I asked.

"What do you mean?"

"I just mean that it's really easy to talk to you when we text or work on our project, but at school it feels like you ignore me sometimes."

Nory seemed to be thinking about what I'd said. I hated the silence.

"I'm sorry," I said. "I don't want to sound whiny."

"You don't. I get what you mean, and I'm sorry if you felt like I was ignoring you. I guess I'm just a pretty private person. The kids at our school like to spread rumors. I like to take things slow."

I knew exactly what she meant. The story of my disability had morphed so many times that I had lost track.

But then I started thinking about how Nory had no problem being seen with Kelvin. I mean, they ate lunch together most of the time, and she'd hugged him in homeroom, in front of everyone. And it wasn't some quick side hug like she'd given me in the hallway.

I wanted to ask why she could do those things with him but not me. But I chickened out. I didn't want to ruin the mood.

"We can take things slow," I said instead. "I don't mind."

She smiled at me, and everything felt all right.

"By the way, do you want to come to Lex's Halloween party with me?" I asked. "Zander is coming, too."

"Definitely. Halloween is my favorite holiday."

Later that night, I went to sleep still not knowing if my day with Nory had been a date. What I did know for certain was that my bed smelled like coconuts.

BLACK(OUT)

ZANDER ARRIVED AT MY HOUSE around six o'clock even though the party wouldn't start for another three hours. He said he wanted to pass out candy but his parents were taking his brothers trick-or-treating, so nobody would be home, and Halloween scared him and he didn't want to be alone. I don't know. Sometimes Zander rambled, making it hard to follow his train of thought.

I love Halloween. My wheelchair is actually a pretty useful prop and has inspired some awesome costumes. One year, my mom cut out and decorated pieces of cardboard to make a replica of the *Greased Lightning* car. We slipped that bad boy over me, and let me tell you, that costume got me a lot of candy.

But it seems that once you turn sixteen, Halloween loses most of its magic and becomes an excuse to throw a party and get drunk or eat a grotesque amount of chocolate. Luckily, Zander and I had yet to reach that milestone, and had spent the night before rummaging through the sale bin at Halloween City. The pickings were awfully slim, and we had to settle for a not-so-cool-looking Batman and Robin. I called dibs on

Batman—not that I really needed to. Zander was all about being Robin. I was thinking about asking Nory if she wanted me to get her a Catwoman costume, but I wasn't sure if that was taking things too fast. Couples costumes seemed like a big step.

Zander and I finished passing out candy with a little boy dressed as a cowboy who asked me where I got my Batmobile. Ollie walked past and noticed our costumes.

"Why are you two losers dressed up?" he asked.

"We're going to a party," I said.

"You two? A party? Is it at Chuck E. Cheese?"

"No. It's at Lex Brockman's house," Zander told him.

"Who the hell is Lex Brockman?"

"A senior on the football team," Zander answered. "You'd love him."

"You guys are going to a senior's house for a Halloween party?" Ollie turned to our mom. He had an expression of utter disbelief. "Did you know Harris and Zander are going to party with seniors from the football team?"

"Yes."

"And you have no problem with that?"

"The house is just down the street, and I think your brother deserves to have some fun. I don't think they're planning on staying for very long."

"Do you know what happens at high school parties, especially with seniors? There's alcohol and drugs and probably some creepy guy who graduated ten years ago. I should know—I'm a senior. You can't let Harris go to the party. He's not ready for all that."

"You don't drink and do drugs, do you?" our mom asked Ollie.

"Oh my God, Mom, no, I'm not an idiot. But kids at these parties do, and they're gonna try to make Harris join them."

"Dude, it's not like I can chug a beer by myself," I said. "Someone would have to lift the cup to my mouth. I don't think that's going to happen, and Zander and I already promised we'd make sure neither of us does anything stupid."

Ollie walked away after our dad gave us a thumbs-up, too.

• • •

Nory arrived at my house right before we were planning to head over to the party, which was about a half hour after it was supposed to start. Zander said we should be fashionably late. He saw that in one of his movies.

Nory's costume was a long-sleeved green leotard under a rainbow skirt, with sparkly wings strapped to her back. I liked that she didn't feel pressure to dress ultra-sexy, like I was sure most of the girls at the party would. She did her own thing.

We didn't hug, but Zander kept making eyes at her and me until I told him to cut it out. Almost every house on the street had spooky decorations and lines of children waiting for their plastic pumpkins to be filled. I was almost tempted to ask Zander and Nory if they wanted to ditch the party and join one of the packs. I didn't think anybody would call us out for being teenagers. Honestly, Zander could've passed for a tall sixth grader.

A few boys were hanging outside Lex's house when we arrived. All the lights were on inside, and I could see the silhouettes of people talking and dancing. Music was blasting, and the bass was rumbling down the whole driveway. Trick-or-treaters with their parents walked right on by. It didn't look like the type of house that had candy.

When I got to the front door, it was my worst nightmare, the reason I never went anywhere: steps. Two small but insurmountable brick steps led up to the porch.

Lex burst outside. He was wearing a very original costume: his football jersey. "Harris, you made it. Good to see you, bro."

"You told me your house is accessible."

"It is." He turned to point like some magical ramp was going to pop out of the ground. "Well, I mean, once you get inside, the house is only one level."

"Yeah, and how am I getting inside?"

Lex stared hard at the entrance. He for sure had been drinking for a while, and I couldn't tell if for a brief moment he'd forgotten what we were discussing or if he'd just realized his house had steps.

"I've got an idea," he said. He ran off toward the garage. "We are getting you into this party, even if me and your skinny friend have to carry your ass around all night."

"My name is Zander," he yelled, "and despite my sidekick costume, I'm not very strong!"

Nory looked around. "I'm going to head inside and check everything out. I'll see you guys in there."

I said okay and watched her walk up the steps and go inside.

"Why do you think Nory just bailed?" I asked Zander.

"I don't know. She probably wants to get her requests in to the DJ. That's the first thing I would do."

Or maybe she didn't want us entering together and starting rumors that we were a couple. Did that mean we weren't actually going to hang out together tonight? What was the point of going to a party with a girl if you didn't actually get to spend time with her? Once again, I wished I knew what Nory's favorite color was. Then I might have some clue as to what she was thinking.

Lex returned and placed a thin wooden board over the steps, supported by two long pieces of lumber. It was the sketchiest ramp I'd ever seen, and if my mom had been there, she wouldn't have let me get within three feet of it.

Lex jumped up and down on it to prove its sturdiness. The board bent under his weight, but less than I expected.

I took a long look at Zander, who shrugged as if to say, *What the hell.*

When my front wheels touched the board, it wobbled, and two guys stepped on it to hold everything in place. Somehow—with the help of God, I think—it didn't collapse. The fall would've been only a foot or so and probably wouldn't have done too much damage, but I was thrilled I didn't have to find out.

Driving up that ramp might have been the bravest thing I'd ever done, but for once, my wheelchair wasn't going to hold me back. In the end, though, the board lost the battle and suffered a considerable crack right down the middle.

"Don't worry," Lex said, "my dad has more in the garage. I'll put another out before you leave. Now, let's have some fun."

I heard Zander breathe a sigh of relief as we entered the foyer, which was between a dining room and a living room. Music poured out of the living room, playing from speakers connected to a MacBook, which was being controlled by some kid trying very hard to look like a DJ.

"Where do you want to go first?" I asked.

"I guess let's head to the kitchen. Maybe there's food."

We went down a narrow hallway that led directly to the back of the house. I was careful not to run over any feet, but it was hard to get couples making out to move out of the way, so in those cases I just hoped I didn't inflict too much pain.

"You want a potato chip?" Zander asked. He held one in front of my face.

"No, I'm kinda grossed out by everyone touching everything. Did you see Nory?"

"No, but you know what? This isn't much of a Halloween party. There aren't any decorations, and we've been here for almost a minute and I haven't heard 'Monster Mash.'"

"I don't think they're going to play 'Monster Mash.'"

A couple of guys from the football team pushed past us to reach a keg. Jameer was with them, wearing his Louis Leakey costume—a shirt, tie, and fedora. I was probably the only person who knew who he was.

"Hey, man. Can I get you a beer?" he asked.

"No, I'm good."

"What about your sidekick friend?"

"I'll take a Yoo-hoo, if there's any left," Zander told him.

Jameer shook his head and walked away.

"Why do you always make it weird?" I asked Zander.

"What? I like Yoo-hoo. I've never been to a party without it. At least, not a good party."

"How do you think they got all this alcohol, anyway?" Zander shrugged. "Do the parents buy it, or is every popular kid connected to an adult who's a bad influence?"

"I think it just appears. Like, the parents leave, and some

party god snaps his fingers, and voilà—beer."

A few girls I recognized from the lunch table walked into the living room. The music had gotten quieter, so I thought I'd be brave and mingle. Maybe I'd find Nory in the crowd. Whatever her favorite color was, I knew it was more social than mine.

"I'm gonna wander around," I said. "You want to come with?"

"No, I'll stay here by the food. I'll shine the Bat-Signal if I need you."

Most of the furniture had been pushed against the walls to make space for dancing. There was only a single couch in the middle of the room, occupied by the girls from the lunch table. Nory was still nowhere to be found. In that moment, I'd never felt so lonely, and I really wished I hadn't left Zander.

"Hey, Harris," one of the girls said. She was a cheerleader; I think her name was Laila. "I never see you at parties."

"Yeah. This is my first one ever."

"Well, you're so brave for coming out," another girl said. "Especially after your accident."

Laila gasped. "Oh, right, your accident. Are you still able to enjoy the circus?"

"Circus?" I asked. "Did someone tell you I'm in a wheelchair because of the circus?"

"Yeah. I heard about how you were at the circus with your family and you volunteered to hang from the trapeze, but you fell when the tiger walked across the tightrope."

The rumors had gone too far. I was going to tell them the truth, I swear, but then Lex appeared.

"I see you girls have met my man Harris!" he yelled like a drunk person. "You know he's a supergenius?"

"No, I'm not. I'm just regular smart."

"He's lying. But you want to know something else about him?" Lex leaned close to the girls to whisper. "He's never been kissed."

Laila and her friends giggled, stood up, and walked toward me.

"What are you doing? I'm fine."

"Come on, Batman. Don't you want to be kissed by Charlie's Angels?" Lex asked.

Never in a million years would I have guessed that's what the girls were dressed as, but the next thing I knew, I had girls on either side of me with their lips on my cheeks and another girl sitting on my lap. Lex snapped a picture with his phone, and then they all scattered.

I wasn't alone for long, though. As soon as I turned to find Zander, a girl almost fell into my wheelchair, then dropped onto the floor in front of me. She laughed hysterically, clearly wasted. I was getting tired of everyone being too drunk to have a conversation with. That was the main reason I avoided parties; it didn't make sense to me for people to get together, then become unable to speak clearly or remember what happened.

The drunk girl smiled up at me like . . . well, kind of like a psychopath. Mascara was running down her cheeks, which I assumed was part of her costume, since I'd seen her at the lunch table and her makeup always looked normal. She was wearing a short white dress and a tiara.

"I'm a sexy bride," she said.

"I can see that. You're really pulling it off."

She laughed and almost fell over again, even though she was already sitting on the floor. "Are you flirting with me, Harris?"

"Nope. I don't think so. Just pointing out that you do indeed look sexy." The girl crawled toward me until her chin was resting on my knee. I tried not to wet my pants. "So, what's your favorite color?"

"My favorite color? Well, right now I'm wearing pink panties." She laughed, hiccupped, and then got very serious and drunkenly slurred, "I saw this video where a guy was paralyzed and he was dying, but before he died, he told his friends he wanted to have sex. But, like, he didn't even know if he *could* have sex. So his friends brought him to Amsterdam or something and hired a prostitute to have sex with him, and he had sex, and then he died."

"Um, I'm not sure what the point of that story is. Are you asking if I can have sex or offering me a trip to Amsterdam?"

Her dilated puppy eyes looked back at me. Then my new friend fell backward, laughing uncontrollably. Eventually, I realized she wasn't going to stop, so I drove away.

"Bro, were you just talking to Tess Santoro?" Lex asked.

"I guess."

"You're on fire tonight. First Charlie's Angels, and then slutty bride."

"I think she's a sexy bride."

"Either way, dude. Keep talking to the ladies. They want you."

I was talking, but I didn't think any of them wanted me. And I didn't want them. I wanted Nory.

I was getting hot in my Batman costume, so I drove toward the kitchen to see if Zander wanted to leave. Then I saw Nory. She was in the dining room playing beer pong, which was pretty shocking. I hadn't pegged her as someone who would actually want to participate in that aspect of high school parties. Worse than that, she was with Kelvin.

Her arm was around him like we hadn't gone to the art gallery. Like I didn't know anything about who she was or who she wanted to be. Like we hadn't eaten chocolate cake off the same spoon. Like she hadn't almost kissed me.

At least I knew now. All the conversations and text messages had meant nothing. And her line about not wanting rumors about us to spread was clearly bullshit. She was okay with being seen with Kelvin, but not with me. I was used to being left behind, but this cut deeper than every other silly crush I'd ever had.

As I watched her with Kelvin, I realized something else, too: Nory Fischer's favorite color wasn't green or yellow or pink or purple. It was black, cold and forgetful of everything it absorbs.

All the party chatter and loud music blended together to form a mind-numbing roar, and I wanted it to stop. Back in my bedroom, I could forget about the person I would never be— that other person who could walk, take care of Nory, sweep her off her feet, and completely, freely do the things teenagers do. But I wasn't in my bedroom. Every public place presented another chance to get crushed and humiliated by the truth.

I wanted to get Zander and leave, but Nory won if I did that, and I couldn't let her get to me. Of course, that was easier said than done.

Just then, Lex waved me over to a couch where he was sitting with Jameer and the Charlie's Angels.

"There's my man!" Lex yelled. "You having a good time?"

"Pretty good, I guess."

"Nah, man. I would say very good. You got kissed, and you're dressed as freaking Batman. What else could you want?"

I was tempted to say Nory, but I wasn't sure that was even true anymore.

"Can I get you a drink?" Jameer asked. "You look thirsty."

"I'm all right. I shouldn't drink and drive."

Jameer laughed. "That's a good one, bro. But if you drive off a cliff, at least you've got a parachute in that backpack."

Before I could remind him that there wasn't actually a parachute in my backpack, Tess Santoro crashed into the group like an exploding bottle of tequila. "Does somebody wanna dance with me?"

"You're too drunk, Tess," Lex said. "I don't need you puking on my parents' carpet."

Tess waved him off and turned to the closest person—me. "How 'bout you, Harris? Sexy bride wants to dance with the Dark Knight."

Before I could spit out the words *No, thanks,* a new song came on, and Tess grabbed my hand and ran toward the dance floor. I followed her, but only because she would've yanked my arm out of its socket if I hadn't.

The bass thumped as Tess twisted and spun in front of me. All I could do was sort of bob my head to the beat, but I was satisfied with just feeling normal. Tess grabbed both of my hands and waved them up and down, and for a moment I understood what it was like to not be seen as disabled. I lost myself in the crappy music and Tess's overwhelming presence.

But then the music slowed, and Tess let go. In less than a second, it was over, and she was dancing with someone who could hold on to her.

Couples around me writhed and grinded on each other while I awkwardly tried not to watch. I saw Nory and Kelvin leave the beer pong table and head toward the part of the house where I assumed the bedrooms were.

All the energy and excitement I'd felt a minute before was knocked out of me. I couldn't bear to think about what Nory was doing at the back of the house with Kelvin. Things I would never be asked to do.

I sped toward the kitchen and found Zander hovering over a bowl of pretzels. The two bowls next to him that had been filled with chips and trail mix were empty.

"Get me a drink," I told him.

"They don't have any Yoo-hoo. I already checked the fridge in here and the one in the garage."

"No, I mean beer. Get me a beer."

Zander dropped the pretzel he was holding. "I thought we weren't drinking."

"I am now."

"Well, I'm not getting you a beer. We promised your parents we wouldn't drink."

"Fine. I'll ask one of my real friends."

I drove back to the living room and found Jameer still sitting on the couch. "I'll take that drink now."

"Hell, yeah, bro."

Jameer poured me a cup from a nearby keg and held it to my mouth. I chugged and immediately felt the buzz from the alcohol. Zander watched, completely mortified, from the opposite end of the room.

"Zander, come over!" I yelled. "Beer isn't that bad. I mean, it's gross, but not that bad."

He rushed over to me. "Harris, what are you doing?"

"I'm experiencing a party, like we said we would."

"Yeah, but that doesn't mean getting drunk."

"Jameer, pour him a drink," I ordered. "This loser is killing my buzz." It was hurtful but true. I didn't understand why Zander couldn't let loose.

Jameer offered Zander a cup, but he rejected it. "I think we should leave."

"Oh, man, that is so typical yellow." The volume of my voice was getting hard to control. "You say you like to have fun, but you don't. You're just insecure, and God forbid someone else has the spotlight."

"Spotlight? I've been eating pretzels in the kitchen. But whatever. If you want to make a fool of yourself, be my guest."

Zander walked away, and for a moment I felt alone, but then I remembered I had other friends. "Another!" I yelled. A crowd formed to watch the disabled kid get drunk.

I sped back onto the dance floor and spun in circles because I'd told everyone I could break-dance, and I guess in my drunken state, I thought doing donuts looked like I was spinning on my head. In my defense, I'd been told I had good rhythm.

At some point, I blacked out.

HOW TO LOSE A FRIEND

WHEN I WOKE UP, my face was in a bucket filled with puke.

One of the strangest feelings is the relative euphoria after a good puke session. You're exhausted, but you feel infinitely better than you did even just a few seconds earlier. I glanced up and saw someone who looked a lot like Miranda holding the bucket with one hand and my head with the other. We were outside, and the autumn breeze felt good against my clammy skin.

"What the hell happened?" I asked.

"You went berserk. That's what happened," Zander said. He was anxiously pacing behind Miranda.

"Well, how did I get here? Where am I?" I could barely speak. Every word burned my throat.

"We're in my backyard," Miranda said.

And then it hit me. She wasn't just a drunk illusion. She was really there.

"You fucking called Miranda?" I asked Zander.

"What else was I supposed to do? You were out of control and could barely drive your chair. Miranda was the only adult I knew who wouldn't kill you."

"Okay, let's all just chill for a sec," Miranda said.

Another wave of vomit came rushing out of me. I was angry and confused and honestly a little scared that a good portion of my memory of the night was gone. I'd become every cliché of every person who ever partied. I was everything I'd never wanted to be, and I had no idea if Nory had pushed me over the edge or if I'd somehow been trying to relate to Miranda's wild side.

"You know what? I'm out of here," Zander said. "I don't even know why I helped you after you ridiculed me in front of everyone at the party."

"You're just jealous because I have friends and you don't." I didn't know if I believed that, but my intoxicated brain did.

"Oh, really? You have friends?" Zander yelled. "All your so-called new friends would've let you sit in a pile of your own vomit!"

"Just get out of here!" I screamed, and Zander stormed off, not looking back.

I didn't need another person in my life who liked the color yellow. My mom was more than enough. And honestly, Zander had said he liked yellow and acted outgoing and friendly, but really he was just as scared as me. I couldn't deal with the contradiction.

A migraine pounded harder in my head with each passing second. I was too tired to move or think or regret anything I'd said. But I was able to notice the full moon glowing on Miranda's skin.

"You're so beautiful," I said.

"Thanks. I look a lot better when I'm not covered in your vomit. I guess you had a fun night."

"Why do you say that?"

"Because I always lost a friend after a fun night." I was too drunk to understand what she meant by that.

"Don't hate me. I'm sorry."

"I'm not your mom, dude. You'll have to answer to her later. I'm just trying to sober you up a little."

"How did I get here if I couldn't drive?" I asked. Another dry heave. I just wanted to die.

"I drove your chair down the sidewalk," Miranda said. "The entire way over here, you sang 'Monster Mash.'"

More vomit. The bucket was almost full. "How long have I been puking my guts out?"

"About twenty minutes. What the hell did you drink?" Miranda asked.

"A few beers. I didn't really want to, but Nory ditched me, and then I saw her with Kelvin, and she acted like we weren't even friends."

I threw my head back against my headrest. My mouth tasted like fermentation.

Before driving my chair and me the rest of the way to my house, Miranda took off my costume and put a clean sweatshirt on me. I caught glimpses of her under the spooky sky. She was in control.

"I love you," I slurred.

WAS I DIFFERENT? OR WAS I ME?

MIRANDA TRIED TO SNEAK ME INTO MY HOUSE, but she forgot that I wasn't a normal teenager. My parents weren't asleep. They were awake and waiting for me, because I needed them to get me in my bed and do my nighttime routine.

"What's wrong with him?" my mom asked. I was slumped over in my wheelchair.

Miranda tried to break the news as gracefully as possible. "Harris had a little too much to drink."

My mom gasped. The sound woke me right up and made me want to be anywhere in the world but there. "You've got to be kidding me. Harris, what the fuck were you thinking?"

"I'm sorry" were the only words I could mutter. I couldn't even look at my parents. "I'm sorry."

"How'd you get him home?" my dad asked Miranda. He was still calm, knowing nothing he could say or yell would change anything. "We didn't think you were going to the party with Harris."

"I didn't, but Zander called me when Harris couldn't drive."

"Well, that was smart of him," my mom said. "At least someone was using his brain."

My dad walked Miranda to the door. "Thanks for your help. We appreciate it."

Mom escorted me into my bedroom, and I braced for a lecture. "Who even gave you alcohol?"

"Jameer. He's on the football team. He's my friend."

She sighed. "I still don't know why you switched lunch tables. What was so bad about sitting with Zander?"

"Can we not talk about this right now? I'm tired."

"I don't care. You fucked up, and you've never fucked up before. The only thing that's changed is who you're hanging out with."

Not to mention the arrival of Miranda—but I didn't say that to my mom. I'd give up sitting with the football team long before I'd risk losing Miranda.

When my dad came in the room, I was already in bed and almost done with my routine. "You could've really hurt someone tonight, driving your chair drunk. Not to mention injuring yourself."

I didn't answer. There was nothing I could say that would stop them from doing the right thing and coming down hard on me. It was the first time I'd gotten in actual trouble, and I had to learn to take it, because I had a feeling it wouldn't be the last.

FORMULA FOR HEARTBREAK

WHEN I WOKE UP THE NEXT DAY, my stomach wrenched every time I thought of how much I'd had to drink and every time my mom looked at me sideways. She'd been silent the whole night when I'd needed her help, and during my morning routine, too. It was way worse than a verbal lashing.

"Mom and Dad are pissed," Ollie told me. We were watching a college football countdown show in my room. I was still in bed because I'd told Mom I wanted to relax, but really I was afraid that if I moved I would puke.

"I know. I'm just surprised they haven't punished me yet."

"I'm not sure if they will. How are they going to punish you? I mean, you don't go anywhere anyway."

"Thanks."

"I'm just saying, it doesn't make any sense that you got so drunk. But I warned you it would happen."

"Can you just leave now?" I wanted Ollie to stop before he bragged about how he never did anything wrong. I didn't either, but when you're trapped in a house with booze, loud music, and heartbreak, there's only one way out.

The rest of the day, I lay low, watched football, hydrated, and did everything I could to forget seeing Nory at the party. The image of her and Kelvin was fuzzy but not forgotten.

A NORMAL TEENAGER

MONDAY MORNING WAS THE FIRST TIME I'd left the house or spoken to anyone other than my immediate family since the party. Miranda and I went through the typical morning motions of driving to school and braving the hallway madness. Every time someone glanced at me, I swear it was like they already knew how big of an ass I'd made of myself.

I dreaded seeing Nory at our lockers, and I thought about not stopping there at all and skipping homeroom, but I wanted answers.

"Hey, why did you disappear during the party?" I asked when she appeared.

Nory slammed her locker shut and looked straight at me. Her face twitched with impatience. "What are you talking about?"

"Wait, are you mad at *me*?"

"You're mad at me," she shot back.

"That's because you bailed on me before we even got inside!"

"I didn't bail. I was getting out of the way so Lex could build the ramp. I told you I would meet you inside."

"But you didn't, Nory. That's what I'm saying. You weren't anywhere near the front door when I got in. It took me fifteen minutes to find you, and when I did, you were with Kelvin. Playing fucking beer pong."

Miranda was standing at my side. She didn't intervene, just watched like some other students were doing. Nory paid no attention to any of them.

"I'm sorry for talking to my other friends," Nory spat sarcastically.

"I don't care if you have other friends. But you tell me you want to take things slow and be private so there aren't rumors about us, but you have no problem drinking with Kelvin and hanging all over him."

Her hands were flaring in the air but not in her usual cute way. "I don't know why you even care, Harris. It looked like you were having a pretty fun time getting kissed by the cheer team and dancing with Tess Santoro."

"Who cares if I talked to Tess for literally less than one minute? We didn't do anything. But I saw you wander off with Kelvin. Can you tell me *you* didn't do anything?"

"Oh my God. Seriously? You're an asshole." Nory turned away like she was going to leave but then quickly turned back. "For your information, I didn't do anything with Kelvin. If you were actually paying attention, then you would've seen that I left that stupid party because I was upset."

"I was upset, too!" I yelled. "I like you, Nory. I mean, I really, really like you, but sometimes it feels like you don't even want to be my friend."

Nory stormed away, pushing through the circle of students

around us. The show was over, and the crowd scattered to homeroom.

I couldn't move. My cheeks felt hot from all the yelling.

"Let's go for a walk," Miranda said.

• • •

It was alarmingly easy for Miranda and me to walk out. Teachers saw us leaving through some random door at the side of the building, but no one said a word.

That's what it's like when you're accompanied by an adult. I could've been driving naked down the hall, and as long as Miranda or my mom wasn't far behind, people would've assumed everything was peachy.

But everything wasn't peachy. For only the second time in my life, I was breaking a school rule, and I honestly wasn't sure if I wanted to or if I wanted to be back in homeroom, staring at Mr. Wormhole. Both options seemed wrong. Where I wanted to be was a place where I had never spoken to Nory like that or gone to a party or been angry and jealous and confused and hopeless and all the rest of those normal teenage emotions.

Normal is a difficult word for me. I would never be normal in the eyes of society. It's all I've wanted, but somehow it chooses everyone else instead of me.

Miranda stayed perfectly in stride with me as we got farther and farther away from the school. I counted the cracks in the sidewalk, and every bump was a reminder that I wasn't where I was supposed to be. Even the autumn leaves couldn't decide what to do—hang on or fall to the ground.

Miranda was my ground. I chose to fall.

"Am I the jerk?" I let the thoughts in my head out. If Miranda didn't have the answer, I hoped the cold air would. "Nory abandoned me and then forgot I existed."

"True. But maybe it felt the same to her? Why are you allowed to talk to other people but not her?"

"That's not why I'm mad. I mean, yeah, I didn't like seeing her with Kelvin, but she abandoned me before that even happened."

"I think you've gotta cut Nory some slack, dude. So she didn't hold your hand going into the party. I think that means she sees you as a capable person."

Maybe Miranda was right and I shouldn't have blown up at Nory. But it had felt good to let off some steam. At the very least, now Nory knew how I really felt about her.

At the end of the street was a playground that saw most of its action after the elementary school let out. We could stay there for hours without being disturbed. The gentle movement of the swings in the wind would remind us that time was still passing.

My wheels crunched over the mulch that covered the ground—extra padding in case a child fell from the monkey bars. It made me feel like I was actually walking.

We stopped at a bench usually occupied by parents. This time it was occupied by me and Miranda—two delinquents. The sun was still rising behind Miranda, shining on her bleached hair like it was the top of a snowcapped mountain.

"Twelve text messages." Miranda held out her phone so I could see the notifications. "Brad sent me twelve texts in the last five minutes."

"Wow. What does he want?"

"Nothing. Just asking where I am and who I'm with and what I'm doing."

"He knows you're at work, right?"

"Yeah. He's just paranoid I'm doing drugs or something."

"Seriously? You're with me."

"Dude, I know. We're just getting kinda serious, and we started talking about what would happen if we had kids, and then Brad brought up my drug use."

"What about it?"

"I don't know. He said that addiction issues can be genetic and he doesn't want that passed down to his children."

"He can't blame you for something like that."

"Maybe. But he brought up a good point. What if I'm selfish deep down? I mean, when I was doing drugs, I really didn't think about anyone else."

"Okay, but you were in pain after Kaylin's death. You were grieving. He said you were selfish?"

Miranda zipped up her fleece and leaned over to do the same to mine. I noticed something written on the inside of her arm that I hadn't seen before. "Yes, he did. And he's right. Mourning isn't an excuse for the decisions I made."

The words coming out of Miranda's mouth weren't her own. I was sure of it.

"Miranda, you can't think like that," I said. "You're clean now and working really hard, and you're going to be a nurse. You shouldn't be with Brad if he can't see how great you're doing."

"I think he just cares a lot about me and doesn't want me to ruin my life anymore, or his."

"Oh my God. He should trust that you're past that stage of your life." I had a flash of guilt. Here I was, shitting on Brad for not trusting Miranda, yet I had just yelled at Nory for hanging out with Kelvin. I had to trust her and give her space. "You deserve better."

Miranda walked over to the swing set and chose the swing

that was right in the path of the morning sun. It only took a few pumps for her to be airborne.

"Tell me about colors," she said. Her voice rang out over the playground.

I drove closer so I wouldn't have to yell. "First tell me what's on your arm."

"A tattoo."

"I see that. What does it say?"

"It says 'This too shall pass.'"

"Why?"

"When I was going through rehab, there were days when all I could do was curl into a ball and cry, and my right arm was always tucked in front of my face. I would say those words over and over in my head until someone found me in my room. They're a constant reminder that however I'm feeling, good or bad, is temporary."

I knew exactly what she meant. In some ways, Miranda and I were the same. We'd both struggled with dark times and had the strength to keep living. Not many people know what it feels like to be on the edge of death, and when people don't understand, they feel pity. Miranda could empathize with me and I could empathize with her because we'd both felt that kind of pain.

I guess Nory had, too.

"When I was younger and always in and out of the hospital, my mom would hold my hand and tell me how she wished she could take away my pain," I said. "She couldn't, of course, but I knew I would get better as long as she was next to me."

"Clare Bear is definitely the best. You're lucky to have her. I wish I had a mom like that."

Not for the first time, I wondered what her mom was like.

She never talked about her parents, and now didn't seem like the time to ask. "I think you're strong enough to cope and survive no matter who's around you, Miranda. And you found something that reminds you why you shouldn't give up."

As for me, I would always need somebody. And because of that, I was afraid I would never change. I mean, I couldn't even tell my mom to stop making me a deli sandwich every day. It's the small things in life that make you realize you're progressing, and Miranda and I were both stuck. She had to eat PB&J to remember Kaylin, and I was still incapable of keeping a friend.

"Now, tell me about colors," Miranda said.

"What do you want to know?"

"Well, to start, why do you care?"

I hesitated because I'd never really tried to explain it to anyone, but I trusted Miranda to understand. "At first, it was just a way for me to find something in common with kids my age. But when I got older, I realized that every time I met someone new or entered a room, people automatically made assumptions about me. They thought they knew everything about me just because I was in a wheelchair."

"Harris, you don't know what they thought about you."

"Maybe not, but I saw their judgment in the way they looked at me, and I heard it in the way they talked to me. Asking their favorite color seemed like an innocent way for me to judge them in return and make my own assumptions. It's how I leveled the playing field. If my wheelchair said everything they needed to know about me, maybe their favorite color said everything I needed to know about them."

"Okay . . . Why do you think people prefer certain colors over others?"

"Because colors make them feel a certain way. Having a favorite color is like unconsciously adopting a personality trait."

"What does it mean if a person likes the color black?"

"Researchers say it means you're trying to protect yourself from something, or you feel a need to be mysterious. Or you're trying to look slim."

Miranda laughed and slowed down on the swing. "So you're saying that if I like a specific color, I have to act a certain way?"

"You don't *have* to, but you will. That's why you chose that color, because you feel a connection to it."

"Interesting." She jumped off the swing midair and walked over to give me a drink of water. Miranda never needed to be reminded about that sort of stuff. Her internal alarms went off whenever it was time for my breathing treatment, and sometimes she even put my mom to shame. Like whenever we crossed the street, she made sure my head didn't fall back while I drove up the curb cut.

My intricacies were becoming her intricacies. We were connected, and it was unlike any other relationship I'd had with a nurse, or with anybody.

"I just like how we can look at something simple and make a prediction," I said.

Miranda turned away. "Yeah, but if it's only a prediction, you can be wrong."

• • •

Miranda and I skipped the rest of the school day. I couldn't find the courage to drive back into a building filled with people who'd seen me make a complete ass of myself, and Miranda was having too much fun trying out all the playground equipment.

It turned out to be a perfect fall afternoon, not too cold, with just the right amount of moisture in the air (which could cause pneumonia, my mom would say). Around lunchtime, a young mom arrived with a toddler and gave us a strange look. I wondered if she thought Miranda had broken me out of my group home—a special adventure for a special kid. She wouldn't have been that far off.

We went to a 7-Eleven to use the bathroom and do my nebulizer. My mom would freak if she found out, but I liked being a rebel all of a sudden, and Miranda was very good at it. For lunch, we split a warm pretzel and a cherry Slurpee. I told her about my home in San Diego, and she shared her favorite memories of Kaylin, whose favorite color was pink.

My whole life, I'd wanted to be somebody's somebody. Maybe I was becoming Miranda's. She'd been my somebody ever since I saw her stepping out of her red Mustang in my driveway.

* * *

It was a perfect day, made even better by the fact that we'd pulled off the perfect crime. Or so we thought. We assumed that if we got back to the school parking lot in time, my mom would never know we had ditched. But it was impossible to get anything past her.

My mom was unnervingly quiet when she picked us up to go home. Once Miranda was in her Mustang and Mom and I had entered the house, though, all hell broke loose.

"Why did you leave school today?" Mom asked.

"I only went out for a little bit," I lied.

"Really? Because Ms. Maszak called to say you missed a laptop training with your teachers, so I checked your attendance online, and you missed all of your classes."

"I'm sorry, all right? I had a fight with Nory in the morning, and I needed some fresh air. We lost track of time."

"I just don't understand what's come over you lately. A few days ago, you got blackout drunk, and now you're skipping school. What the hell is going on? Is this because of Miranda?"

"No, don't blame her. All of those choices were mine."

"Well, you better get your shit together. I hope this isn't what you had in mind when you said you wanted to reinvent yourself."

She was right. This wasn't who I wanted to be, but I also had no idea who I *did* want to be or what that person looked like. I knew I wanted friends and maybe a girlfriend and for people to stop seeing me as disabled. I think my subconscious was telling me that none of that was possible.

THOUGHTS OF A BOY ALONE

THE DOOR TO MY BEDROOM was cracked and let in just enough light to cast shadows on the wall next to my bed. Silhouettes overlapped and formed shapes that didn't make much sense but were still terrifying to look at. I found comfort in counting the empty spaces in between.

That's what I'd been doing since my mom had finished my nighttime routine, turned on my breathing machine that I used to sleep, and said good night. Only thirty minutes had passed, but they'd dragged on like hours.

I closed my eyes. I saw Nory at her locker wearing the green headband she'd worn the first time she smiled at me. I wanted to remember her that way, not as the person who'd called me an asshole. Was I an asshole? Maybe a little, and now even more so because I kept picturing her in that freaking dress, which sexualized her in a way she didn't deserve . . . but I was a teenage boy who liked when girls wore short dresses. It didn't help me sleep.

Sweat dripped down my forehead. The straps from the breathing machine were pulled over my cheeks and itched from the moisture underneath. I wiggled my face, but it didn't help.

"Mom?" I yelled.

I heard her set her reading glasses on the kitchen table. Less time had passed than I thought. When she entered my room, the light from the hallway flooded my blue walls. "What?"

"Can you turn me?"

"Already? I just put you to bed."

"I can't sleep. I'm too hot."

My mom walked around to the right side of my bed and rolled my body so that I was lying on my left. She yanked the comforter down below my feet.

"I'll turn up the AC," she said. "Get some sleep."

Except it didn't help. I couldn't stop thinking about Nory.

I was afraid I'd ruined any chance of her being interested in me and probably any chance of her even being my friend. All because I had decided to go to that party.

Sometimes I really hated how my disability held me back from the small things. Like, when I pictured Nory in her sundress, I also pictured myself next to her. But I wasn't in my wheelchair. I was standing, and my working arms reached for her waist and pulled her body tight against mine so that our chests touched. I felt the warmth of her skin. I brushed away the hair that had fallen in front of her eyes. Then we kissed. We kissed because I could hold her and make her feel safe, and we kissed because able-bodied Harris was brave.

I finally fell asleep at some point. When I woke up, the gears in my head had stopped turning.

I called my mom again so she could turn me back to the original side. She sent my dad, who must not have received the memo that I was hot because he pulled the comforter up to my shoulders, but he was not to be conversed with late at night.

Beams of sunlight were sneaking through my bedroom window the next time I opened my eyes. Soon Miranda would be talking to me from the passenger seat of Black Hawk. Maybe she could help me figure out what to do about Nory.

MORNINGS ARE ALWAYS
THE HARDEST

AT MOST I GOT FOUR HOURS of sleep that night, and my mom didn't stop buzzing from the moment she woke me up. She complained that it was raining outside and that Ollie wouldn't wear a raincoat and he was going to ruin his school uniform, et cetera. Occasionally, we have mornings where crap just keeps piling on top of more crap. That morning, it was almost like the universe had slept poorly, too, and was throwing a giant hissy fit as a result. It took my mom five minutes to figure out that the car keys were in the same place they always were, but if I'd mentioned the keys' obvious location, she would've accused me of moving them. She needed to find the keys on her own.

"Where the hell is she?" Mom asked.

We'd been waiting in the car for less than thirty seconds before she started in about Miranda's tardiness. My brain was dead, so her freak-out made my head pound harder than usual.

"I really hate her being late, Harris," she continued. "I really hate it."

"I'm never late to homeroom, and you have nowhere to be, so it doesn't matter."

"That's not the point. Do you not understand that? If we tell her to be here at a specific time, then she should be here."

"Calm down. It's raining, so I'm sure she hit a lot of traffic. Remember how she drives a Mustang? It probably doesn't do well in this weather."

Mom fished around on the car floor for an umbrella to use once we got to school. "You need to tell her that she has to start leaving her house earlier. I can't take the stress. I'd rather go to school with you than worry about whether she's going to show up."

"She'll show up."

And she did, exactly two minutes after I said she would. No one said a word the entire ride to school, which made for an even worse morning. I really wanted to talk to Miranda, but the tension was palpable.

I guess the world was flat-out against my mom that morning, as all the handicap parking was taken.

• • •

Nory's seat next to me in homeroom was open, but she sat in the back with Kelvin. Mr. Wormhole went on and on about World War II, apparently thinking we were in his AP history class rather than homeroom. He was crashing early in the year. An argument could have been made for forced retirement.

Miranda caught me looking at the empty desk. "You're gonna have to apologize to her."

"No way. She's over me, and I'm fine with that. Besides, I have too many issues in my life to have a girlfriend."

"Harris, you need to get over what happened. People get drunk and fight. Unfortunately, that's most of being an adult."

This didn't seem like very sound relationship advice—my parents never got drunk and fought, though they did sometimes drink and sometimes fight—but I hoped she was just joking. "Whatever. I'm still not apologizing."

"Fine. I'll do it for you. I have a plan anyway."

"What is it?"

"I'm not telling you. You'll ruin it."

Finally, Wormhole realized he just had to take attendance and shut up. I monitored the rise and fall of his stomach to make sure he didn't stop breathing.

"My mom is pretty pissed that you're late all the time," I said.

Miranda sighed. "I know. Tell Clare Bear I'm sorry. I ended up moving in with Brad, and it takes me longer to get ready in the mornings now that I don't have my own bathroom. But I'll try to get up earlier."

"Listen, Brad is not a good guy. You need to break up with him."

"Why? Because he texts me all the time? He just worries about me."

"He doesn't trust you, Miranda. Like, at all. That's not healthy. The guy is basically stalking you."

Miranda ignored me and picked at her black nail polish. I felt horrible for bringing up her late streak now that I knew the reason for it. To me, it wasn't a big deal if Miranda arrived five minutes past seven, but I was tired of my mom complaining.

"By the way, you look terrible today," Miranda told me.

"Thanks for noticing. I couldn't sleep last night. I kept thinking about Nory."

"Were your sheets dry this morning?"

I blushed. That was my answer.

THRIVING, NOT THRIVING

NORY'S SEAT IN PHYSICS STAYED empty until the last possible moment. I'd figured that I repulsed her so much she'd transferred to another period. But then, in her normal awkward fashion, she slid onto the lab stool. Mrs. Ivavych gave her a pretty vicious Russian interrogation stare. I wanted to turn my head and watch Nory frantically rummage through her backpack for a pen and notebook, but I didn't want her to know that was the best part of my days.

Halfway through the lecture on Newton's third law, she finally got settled. A couple of times, our hands bumped when she turned the page of her notebook, and she didn't move farther away when it happened. That had to be a good sign.

Miranda—who was supposed to be taking notes for me—was busy writing something on a piece of ripped notebook paper.

"What are you doing?" I whispered.

"Don't worry about it."

"Don't do anything stupid."

"Stupid is where I thrive."

Miranda slid the folded piece of paper across the table and dropped it in front of Nory. She didn't open it or even acknowledge its existence for practically the entire period.

Finally, while Mrs. Ivavych was writing our homework on the whiteboard, Nory opened the note. She read it a few times but had no reaction. My heart was pounding. I had no idea what Miranda had written.

Eventually, Nory placed the note in front of me, and Miranda snatched it away, as if I actually had the ability to open it myself. The bell rang, and Nory left class, making it the first school day in a month that we hadn't spoken to each other.

"You have a date on Saturday," Miranda told me. She held the note open for me to read.

It said *Sorry I'm an asshole. Want to go to a concert?*

Nory had checked off *yes.*

The idea of going to a concert with Nory scared the hell out of me. It felt like I was starting over with her, which might be a good thing. I wanted to understand Nory the way I understood Miranda and have Nory understand me the way Miranda did. There had been glimmers of that, like when I noticed the glitter in her eye shadow and when she put the napkin in my lap. But clearly we had a long way to go.

Part of me wished we could *truly* start over, rewind to the first moment we'd met and take it from there. Then I might find out her favorite color.

#FF1100 + #0000FF = #800080

"WHAT'S THE BAND'S NAME AGAIN?" I asked.

"A Band Called," Miranda answered.

"A band called what?"

"A Band Called. That's the name of the band. A Band Called."

"This is like a 'Who's on First?' kinda thing."

"What's that?"

"Never mind."

Miranda was wearing a leather jacket, a crop top, and skin-tight jeans, all pulled together by a pair of spike heels. It was the perfect outfit for a punk concert. At least that was the type of music I assumed the band played, considering the name of the venue was Dirtbag's.

She was helping me pick out something to wear, but all my clothes said *My mom shops for me*. We'd gone through each item in my closet twice, and Nory was due at my front door any minute.

Miranda pointed to a shirt on my bed. "How about that black polo, and I'll roll up the sleeves and spike your hair?"

"That would be cool," Mom said.

"No way," I insisted.

"Dude, you've got no other choice." Miranda grabbed the shirt, and I reluctantly followed her into the bathroom. "I'll show you."

She helped me put on the polo, which was a little snug, since my mom had bought it when I was twelve and it had been collecting dust in my closet ever since. Then she cuffed the already-short sleeves in a way that appeared intentional but also like I didn't care.

Miranda popped the collar. "Too much?"

I nodded.

"Fair enough."

She scooped up a considerable amount of hair gel and played with my hair, trying to give it some edge.

For a moment, I felt like I was hers and she was mine. We were just an average couple going out on the town.

"I think that's enough gel," I said.

"Chill. I'm trying to make you look handsome for Nory."

I let her continue playing with my hair, because in that moment I didn't want to look handsome for Nory. I wanted to look handsome for Miranda, or however she wanted me to look.

After a few more tugs at my hair, she stepped back so I could see myself in the mirror. At first, I didn't recognize the kid in the wheelchair who was staring back at me. He had somewhere to be on a Saturday night. Not to mention enough hair gel to withstand a tornado.

"I look like a poser," I said.

"Perfect. You'll fit right in. Are you excited about your second date?"

"This isn't a date. You'll be there."

"Hey, don't let me cramp your style. If you and Nory want to sneak away to the bathroom during the concert, I won't stop you."

"I doubt that will happen. And you're sure this place is accessible?"

"Yup. I used to go to shows at Dirtbag's all the time."

My mom and dad were waiting for us in the living room. Turns out I was wrong about them not allowing Miranda to drive Black Hawk too far. They'd agreed to let her take Nory and me, if only to make sure I didn't get drunk again. One bad choice, and I'd changed my parents' entire perspective on me.

There were three knocks on the front door with no discernable rhythm. Only Nory would knock like that.

I went with Miranda to answer the door, but the sweat on my hand made it almost impossible to grip the joystick. I hated how nervous I was about a simple thing like going to a concert. My body was acting like I was the one who had to perform.

"I like your black lipstick," I told Nory. "Looks like you got the memo."

"Thanks. Nice hair."

I yelled to my parents that we were leaving, and my mom answered by telling me to take a jacket, which I didn't. Nory sat shotgun, and every few minutes, she'd turn around to see my reaction to whatever she'd said. I tried to be cool. You know, not laugh at my own jokes, only smile if she smiled. Stuff like that.

The venue was an hour away, so there was ample time to talk about anything other than Kelvin and the party and me being an asshole. Miranda barely spoke. She concentrated on driving because she knew she'd be in deep shit if anything happened to Black Hawk.

"So, Harris, where'd you hear about this band?" Nory asked.

"Miranda told me about them, actually," I said.

"The lead singer is a cousin of one of my friends," Miranda added. "I'm surprised you've never heard of them. They're big in the North Jersey scene."

Nory bounced up and down in her seat. "I'm pumped. I've never been to a concert before."

"You've never been to a concert?" I asked.

"I guess technically I have, but it was a Journey reunion show that my dad brought me to. I've never seen an actual touring band. Have you?"

"No."

"Then why'd you sound so surprised?"

"I don't know. You just seem like someone who's been to a lot of concerts."

"Is that based on my favorite color?" Nory smiled.

"No, since I don't even know your favorite color."

She smiled again. "That's just the way I like it."

• • •

Hundreds of rowdy college-age-looking people stood in line, waiting for the doors to open. The parking lot was small and covered with gravel that crunched under the car tires. Our mode of transportation was a dead giveaway that we didn't belong. Maybe Miranda did, and I was sure she could handle herself in a place called Dirtbag's, but I started to think that Nory and I were in over our heads.

"Try to keep your heads down," Miranda said while we were in line. "I'll handle everything when we reach the bouncer."

I had no idea what she meant, but Nory listened and stared at the ground. Someone behind us was smoking, and the smell made me nauseated and concerned that I should've done a breathing treatment before getting out of the car. I also couldn't help but notice that everyone in line seemed like they could've killed us for fun.

"IDs," the bouncer demanded.

"We have to be twenty-one?" I asked Miranda.

She ignored me. "We're actually friends of Renzo's."

"I don't care. No IDs, no concert."

Nory looked jittery. I wondered if the chaotic energy was reminding her of the Halloween party. IDs meant drinking, and we'd both become different people around alcohol. And if we couldn't get in, I'd feel terrible that I'd promised her a good time but instead delivered two hours in an accessible van. Miranda should have known we needed to be twenty-one.

Then, out of nowhere, a group of guys stumbled out of the building to smoke cigarettes. One of them saw Miranda and did a double take. I thought what happened next only happened in movies.

"Miranda Gilsip?" he shouted. "Holy shit!" Cigarette between his lips, he walked over to give her a hug. The people behind us were getting impatient. "I never thought I'd see you here again."

"Renzo texted me that you guys were touring again. I thought I'd introduce my friends here to a kick-ass band."

"So what's the problem, then? You guys coming in?"

"We're trying, but Johnny Rain Cloud here isn't having it." She nodded toward the bouncer.

Miranda's friend slapped the two-hundred-pound bouncer on the arm. "They're cool. They're with the band."

Nory looked at me, and I looked at her. We both shrugged.

The bouncer stepped out of the way so I could fit my wheelchair past his muscles. Inside, the stale stench of cigarette smoke floated through the bar and toward the small stage. It didn't mix well with the smells of burnt popcorn and beer. I was careful not to drive through any suspicious stains on the wood floors.

"Who are your friends?" The guy who'd gotten us in had stuck with us.

"This is Harris and his friend Nory. Harris and Nory, this is Cullen. He plays drums in the band."

"Awesome to meet you both," Cullen said. His hands fiddled with the backward baseball cap on his head and then fell into his pockets. "How do you know Miranda?"

"She's my executive assistant," I said.

"Dope. Sounds like a sweet gig. So, you guys want to watch from up front? Might be difficult to see from the back."

"Sure," Miranda said.

"Awesome. Let me make a path in the pit for you." Cullen looked at Miranda. His expression softened. "Renzo and I thought we'd lost you along with Kaylin, but you're a fighter. We love you, girl." He hugged her again and then escorted us toward the stage.

The opening act was some nerdy white guy who thought he could rap. Me in a parallel universe, maybe. People were still jumping around to the terrible rhymes and overhyped beats. All the movement made it difficult to navigate the tiny path that Cullen had made for us, and the butt of a screaming girl hit my driving hand, forcing my chair to the left. My tires bumped over what I assumed was someone's foot.

Miranda turned back to see where I was. "Why'd you stop?"

"I think I ran over somebody."

"Knowing this crowd, they probably deserved it. Just keep driving forward."

She repositioned my hand and gave me a look that said I could get through this, that everything was fine and she was there for me. Nory didn't look back or even notice that anything had happened. She was already at the stage, and it felt the same as when she'd gone into the party and left me outside Lex's house.

Maybe she had let her guard down because Miranda was with us, but that still didn't explain the Halloween party. Honestly, neither of us had really apologized or talked about what had happened. Suddenly, going to a concert and acting like everything was fine seemed like it probably wasn't the best solution.

I just wanted the same Nory who'd helped me up the ramp at the art gallery and flipped off the coffee shop that wasn't wheelchair accessible. I wanted her to be more like Miranda, who never wavered in how she acted around me.

I liked that. More importantly, I needed that.

We made it to the front of the pit, and Miranda took a spot on my left while Nory stood to my right. Cullen somehow escaped the commotion and returned in less than two minutes. He handed Nory and me each a shirt, as well as a copy of the band's latest album. "Some merch," he said. "On the house." The opening act was wrapping up, so Cullen headed backstage, but not before giving Miranda another hug.

She twisted her hips from side to side, dancing to whatever song was playing in her head. She was in her element, and I found comfort in that, even though everything was new and overwhelming to me.

"What are you doing?" I asked. "There's no music."

"I'm just excited. You're going to love them. Renzo is a killer front man."

"So you've known the band for a long time?"

"Oh, yeah. Renzo and Kaylin used to date."

I didn't know what to say to that, and I was starting to feel like I was neglecting Nory, so I turned to her and asked, "Do you like punk music?"

"It's all right. I'll listen to pretty much anything. And I'm just excited to feel the energy in the room."

"Yeah, it's going to be way different from Lex's party."

I could almost feel my foot in my mouth. I'd told myself a thousand times not to bring up the party, but almost every time I talked to Nory lately, I struggled to find the right things to say.

There was a long silence, and then Nory broke it. "I'm gonna get a snack. Do you guys want anything?"

"I'm fine. Do you need money? My parents gave me some."

"No, I'm good. Thanks."

Nory shuffled through the crowd, which had thinned between acts. Miranda knelt next to me.

"I think the night's going well," she said.

"I just brought up the Halloween party."

"That was bad, but at least you were talking to her. Keep it up."

"How? It's loud in here, and the band hasn't even started playing yet."

"Harris, as long as you have fun, Nory will, too. Just enjoy being out with a girl."

And so I tried to embrace the atmosphere and the smoke that stank up my clothes (which would be thrown out by Mom later that night) as I watched the crew scurrying around, setting up drums and extra amps. But it was a far cry from having fun.

I thought the problem was that the concert hadn't been my idea. Going to Dirtbag's wasn't how I wanted to repair things with Nory, and I felt like we were both struggling to get comfortable with each other again.

Nory returned with a gigantic pretzel in one hand and a huge bag of popcorn in the other.

"I may have bought too much," she said. "I forgot there's nowhere to put anything."

"You could set it on the stage," I said. "The show probably won't start right away."

"No way, the stage looks filthy." Then she smiled at me in a way she never had before. She was gently biting down on her tongue with her front teeth. "Can I sit on your lap? Then I can keep the food on my legs."

I looked at Miranda, and she literally winked at me. "Um, s-sure," I stuttered.

Nory didn't hesitate. She gently scooted into place on top of my legs. I liked the feeling of her weight pressing down on me and the cloud of coconut perfume that now enveloped both of us. Honestly, I was a little concerned that things could get awkward fast. I mean, except for that brief moment with one of the Charlie's Angels at the party, I had never had a girl literally on top of me.

"Pretzel? Popcorn?" Nory asked.

"Pretzel."

Nory stuck a bit of pretzel in my mouth and took a handful of popcorn for herself. She wrapped her arm around my neck for balance, and I could finally see her face. It felt like we were one person, and when she smiled, I smiled. Was she pretending everything was okay between us? Or was I just overthinking, and people moved on from arguments faster than I thought?

"Don't choke," Miranda said. "I know you're probably having a hard time concentrating."

"I'm fine." And I really was. For some reason, I was able to control the part of my body that should've loved having Nory on my lap.

Nory swallowed her popcorn. "What types of music do you like?"

"I used to be really into rap," I said.

"Is that what your mom was talking about? When she said you wrote songs?"

"Yeah. I thought I was going to be the next Eminem."

"Seriously? That's cool but also really funny. No offense. How old were you?"

I shrugged. "Nine or ten."

Without asking, Nory fed me another bite of pretzel. "So, old-school rap and what else?"

It took me a minute to chew. I wished I had some water. "Pretty much anything except country. I'm a big fan of Frank Sinatra."

"Same. My dad has all his records on vinyl."

Four guys casually walked onto the stage. Three of them held guitars, and Cullen sat at the kit in the back. The crowd cheered like crazy before a single note was played. As best I could, I cheered with them.

"I'm gonna stand," Nory said. "I don't want to block your view."

She climbed off my lap. Part of me wanted to beg her to stay, and part of me was relieved to have her off me. It was the weirdest thing.

"Hello, Dirtbag's," Renzo said into the microphone. He looked like the typical punk singer with long hair and a collage of tattoos that covered both his arms. "Welcome to the show. We are A Band Called."

Without further ado, one of the guitar players broke into a high-pitched riff, then Cullen's drums kicked in, then the bass, and finally Renzo's massive voice. Their music wasn't ridiculously loud, thankfully, plus the harmonies were decent and the lyrics were catchy. After only a few seconds, I was singing along to the chorus.

The set went on for over an hour, and each song transitioned perfectly to the next. Renzo wasted no breath making chitchat and let the music do all the talking.

Nory bounced next to me, and a few times, we caught each other's eyes and smiled. During one of the slower songs, she put her arm around my shoulders and we swayed. Miranda also didn't stop moving the entire night, jumping and dancing and screaming and looking beautiful through all of it.

ALL THE THINGS
I SHOULDN'T KNOW

MY EARS RANG DURING THE ENTIRE RIDE to Nory's house, and my heart was still thumping like Cullen's drums even after we got back home. It was past midnight, but the rush from the concert kept me wide-awake. I wanted to feel that feeling every day of my life.

My parents were waiting for us in the living room. Dad was barely awake and only opened his eyes enough to see that I was in one piece. Mom couldn't stop talking, and her endless questions exhausted me. I had to keep reminding her that I was fine and alive.

"You should text Nory and thank her for coming," she said.

I asked Miranda to send the text. A minute later, Nory answered saying she'd had a great time and we should do it again.

I started to come down from the high, and every little movement felt like I was trying to lift two pounds. (For an able-bodied person, that would be like lifting a hundred pounds.)

"Your face is red," Mom said. She put her hand on my forehead. "Do you have a fever?"

"I told you I'm fine. I'm just hot from the concert. There were a ton of people there."

Mom was undressing me in my bedroom. Miranda had stuck around to help and had brought in the night's souvenirs. I wondered whether she thought she needed to stay or if she was just reluctant to go home.

"I can open a window if you want," Miranda said.

"We never open the windows," Mom answered.

I groaned. I was too tired to argue. "Just for a few minutes. I need the fresh air."

Next thing I knew, I was on my side wearing my breathing machine, and the lights were out. I must've dozed off while Mom finished my bedtime routine. Someone whispered about how cute I looked falling asleep.

• • •

Hours later, I felt something shift on my bed, and my dream told me to wake up.

At first, all I saw was the blackness of my room. Everything was still except two bright little specks. I blinked and refocused. They blinked, too.

"Hey."

"Miranda? What are you doing here? What time is it?"

"Almost three. Your mom's right. You do look like a newborn baby when you're sleeping."

I kept blinking, thinking I'd woken up in another dream. Miranda just stared, our noses almost touching.

"How did you get in here?" I asked. It was the first of many questions I had.

"The window's still open. Your bed is really comfortable."

"Stop changing the subject. Why are you here?"

"Harris, can't you just lie with a girl and not ask so many questions?"

"No. I've never been in this situation before."

But apparently I could. We were silent for one rotation of my air-pressure mattress, which cycled every five minutes. Miranda couldn't hold still. Her mouth twitched. Her hands played with the ends of her hair, then brushed mine back from tickling my eyebrows.

Miranda was energetic like orange and burned like red. I hovered like blue. Together, we made purple.

What was she thinking about? Was I supposed to do something? I couldn't touch her. At least, not on my own.

"Is the air from my BiPAP blowing on you?" I asked.

"It's fine. It's kinda relaxing."

"Do you want to get under the covers? It's pretty cold with the window open."

Miranda lifted the comforter and slid her legs under, tangling her frozen feet with mine. I had no clue what to say. I wanted to tell Miranda she was the most beautiful girl I'd ever seen, but the whole situation felt strange. It felt wrong and it felt right.

"Did you have fun tonight?" Miranda asked.

"Yeah. I think I'm back on Nory's good side." But I didn't want to think about Nory right then.

"I think she really likes you. I mean, she sees you," Miranda said. "She doesn't see your disability and the things you can't do. She just sees you."

"I know. It's just like how you see me."

Miranda smiled. I almost fell asleep looking into her eyes.

"Brad kicked me out." She said it like it was yesterday's

news, but I suddenly felt much more awake. "He texted me after I left your house. He was pissed that I went to the concert. He said I keep putting myself in potentially harmful situations and he's tired of looking after me."

"Are you sure you're not dating a toddler?"

"I think we're done for good. I just don't have anywhere to go."

"Why didn't you go to your parents' house?"

"They're in Connecticut, visiting my aunt. I can't be alone tonight."

For a moment, I let the fantasy play out: Miranda curled up next to me all night, her cold feet staying tangled with my perpetually chilly ones. But I knew it was just that—a fantasy. "Miranda, I'm sorry, but you can't stay here. My mom will wonder why I'm not calling for her, and she'll freak when she eventually comes in."

"Fine. I'll leave when you fall asleep again."

I fought to stay awake. I focused on Miranda's eyes and the synchronization of our breaths.

"I'm really comfortable around you," Miranda said. "Like I can tell you anything."

I wanted to tell her I felt the same way, but my brain was so tired from the concert that all I could do was nod. I nodded slowly, maybe once or twice, and was on the verge of slipping back to sleep. This time with a beautiful girl next to me.

Then Miranda's voice floated through the darkness. "I let Kaylin die."

My eyes slowly opened, and I looked at Miranda, who hadn't moved. "What are you talking about?"

"I lied to you. I was at the party that night. I saw her passed out on a couch and went to dance. An hour later, I came back, and she was still unconscious. I shook her, but she wouldn't wake up." Miranda wiped away tears. Her voice was quiet and shaky. "She wasn't breathing, and I have no idea when she stopped. But it doesn't matter. I let my best friend die at some random fucking party in the basement of some random fucking house."

"You can't blame yourself. There was nothing you could have done."

"Yes, there was. I could've stayed with her. I could've stopped her from going to all those parties. I should've checked on her when I saw her passed out."

We were silent for a long time. I let Miranda's words sink in.

From my experience with nurses, it seems like knowing what to do in an emergency situation is an instinct. Taking control and remaining calm can't be taught in a classroom. Miranda was right; she should've done a lot of things differently. But I had to believe that she was so high then that she didn't know how to save Kaylin. I had to believe that she was a different person now.

"You're the first person who's heard the whole story," Miranda said. "It feels good to get it out of my head."

"You've seriously never told anyone all of this?"

Miranda shook her head.

People rarely confided in me. This was a secret I planned to keep to myself. For Miranda and for Kaylin.

Miranda's mouth curled into a smile. "What are you looking at?"

"Your eyes. I've never seen that color anywhere else."

She laughed softly. "What are you talking about? It's too dark to see that."

"Maybe. But I know the color well enough that it's like I'm seeing it now, even in the dark. Sometimes they're blue and clear, like your pupils are floating in tropical oceans. But then sometimes your eyes are green and hazy. They morph a lot."

She was quiet for a moment. "And what do you think it means?"

"That you're in pain."

Miranda lifted her head and kissed my cheek. "Always."

My eyelids eventually became too heavy to keep open. No matter how much I fought, exhaustion swept over me, and as I drifted back to sleep, I heard her say, "I love you, too, Harris."

The words echoed in my head and conjured the hazy memory of my drunken confession the night of the Halloween party. My world contracted until it was just me and Miranda. Nothing else mattered.

When I woke up, she was gone, and my mom was turning me onto my left side. She shut the rebellious window.

THE ART OF FALLING

"**I DON'T KNOW** why we had to open that window," Mom said. She paced around my bedroom. "Now you're sick."

"It's not from the window. And I'm not sick."

"Then what are you, huh? Because you have a fever and can barely breathe."

Her energy was making me nervous. The day after the concert, I had felt excellent. But by the time Sunday night rolled around, liquid was pouring from my nose like it was fucking Niagara Falls. Then it found my lungs, and Mom stayed up with me to run extra nebulizer treatments and listen to me cough my guts out.

I hadn't slept a wink two nights in a row, which for sure helped whatever was trying to kill me. We were awake so early that my dad was able to check in before leaving.

"How are you feeling?" he asked.

I was going to say okay, but then Mom interrupted. "I haven't stopped suctioning him for the past eight hours. And I don't even know who to call. I haven't found him a new pulmonologist."

"We've been here for almost three months."

"Yes, I understand that, but I've been a little busy dealing with the move while you're at work."

Dad remained calm, like he always did when my mom was in panic mode. He was the rock for both of us.

My chest wheezed with every inhale and exhale. I coughed, and my mouth filled with mucus. Mom rushed to flick on the suction machine and shoved the tube between my lips, pulling out whatever was inside. I could breathe again for a little longer.

"Oh, jeez." Dad sighed. "You're in bad shape."

"This has been my entire night," Mom said. "Thankfully, the secretions aren't green or anything, but he still needs to see someone."

"Do you want me to stay home and drive you to a doctor?"

"No. Miranda will be here in a couple of hours to help. Right now I just want Harris to rest."

She slipped the BiPAP mask over my face so I could relax and breathe easier. It was going to be a long week.

•   •   •

I saw two blurry faces at the foot of my bed. The sun was finally up, but the burning in my lungs hadn't subsided.

"Hi, sweetie. Did you have a nice nap?" Mom asked. "Miranda's here."

"Hey, dude. You're not feeling so hot?"

For some reason, I couldn't conjure any words. All I could do was nod. I hated that Miranda was seeing me sick, even though it was her job. Healthy Harris wearing a breathing machine was somehow cooler than sick Harris wearing a breathing machine. At least I thought so.

"Do you want to take your BiPAP off and see how you're feeling?" Mom asked.

I nodded again.

Mom lifted the mask off my face, explaining it all to Miranda as if she'd never seen it before. Little did she know.

As soon as the air stopped flowing into my nostrils, I gasped hard for each breath. I tried sucking in as much oxygen as I possibly could, but my chest was too heavy, and my lungs barely filled. I choked on the exhale.

"Let's do another neb," my mom said. She handed a vial of medication to Miranda, who seemed totally unfazed. The mist from the medication started breaking up all the crap that had settled in my lungs. Each inhale was a struggle. Each exhale was a cough, an attempt to clear my lungs.

But I couldn't do it by myself. SMA limits extremity movement and the ability to properly cough. I really was a non-walking catastrophe.

Mom yanked the nebulizer mask off my face and placed another, larger one over my mouth and nose. She flicked a switch on a different machine, and air rushed into my lungs and then shot out.

"This is a cough assist," she told Miranda over the noise. "It helps Harris get the mucus out." A few more involuntary coughs, and then Mom suctioned my mouth.

"Can I try?" Miranda asked.

Mom handed her the suction tube, and she stuck it in my nose. It was pretty gross, but at least I could breathe. "You have to be a real nurse now," my mom said.

My coughing fit ended, and Mom left us so she could take a shower. Miranda sat in the chair next to my bed while

I watched the morning talk shows. The concert felt like it had happened in another life.

"Sorry," I said.

"For what?"

"I don't know. That you have to see me like this and do a bunch of extra shit."

"I'm actually pretty excited. I get to learn and take care of you. And we're still hanging out. I'm sure you're not going to school anytime soon."

"Yeah, I'll probably miss the entire week. Maybe more. I recover slowly."

"Well, I'm here, and so is your mom, and we're going to get you better."

"I know, but it sucks. Five steps forward and eight steps back."

I coughed up some more mucus on my own, and Miranda was ready with the suction. I didn't even ask. "That's just life. It has nothing to do with your disability."

Mom came back and placed a cup of water on the shelf. Sticking out of the top was a large syringe.

"Harris needs to stay hydrated," she said, "but it's hard for him to use a straw when he's sick. Just suck some water into the syringe and push it into his mouth. I want the cup finished in a half hour."

I was used to the sick routine. My mom should've been, too, but she acted like every decision was life or death, and honestly, she could've been right. Fortunately, we'd never found out.

Miranda followed her directions, and every couple of minutes she filled my mouth with a few ounces of water, which tastes pretty disgusting when you're sick. All I wanted was for her to lie next to me. She never did. I wanted the warmth of her hands next to mine, but hers were busy texting. I didn't have the energy to ask who she was talking to, or—more likely—I didn't want to care. In my delirious mental state, I truly believed that once someone sneaks into your bedroom, you become theirs, and they become yours.

We spent the day watching the TV shows nobody cares about. Around noon, I had another coughing episode that Miranda handled without any help from my mom, who was taking a nap so she could be awake for the night shift.

Things were going to get worse before they got better. Life always works that way. I knew that. Miranda did, too. But when you're falling, it's hard to think. You just aim for the ground, I guess.

IT TAKES TWO

I COULD HEAR MY PARENTS talking in the other room after my dad got home from work, but I couldn't hear exactly what they were saying. They whispered, not wanting Ollie and me to think any of it was serious, and their words faded into the walls. I had already spent an hour watching ESPN highlights with my brother, who was twitching his legs and biting his nails and doing anything else to distract himself from the fact that I need a machine to breathe.

Ollie and I didn't say anything to each other, and we didn't need to. It was in those moments when I truly understood how terrified my family was to lose me.

My phone buzzed, and Ollie picked it up. "It's a text from Nory. She asked if you're okay."

"Don't answer," I said.

He set my phone back down. "So, are you feeling better?" he asked.

"I don't know. Today was pretty rough."

"Yeah, I saw this morning before I left for school. Mom says you're sick because you left your window open or something?"

"That's not why I'm sick." I paused to adjust my tone; I sounded too defensive. "I wasn't feeling well before that."

"You mean when you went to the concert?"

"Yeah."

"Then you shouldn't have gone. That was just stupid."

"I'm not stupid. I always get sick around this time of year, so better to get it over with."

Ollie shook his head.

Our dad shuffled into my bedroom and pointed at Ollie. "Mom needs to see you."

He left without arguing. We both knew Dad also wanted him out so he could sit with me alone.

"I haven't seen Zander around in a while," my dad said. "How's he doing?"

"I don't know. I haven't talked to him."

"Why?"

"Just because I was friends with him at one point doesn't mean I have to be friends with him forever," I said.

"You're right, but friendships don't usually end that fast. I fight with my friends, and sometimes we go years without talking to each other . . . but when we do talk, we always pick up right where we left off like nothing happened."

"I don't know what you want me to say."

"You don't need to say anything, at least not to me. What I'm trying to tell you is that friendship is a two-way street."

"Zander and I are on completely different streets."

Dad sighed. He was getting frustrated, but I didn't care. There was no changing my mind. "Harris, he texts you every day and asks how you're doing. He's showing he cares, which is more than any of your other friends have done."

"Miranda cares."

"It's Miranda's job to care."

We were silent. I didn't appreciate the implication that Miranda wouldn't care if she didn't have to.

"How are things going with her?" my dad asked.

"Good. She's doing a good job."

"Yeah? And you feel safe with her?"

"I mean, she's helping take care of me through all of this, and I'm not dead, so . . ."

"All right. Mom and I just want to make sure you're comfortable."

My dad has always been the more levelheaded parent. Sometimes it's hard to separate my mom being a mom from her being my caregiver, but it's easy for me to see my dad as just my dad. When my mom and I fight, he always swoops in to have the same conversation with me, but as a discussion and not as a fight.

It's those times—and watching football with him, honestly—when I've learned how to deal with difficult situations. But sometimes my stubbornness gets in the way of fully appreciating the lesson. That evening was one of the moments when I refused to listen.

HARD TO HANDLE

THE NEXT DAY, I COULDN'T take my BiPAP off at all. My breaths were shallow, and every one ended in a weak cough.

We ran nebulizer treatments more frequently to minimize additional congestion. There were good minutes, but mostly there were bad hours when I coughed so much that tears dripped down my face. Sometimes I tried to cough and nothing happened, like I'd forgotten how to do it.

Miranda was next to me through all of it. I keep saying that because it's what I remember most. I remember the fuzzy image of my mom standing over me and Miranda's calming presence at my bedside, sitting and watching. Steady.

She pushed another syringe of water into my mouth. "When was the last time you were sick like this?"

"A while ago," I mumbled. "I used to get sick a lot when I was a child. My mom spent every Christmas break with me in the hospital."

"Clare Bear is the best."

"She is. Although she stresses too much, especially about me."

"I don't blame her. You're her baby. I wish my parents cared half as much about me."

I started to talk, but my mouth was filled with spit. Miranda suctioned me so I could speak clearly. "You never talk about your parents."

"Not much to talk about. They do their thing, and I do mine."

"How did they feel about Brad?"

"They loved him, of course. They thought most of our problems were caused by me."

"How could they say that?"

Miranda shifted in the chair so her legs were tucked under her butt. She leaned to the left and rested her head on the edge of my bed.

I liked that she wasn't afraid to be near me. Sometimes I wondered if strangers and even close friends were afraid to get physically close because they thought they would hurt me. To Miranda, I wasn't different. I was just another friend she could lean on.

"My parents are old-fashioned," she said. "They chose not to see the bad parts because their own relationship is fucked up. My dad controls my mom, so to them, Brad wasn't doing anything out of the ordinary."

"Do you think Brad was controlling?"

"I don't know. Some of my friends thought he was, but maybe my parents were right that he just wanted the best for me."

"No, Miranda, your friends were right. You deserve to be with someone who respects you and trusts you."

"Maybe. But my options are pretty limited. Not many guys want to be with a recovering addict."

"I would want to be with you."

Mom chose that moment to check on us and drop off another cup of water. It would be my third of the day. I'd already peed like five times.

As soon as she was out the door, Miranda grabbed something from her purse. "I brought movies. Wanna watch one?"

I chuckled. "You still own a DVD player?"

"Yes, and so do you," Miranda said, nodding toward my Xbox. She held out the options, which were *The Girl Next Door* and *Harold & Kumar Go to White Castle*. "Kind of dated, but two of my favorites. Your parents are cool with R-rated movies, right? They seem like they are."

"Yeah, we watch them. Usually I just close my eyes if there's nudity."

She laughed. "You're fifteen years old. You don't have to close your eyes. Besides, if there's ever a time to see a boob, it's after the week you're having."

"You could just show me yours."

"Nice try. You couldn't handle them anyway."

I chose the first movie for the sole reason that the girl on the cover was really hot. I guess that was the point. Miranda popped the DVD into the Xbox. We made it through half the movie before my mom came back in to check on us. Actually, she walked in during a scene where the characters were at a porn convention, which was unfortunate. She didn't seem to care, though.

She told us that she'd made an appointment with the new pulmonologist for the following morning. I argued that I wouldn't have enough energy to sit in my wheelchair, but there wasn't another choice. I had to be seen.

REAL FRIENDS CARE

SURPRISE, I HAD AN UPPER RESPIRATORY INFECTION.
We waited twenty minutes in a depressing doctor's office to be
told what we already knew. We got no instructions except to
stay hydrated and do additional nebulizer treatments, both of
which we were already doing.

Honestly, I was right that the whole morning would be
a waste of our time. Doctors poke and prod and mumble a
bunch of nonsense that usually translates to, "Yup, you're sick.
Good luck out there."

I bet I coughed up half a gallon of mucus during the useless excursion. When I got home, all I wanted to do was get in
my bed and die.

"Zander texted you a few times while we were out," Mom
said. She held my phone in front of my face so I could see the
messages.

> **ZANDER:** Where are you? You've
> missed five days in a row

ZANDER: Nory said she texted you
but you didn't answer

ZANDER: Are you ok?

It was strange that he cared after what we'd said to each other at the Halloween party.

"What do you want to say?" Mom asked.

"I'll answer him later. I'm too tired right now."

Mom put my BiPAP on me, shut off the lights, and led Miranda into the living room so I could take a nap. When I woke up, it was dark and Ollie was in my room watching ESPN. Miranda and I had barely spoken to each other the whole day, and I never responded to Zander.

• • •

Thursday ended up being the worst day of the entire week. When Miranda arrived at nine o'clock, I'd been awake for more than two hours. Both of my parents spent the early morning watching me struggle to breathe. One would suction while the other alternated between using the cough assist machine and running nebulizer treatments.

I felt like death—or at least neighbors with death—but I kept telling myself that I always made it through. It wasn't my first time being that sick, and it wouldn't be my last.

What I hated was seeing Ollie watch me from the hallway.

Miranda took over my dad's duties after he left for work. She marched straight onto the battlefield without hesitation. The last several days had engraved the process into her brain. Cough, then suction. Cough, then suction.

I focused on her eyes. There was a new intensity there.

"You're a fighter," Miranda told me.

"I'm used to it," I said.

"Well, you shouldn't be used to struggling to breathe without choking. Life sucks, though."

"Miranda, I'll be all right. In a few days, this will be in the past, and unfortunately, we'll go back to school like none of it happened."

Miranda placed her hand on top of my upward-facing palm. Her index finger traced the creases. "Just don't die."

"I'm not planning on it. Besides, I can't die when the only girl I've ever kissed had a boyfriend. I don't want to be buried as a mistress."

"But you're a guy. You're just my sidepiece."

"Either way."

My mom announced that she was going to the grocery store to get something for lunch. That woman does not understand the definition of *rest*.

I find that while I'm sick, I spend most of my time worrying about the people caring for me. Like, Miranda seemed genuinely concerned that I might die, but I had to be brave for her and for my mom, who wouldn't sit down for more than two minutes.

"You want some water?" Miranda asked.

I nodded, and she emptied a syringe into my mouth. Another short coughing fit hit me, and the rumble in my chest was audible even without a stethoscope.

"Man, you really sound terrible," Miranda said. She frowned and reached for her purse and started digging through all the junk. It seemed to be filled with as much crap as my lungs. Finally, she pulled out a short, skinny tube. "I brought this for you. I think it might help."

"A vape pen? I didn't know you vaped."

"Not very often—Brad hated it, obviously—but it's something I do from time to time to help me relax."

At first I thought I was hallucinating from some kind of sickness delirium, but I watched Miranda take a puff. This was no dream. "And you want *me* to try it? No way." Sometimes Miranda let her red side come on too strong; this was definitely one of those times.

"We've been learning about alternative medicine in my class—mostly about how a lot of the stuff out there is a total farce—but apparently, marijuana can help with breathing issues."

I looked at her again like she had lost her mind. Thank God my mom wasn't home.

Miranda took another quick puff to demonstrate how it worked. "It barely has any weed in it, but it should be enough to open your airways."

Let it be known that I willingly took medical advice from an unregistered nurse. Maybe it had something to do with my lack of rest, or how beautiful she looked sitting next to me and the way her eyes searched for an answer. Or maybe it was because she had told me a secret, which meant she trusted me, and I wanted to show her I trusted her in return. Or maybe it was because I felt like death, and when you feel like death, there's not much to lose.

I wrapped my lips around the vape pen and inhaled. Miranda told me to hold it for a moment, and I did. When I let it out, I coughed, but overall I didn't feel any different.

"Just give it a few minutes to see if it worked," Miranda said.

My phone buzzed again. I should've known it would take nearly dying to become popular. There were two emails. One was from all my teachers except Mr. Bavroe, who still refused to scan in my homework so I could do it on the computer. He wouldn't even accept an electronic submission if I scanned the documents myself. He claimed reading on his computer gave him a headache, and apparently he didn't know how to operate a printer. The guy was the very definition of entitled.

The other email was from Nory with the history assignment.

"She says she hopes you're feeling okay. Do you want to answer her?" Miranda asked.

"Just leave it," I told her. "I don't want to answer."

And then I coughed. I mean, I coughed *hard*, and I kept coughing until tears raced down my cheeks. Miranda stood next to me, suctioning and holding the cough assist mask over my face. But nothing helped. I coughed and wheezed and gasped while the look in Miranda's eyes morphed from confident to concerned—and then to terrified.

"I think I'm gonna throw up," I said, barely getting the words out.

Miranda ran into the bathroom and returned with a metal bowl, and I tried to puke, but my stomach wrenched and my chest tightened, and the only thing that came out of my mouth was more mucus. This was way different from my drunk puking.

The room began to spin, and through all the blurriness, I saw Miranda reach for her phone and dial.

RED BLUE RED BLUE

When I opened my eyes, I was in the back of an ambulance. Two EMTs were monitoring my vitals, and every couple of seconds, one of them yelled to the driver to drive faster.

Miranda was next to me, curled up and staring at the tattoo on her arm. "I'm sorry," she said. "I'm sorry." She wouldn't look at me, and I probably would've felt some way about that if it weren't nearly impossible for me to breathe without pain.

Through the back window, I watched the red-and-blue lights flash, a warning to everyone else on the road. They reminded me of Miranda and myself—two opposite colors. One was calm and the other loud. When put together, they can't be missed.

"I'm sorry," Miranda said. "I'm sorry."

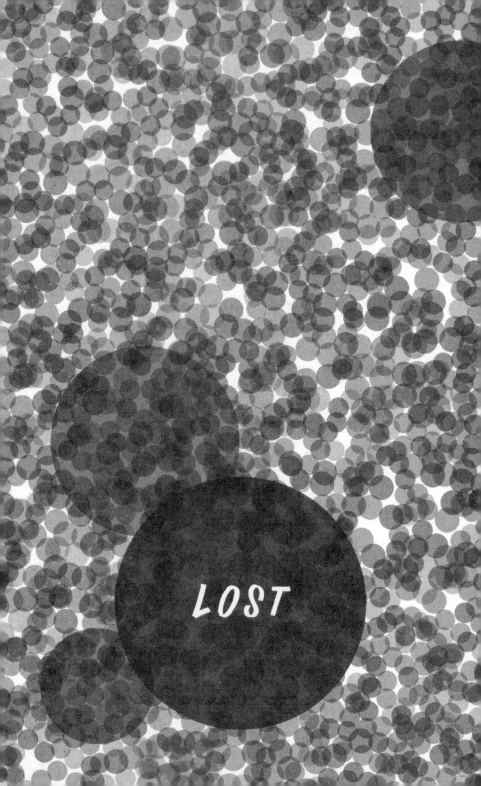

SAY ANYTHING

ME: I'm doing ok and should be leaving the
hospital in a few days. You shouldn't
feel bad. The doctors think my upper
respiratory infection became bacterial.
There's nothing you could've done

ME: Come visit me!

ME: You're way better than any of the
nurses in this hospital. We miss you

ME: Why aren't you answering?

• • •

NORY: Zander's mom said you're in the
hospital now?! We tried to come
see you but they said you don't
want any visitors. Feel better! 😞

NORY: Also I promised I would cook you someing the next time you were sick. I'm going to make sopa de fideo. It's the soup my mom made me when I got sick. Let me know when you're home from the hospital and I'll drop some off <3

ZANDER: The gift shop should've delivered a balloon to your room. Did you get it? Hope you're feeling better. School sucks even more without you

• • •

ME: My infection is all gone! I should be getting out tomorrow if you want to come work

ME: BTW I got your get-well card. You don't have to apologize. We don't blame you for anything. My mom was actually glad you thought to call an ambulance

ME: Haven't heard from you in a few weeks. My mom doesn't think you're coming back

ME: I don't understand what happened

ME: Are you with Brad?

ME: I'm going back to school tomorrow

ME: Mom wants to know if you're coming

ME: I guess that means no

ME: I had my mom bring me to your parents' house. They said they haven't talked to you in a month and don't know where you are

ME: I'm really worried about you. Please answer me

● ● ●

NORY: Glad to see you back in school. Do you feel up to working on the project is week?

● ● ●

ZANDER: Hey! I saw that you were looking for a table now that the football team is eating off campus. Your spot at the Refuge for the Lost is still reserved if you want to come back

ZANDER: You know I'm not mad about the Halloween party anymore, right?

• • •

ME: Hi Miranda! Merry Christmas! 🎄🎁

ME: Happy New Year! 🎉

• • •

NORY: Hey Mrs. Ivavych wants a draft of the textbook section of the project next week. Do you want to work on it this weekend?

• • •

ME: So I guess I'm never going to see you again. I really don't understand what happened. Why did you disappear? I trusted you and now you're gone and nothing makes sense

ME: I don't blame you. Please come back

EPISTEMIC AMBIVALENCE

I UNDERSTOOD THAT SHE WAS OUT OF MY LIFE. I understood the reality of that. But I still had my memories, and they pulled at me. It's like they wanted to know why they'd been made in the first place. They wanted to know what makes someone disappear. They wanted to know who to blame. They asked for an explanation every day.

It was more torture than my body had ever endured.

THE NEW OLD NORMAL

OLLIE HADN'T BEEN HOME MUCH since lacrosse season had started. I usually saw him—or heard him, really—around ten o'clock at night, when I was already in bed. I couldn't fall asleep until I knew he was inside the house, and then I'd close my eyes to the sound of him heating up his dinner in the microwave and telling Dad about his day.

Mom was never up at that hour. Now that she was going to school with me again, her bedtime was right after dinner. Some nights, she couldn't even stay awake long enough to eat.

The nursing agency had nobody to send. Well, not nobody. What I mean is nobody like Miranda, which was probably for the best.

Because Miranda had fallen off the face of the earth, my school days now started an hour earlier so my dad could help me get ready.

"Get his armpits," my mom directed one morning during a shower.

Dad pointed to the soap bubbles. "What do you think I'm doing?"

"But I mean *really* get in there. He's been sweating a lot now that it's warmer outside."

"Giving Harris a shower is not a two-person job, hon. Either I do it or you do it."

I sat naked in the shower while my parents fought about how to bathe me. It was the same argument every day. I wondered whether my dad's help was actually helping or if he was just another person for my mom to yell at in the morning.

"What are you doing?" Mom asked me later as she slipped on her shoes. I was in my wheelchair, head slumped over, trying not to vomit.

"I hate waking up this early. It makes me feel really sick."

"We'll eat something when we get to school, and you'll feel better."

She told me that every morning, but it was never true. Food didn't stop my stomach from trying to climb up the back of my throat. It only made things worse. I gagged every time I attempted to swallow a bite of granola bar.

Most days, there wasn't so much as thirty seconds to choke down breakfast. Even with the head start, I barely rolled into homeroom before Wormhole finished taking attendance. I wanted to point out to my mom that Miranda and I had never been late, but of course I didn't.

The only positive thing about being late was that I got a quick peek at Nory as I entered the room. She still sat in the back with Kelvin, whom I didn't hate. I just strongly disagreed with his stupid face.

Nory and I hadn't spoken since before Christmas break, when she quickly wished me happy holidays while walking past me in the hallway. After that, I would catch her glancing at me in class or by our lockers. Sometimes she'd smile.

Sometimes I'd smile back, but the days she looked at me were actually more miserable than the others.

Her face reminded me of all the things I wasn't able to tell her, like why I stopped answering her texts and why I wouldn't let her visit me in the hospital. The only words we had exchanged in months were when I'd emailed her the first draft of the physics project. I had finished the remaining two chapters by myself for no real reason except that I felt bad.

I could've blamed all this on not knowing her favorite color, but I realized I knew Miranda's, and that hadn't helped me much. We had both disappeared with no explanation and no warning.

I THOUGHT I KNEW

"ZANDER IS AT YOUR REGULAR TABLE," my mom pointed out from the lunch line. We bought the disgusting cafeteria food now since there wasn't time for my mom to make lunch. "You want to sit with him?" She waved.

"Stop waving. We're not friends anymore."

"What happened, anyway? You haven't spoken to Zander in months."

"Yeah, well, sometimes people just stop being friends." It was the same answer I'd given my dad.

Mom carried the tray to the outdoor patio. Early spring had melted the snow, but the ground was still stained white from the salt. A dozen round picnic tables were scattered about, most of them empty. Nobody ever sat outside at this school, as far as I could tell. Not even during beautiful weather or when there were rumors about a lunchtime fight.

"So you're never going to talk to Zander again? Another friendship just thrown away?" Mom asked. "And let me guess—you've convinced yourself it's all about colors?"

To be honest, I'd kind of given up on the whole color thing

since Miranda, but I didn't feel like telling Mom that. Instead, what I said was, "Well, if I have, that's your doing."

"How is it my fault?"

"After my first day of kindergarten, I came home and told you that the other kids wouldn't talk to me. You said I should ask what their favorite colors were, so the next day I went to school and started asking everyone."

"Jesus, Harris, I just meant it as a way to start a conversation or find something in common with a classmate. You weren't supposed to assume you knew everything about someone just because you knew their favorite color." She smiled at me sadly. "You have to stop finding reasons to push everyone away."

"I didn't push Miranda away, and yet she still left." I chewed slowly on my lunch, pondering whether I should voice the thoughts in my head. "Did you know she was my first nurse to like red and orange? Our colors were supposed to complement each other. Miranda felt like the only person who actually cared about me."

"She's gone now, for whatever reason, and you need to move on." Mom swatted a bug away from our food. "I never should've let you get so close to her. This was a job, and we should've left it at that." She pushed my long hair back from my forehead; my hair was another thing we didn't have time to take care of. "I love you, honey."

My parents didn't know most of what had happened between Miranda and me. They only knew the good stuff, like how she had saved me when I was drunk and called an ambulance when I stopped breathing. I had never told them about Kaylin or Miranda's addiction or the time she'd crawled into my bed. I had never told them how she'd kissed me in the bathroom before my date with Nory or how we'd told each other "I love you," only I'd meant it in a way she hadn't. I'd never told them about the vape pen.

All they knew was that Miranda was there, and then she wasn't. At the end of the day, I guess that's about all I knew, too.

MOM'S BREAKING POINT

WHEN I'D BEEN WITH MIRANDA, school hadn't been important. I went to class and did the homework, but that was just a reflex. Teachers taught, and I listened . . . partially. Now, teachers taught, and I listened—partially—while thinking about where Miranda possibly could've gone.

My mom didn't allow those thoughts to linger. She made sure I paid attention and had copious notes and that my teachers sent work to my laptop. All of them obliged except Mr. Bavroe.

Since my mom had returned to school, we'd had countless meetings with Ms. Maszak, Mr. Bavroe, and someone from IT to train my geriatric history teacher how to electronically send and receive my homework. At the end of every meeting, Mr. Bavroe seemed to think he was Steve Jobs, but when it came time to pass out homework, he always handed me a worksheet just like everyone else. He also still refused to accept my work if I emailed it to him and would mark it as incomplete.

I wasn't mad that he was an unaccommodating asshole, because I expected it. But over and over, Mom gave me an earful about how I should've taken care of this at the beginning of the year, then marched into Ms. Maszak's office and demanded that Mr. Bavroe be fired.

"I can't fire a faculty member because you don't get along with them," Ms. Maszak said to my mom this time. "Besides, Mr. Bavroe will be retiring at the end of the year, and—"

"*Get along* with him?" Mom laughed. "Do you hear yourself? I don't want to be friends with Mr. Bavroe. Neither does Harris. What I want is for him to do his job."

Dr. Kenzing sat behind Ms. Maszak, her arms folded. She never said much during the meetings until the very end, when she'd sum up what we already knew and act like everything was fabulous, even when everything was obviously not fabulous.

"Let's get Mr. Bavroe in here and see if we can't figure out a solution," Ms. Maszak said. She dialed her office phone and spoke quietly to the person on the other end.

Mom sighed. "Go ahead. But we've been going at this for months now with no action."

A few minutes later, Mr. Bavroe sauntered into the tiny office. "Hey, buddy," he said to me. I didn't answer.

"We started having these discussions in September." Mom wasted no time getting to the point. "Now it's April. What's the problem?"

Mr. Bavroe stared at my mom like he had no idea who she was or what she was talking about. Then he shrugged. "I don't see a problem. Harris is a great student, and he's easily passing my class."

"So was he *easily* passing your class when you gave him an incomplete on his last three assignments?"

"He never turned them in."

"He did!" Mom yelled. "On his laptop!"

Ms. Maszak motioned for my mom to ease up. "Please, Clare, don't raise your voice. We're all here to help Harris."

"But you're *not* helping him. The school year is almost over, and I'm still doing everything for Harris. Some of his teachers have been accommodating, and history seems like it would be the simplest to make electronic. It's just worksheets that need to be scanned in."

"I'm teaching three AP classes, two honors, and a college prep," Mr. Bavroe announced. "I don't have time to scan and email every assignment."

"I want Harris switched into another history class," Mom told Ms. Maszak. "He deserves a teacher who cares."

Ms. Maszak hesitated. She looked at Dr. Kenzing, and the two stared at each other as if they were communicating telepathically.

I watched it all unfold in silence. I knew that after this meeting, my mom would lecture me about not sticking up for myself. But I didn't care. I just wanted out. I wanted out of that office and that phony school. I wanted out of Mr. Bavroe's history class and out of my wheelchair. I wanted out of my memories of Miranda.

"All the other honors history classes are full," Ms. Maszak finally said. "Fortunately, Harris isn't required to take history this year, so we can transfer him into a study hall, and he can make up the credit next year." She smiled at Mr. Bavroe. "As Mr. Bavroe will be retiring in just a few weeks, Harris will of course have a different teacher for history."

Everyone looked at me for approval. I hated being complacent, and I knew my mom did, too. Usually we wouldn't give up so easily, but I saw how tired my mom was of fighting, and honestly, I didn't care as much as I thought I should about wasting a whole year on a class that wouldn't count. So I shrugged convincingly enough that Ms. Maszak printed me a new schedule.

"I'm thrilled about this plan," Dr. Kenzing said. She was just as horrible after nothing was accomplished as she was before.

"Why?" I asked. "You just gave me a free hour to slack off."

WE'RE STILL DOING THIS(?)

THE RIDGE PREP LACROSSE FIELD was adjacent to the sports training complex and behind the academic building. Yes, Ollie's private school had an entire sports complex, detailed with maroon and silver for the Ridge Prep Raiders.

His first game fell on the hottest day of spring so far, and you could actually see the heat rising from the field, accentuating the stench of rubber and artificial turf. It was unseasonably warm, but as I was learning, that was New Jersey weather.

"How'd the meeting go the other day?" Dad asked Mom. Family catch-ups happened at random times, since every other moment we spent together involved getting me ready for school or ready for bed.

"Oh, you know." Mom shrugged. She watched the teams run up and down the field.

"No, I don't know. I wasn't there. That's why I'm asking."

"Well, I explained how ridiculous it is that Mr. Bavroe is the only teacher who refuses to use the laptop."

Dad looked at me. "All your other teachers use it?"

"Yeah, mostly. Sometimes it's hard to do math homework on it, but all my other classes are fine."

"I don't understand what the problem is for that one teacher," Dad said.

"That's what I said to Ms. Maszak and Dr. Kenzing," Mom said.

"And who are they?"

"Harris's accommodations manager and the principal of the school. You've met them."

"Oh, right. And what'd they say?"

The bleachers erupted with applause. The Ridge Prep Raiders were up one goal, thanks to a shot by Ollie. Our parents had missed the action but clapped along with everyone else, not realizing their son had scored.

Ollie looked up from the field and pointed at me. I smiled like I always do after every goal, because that's our thing. I promised to never miss a game, and he promised to never miss a goal.

"They called Mr. Bavroe and asked him to join us," Mom told Dad. "So he comes to the office and right away starts saying how he's not going to bother with the computer because he's too busy and that we should just go to hell."

"That's not what he said," I corrected her.

"Well, that's what he meant. So I said I wanted Harris switched to another class with a teacher who actually gives a shit."

"Good." Dad nodded. He was half watching the game. "Did they switch him to a new class?"

Listening to a play-by-play of a meeting that had been miserable the first time was inexplicably nauseating. Like, I just wanted to drive my wheelchair through the bleacher railing. There was no reason for my mom to recount every second of the conversation. My dad had asked how it went, and she could've answered, "It was a shit show, per usual."

The Raiders scored again. Ollie got the assist, and the team was leading by four.

"All the history classes are full, so Harris is getting a study hall period instead," Mom said.

"That's bullshit. The lazy teacher shouldn't get out of doing his job. Study hall isn't a solution. His teachers need to be held accountable."

"Hon, I agree, but there's only so much energy I have to fight with them every day. You should've come to the meeting like I asked."

"I can't just leave work in the middle of the day. I'm two hours away, and then it's two hours back to the city. I would've had to take the whole day off."

"Yeah? I take the whole day off every day to go to school with Harris. It's what you do."

Dad ignored Mom and focused his attention on the game. They always talked about me as if I wasn't sitting next to them.

I didn't like watching my parents get snippy with each other. Sure, they fought and yelled from time to time like married people do, but it usually resolved itself in a few hours. Ever since Miranda had disappeared, though, it was tense all the time. I think everybody was tired.

Honestly, I had stopped caring whether Miranda ever came back. I hated her for putting even more of a strain on my parents.

During halftime, Dad asked me, "Are you all right with being in study hall? It's up to you, bud. Mom and I can fight it if you want."

"I think it'll take away the stress of dealing with Mr. Bavroe."

"Don't worry about him. If you want to take history, then we'll make it happen."

I thought about it. "I guess it would suck to repeat the class next year."

"Okay, I'm going to take off work tomorrow so we can rectify this," Dad said to Mom. "I'm sorry for not being around as much as I promised I would. I'm going to fix that."

He kissed her on the head, and for a moment, we felt like a family again.

• • •

We waited for Ollie outside the locker room. Somehow, he always managed to be the last player to leave.

"Four goals and three assists," he boasted. "Not too bad for the first game."

"Could've been five if you'd taken that extra step from the wing," I said.

"Shut up. Why's your face so red?"

"Sunburn." Which was the result of our family underestimating the strength of the New Jersey sun. I didn't mind, though. I'd gotten sunburned almost every day in California, so the sting on my cheeks felt normal. Just like Ollie's bragging and our parents trying to fix everything.

I THOUGHT I'D FOUND A WAY

EARLY THE NEXT MORNING, we had another meeting with Mr. Bavroe, Ms. Maszak, Dr. Kenzing, and my dad. My dad pointed out, as my mom and I had during earlier meetings, that none of my other teachers had a problem with taking five minutes out of their day to scan in worksheets and email them to me. My dad even demonstrated how simple it was. Mr. Bavroe didn't say much during the hour, because there was nothing for him to say. He'd already gone through the training with the IT team, so it wasn't like he didn't know how to do it. The lazy old man just wanted to coast toward his retirement.

By the end of the meeting, he still wouldn't budge. Mr. Bavroe was convinced he had no free time during the day. My dad recommended he do it during his lunch break, but that didn't go over well.

Either way, we eventually came to a compromise. Mr. Bavroe would allow me to leave class ten minutes early to scan in the homework myself and promised to accept it by email. My dad also insisted that Ms. Maszak and Dr. Kenzing be copied on all homework submissions so Mr. Bavroe couldn't claim

I hadn't sent it. From the look on Mr. Bavroe's face, I could tell he didn't like that idea, but he couldn't reject it without sounding like a total ass.

After the meeting, I was feeling pretty good, like maybe my life was moving forward again. Like maybe Miranda disappearing was a good thing. I had so much confidence after my morning with Mr. Bavroe that I was even thinking about approaching Nory.

All this time, I had been waiting around for her to say something, but I was finally ready to admit that it was on me to make the first move. I was the reason we hadn't talked. I had disappeared just like Miranda—without explanation or warning. Nory deserved better than that.

She deserved someone who didn't care about whether their colors blended into something beautiful, the same way I knew she didn't care that I was in a wheelchair. All that mattered was the way we felt when we were together. It had just taken my life falling apart and Miranda being out of the picture for me to understand that.

Nory was at her locker when I got to mine, but somehow she felt miles away. The thing about isolation is that it can happen so quickly, you don't even realize how far you've drifted. You can see the rest of the world, but you can't get close to it. Probably because I hadn't even apologized for the things I'd said after the party or for disappearing after Miranda left. Besides, I still didn't know what I wanted with Nory.

But maybe I didn't have to know. I just had to start talking and hope that was enough.

Her eyes flickered at the sound of my wheelchair as I pulled closer. We shared a look.

"Hey," I said.

"Hey."

Then Nory shut her locker and walked into homeroom.

That cut deeper than her calling me out in front of everyone in the hallway. And this time, I knew it couldn't be fixed with a stupid note slid across a classroom table.

I'd thought I had nothing more to lose, but it turned out I did.

I lost all hope.

GROCERY STORES RECONNECT YOU

DAD STARTED WORKING FROM HOME on Fridays so he could be around more to give Mom a break. After Ollie got home from school, the three of us went to the grocery store to stock up for a couple of weeks. Our fridge and pantry had been pretty empty since Mom had started being with me full time. Occasionally, we picked up odds and ends, but never enough to make more than a few meals during the week, and Mom was usually too tired to go shopping over the weekend.

The grocery store on a Friday evening was the worst place to be. Toddlers wreaked havoc in aisles that were too narrow for shopping carts, let alone a wheelchair. I felt like I was constantly in somebody's way.

When my mom went to the market, I usually stayed home, but Dad didn't give Ollie or me a choice. Mom gave him a shopping list, and we followed him like ducklings. We zigged and zagged, squeezing and sniffing various fruits. When Dad finally made a choice, he'd grab a plastic bag from the dispenser and blow into it so it would open. That really grossed me out, hearing his breath hit the flimsy plastic. But everything bothered me: Ollie standing too close or my dad taking too long to pick a ripe avocado.

I knew we'd buy a cart full of food and that half of it would go bad. Mom would cook over the weekend, but once Monday came, her ability to function would deteriorate. Dad was only capable of preparing boxed mac and cheese or something frozen.

"Ollie, do you need any Gatorade or water bottles for practice?" Dad asked.

"No. The school gives us that."

"All right. I'm just asking."

For a moment, we felt like a normal family again. Ollie was being snotty, and Dad was being Dad. But I couldn't enjoy any of it. All I could think about was how the only reason our lives needed fixing was that Miranda had broken them.

And I couldn't wrap my mind around it. How had she made such an impact? My family had overcome so much worse than being ghosted by one of my nurses. But a part of me still wished she'd come back. Miranda would know how to fix things with Nory or at least give me the confidence to keep trying. She had already partially done that before.

A voice down the aisle interrupted my thoughts. "Hi, Jacobuses." It was Zander's mom.

My dad waved back, and we walked toward a woman who looked identical to her son. Basically, if you put a wig on Zander, that was his mom.

"How are you guys?" Zander's mom asked.

"Eh, okay," Dad answered. "Just trying to catch up on grocery shopping."

"You know, I haven't seen Clare here in a while."

"Yeah, she's been at school every day with Harris. His nurse vanished into thin air."

"Oh, no. I remember you really liked her."

"Yeah, well, life happens. This isn't our first rodeo."

"We're having problems with Zander's older brothers," Zander's mom said.

"What's going on with them?" Dad asked.

"They're aging out of their school, and we're just trying to figure out what's next."

"What do you mean?" I asked.

"Zander's brothers have autism. He never told you?"

"No," I said.

"Well, I'm not sure about the specifics in New Jersey," Dad began, "but every state offers a ton of day programs for high-functioning adults. If you need help, Clare is great at finding info like that."

"That'd be amazing. And let me know if there's anything I can do for you guys."

We started to walk away when Zander's mom turned to me. "Zander's just been sitting at home. I think he misses you."

I nodded, though I didn't know what she wanted me to do about that. What could I have said? *Sorry I treated your son like dirt even though he was my only friend*?

. . .

Ollie and my parents unloaded the bags of groceries, and I watched from the front hall, trying to take my mind off the fact that I couldn't help. It was this sort of stuff that reminded me of my disability more than strangers staring at me in public. Not being able to contribute made me feel empty. Then I'd start to hate myself for being overly dramatic. It was a twisted cycle.

Dad struggled to carry the last two bags through the door, then Ollie took one from him. "How do you like the guys on the lacrosse team?" Dad asked.

Ollie shrugged. "They're still assholes, just like I said at the beginning of the year."

"And why are they assholes?"

"I don't know. They won't pass me the ball, crap like that."

"Then let them be assholes. But if you get the ball, you should pass and get the assist. It's still a point for your team, and it shows you're not bothered by their immaturity."

Ollie didn't answer. He just nodded and finished unpacking.

"Have you heard from the Virginia coach?" Mom asked him.

"Yeah. He's coming to watch a game in a few weeks."

We ate salmon for dinner, and although we all complained that the recipe was salty, it was the first nice meal we'd had since Miranda had left. I tried my best to enjoy each moment, especially when Ollie did his secret routine of flipping me off from across the table and Mom caught him and grabbed my hand to help me return the brotherly sentiment. We all laughed. It was nice.

SOUR GUMMY WORMS
FIX EVERYTHING

I HADN'T SAT AT ZANDER'S LUNCH TABLE IN MONTHS, but there was still an empty spot without a chair, an open invitation for me to come back. I only realized that after seeing Zander's mom and understanding that he wasn't mad at me and that I really had no reason to be mad at him. I guess I'd always known that but refused to accept the truth, since it meant I was the only thing holding us back from being friends again.

And so I sucked it up and drove over to the empty spot next to him. "Can I sit with you?"

Zander shrugged and buried his face in a tuna fish sandwich, so I stayed, and Mom unpacked our lunches. Thanks to the trip to the grocery store, it was the first time in months that we didn't have to buy crappy cafeteria food.

"Hey, Ms. Clare," Zander said, still not looking at me.

"It's good to see you, Zander." I knew my mom wanted to say more or joke around like we used to during lunch, but she was waiting to see what I was going to do.

"I saw your mom the other day," I said to Zander. "She told me you've become a hermit."

"I've always been a hermit. Isn't that why we stopped being friends?"

"My dad told me that people don't just stop being friends. I guess they just get pulled apart by all the things they don't have in common anymore."

"Let me get this straight. We didn't have enough in common because I refused to party?"

Mom kept trying to force food in my mouth, but I shook her off so I could talk. I think she wanted the opposite. "No, we didn't have enough in common because you refused to grow as a person and try new things. I didn't care if you got drunk, but you didn't even try to mingle at the party. You just hid in the kitchen. We might as well have stayed home and played video games."

(Who else had to talk about getting drunk in front of their mom? I had a pretty weird life.)

"I liked hanging at your house and playing Xbox all night," Zander said. "It was the only time I got to relax and be in a quiet place. You took that away."

The two other boys at our table kept trading cards as if nothing remotely important was happening in front of them. But maybe Zander and I were making a bigger deal of it than we needed to. Or maybe he was feeling the right amount of outrage and I was being a jerk again.

I have a tendency to downplay stressful situations. My mom does most of the worrying, and I knew, based on experience, that everything that needed to work out would work out. I mean, I'd been on my deathbed or stranded in a broken wheelchair enough times to understand that circumstances would get resolved and I would move on with my life.

The problem was that those resolutions were almost

always a result of my parents' heroics. My friendship with Zander could only be repaired by me.

"I didn't know about your brothers," I said.

Zander sighed. "There's a lot you don't know about me, because you never ask. I mean, I get it—you aren't able to come to my house, so you don't see what goes on in my life. But you could still take an interest."

My mom glared at me. Zander was saying the same thing she'd been telling me my whole life—that I never took an interest in other people. For some reason, Miranda had been the exception. She'd survived her own dark past, so I'd thought she could empathize with mine. But I wasn't sure I'd understood her. And I wasn't sure she'd actually understood me, either.

"Then tell me now," I said. "What don't I know?"

"Well, to start, my stepdad is the football coach. Did you know that?"

I shook my head. "I guess that's why you hate going to the games and hide when we're on the field."

"Yup. He accepts that my brothers have autism, but it was a big disappointment when he found out his other son was nerdy and unathletic."

"Why didn't you tell me that?"

"I tried, but you were always blabbing about Miranda or Nory. And then you disappeared."

I knew Zander had nothing against Miranda, but we both knew that after she'd showed up, I'd spent my time trying to become someone else.

When you're young (and probably when you're old, too), it's easy to lose yourself in the excitement of something new. An innocent example: you get the superfast bike you wanted for your birthday, and the world's your oyster . . . until you take a bad fall. And then another. And then another. It's obvious you're not ready for it, but you're too enthralled to admit it. So you keep falling. And meanwhile, your old bike gathers dust in the garage.

That was my relationship with Miranda. She'd taken me places I'd never have been able to go on my own, but I'd fallen way too hard, way too many times. At some point, I needed to stop blaming the bike and start blaming myself for getting back on. At some point, I needed to remember where I'd started.

"I brought you something," I told Zander. I nodded at my mom to take the package out of my backpack.

He looked at the jumbo pack of sour gummy worms and smiled. "For me?"

"Well, I don't expect you'll be able to eat all of them yourself, but yes, they're for you."

"You underestimate me, good sir."

Zander ripped the bag open and began devouring entire handfuls. In a split second, we were back to our old selves, but I still felt the weight of abandoning him. I hoped it would pass.

"You boys crack me up," Mom said. "One bag of gummy worms fixes everything?"

"It sure helps," Zander answered. "But I actually forgave Harris a while ago. I texted him, but your son never answers his phone."

I saw Nory watching us from her table on the opposite side of the cafeteria. She was sitting with Kelvin and some of his friends. Zander noticed her, too.

"She told me you tried to talk to her," he said.

"Yeah, and I probably messed things up even more."

"I don't think so. If you did, then why is she looking over here?"

"She's probably wondering why you want to be my friend again."

"I'm wondering that, too," Zander teased. "But dude, Nory doesn't hate you. She just moved on."

Zander shoved more worms into his mouth. The bag was already a quarter empty. "I wish we could all get along like we did in middle school. I wish I could bake a cake filled with rainbows and smiles and everyone would eat and be happy."

"*Mean Girls*?" I asked.

"Duh."

I started to feel comfortable at the table again, like old times. Even with the Pokémon boys playing cards and Miranda's and Kaylin's initials carved underneath, it belonged to us. As long as we were students at East Essex Central, we would always have somewhere to sit.

APPROACH

THE SKY IS ALWAYS BLUE

A WAVE OF SPRING RAINSTORMS trapped us in the house for days. The heavy clouds rolled in on a Monday and seemed to just sit there, hovering over the city. Sometimes, I'd peek out the window and catch a sliver of blue before the clouds shifted again and covered it up. It was sort of a torment at first, like the storm was following us and letting the sun shine down on everyone else. And it was during one of those moments that I realized the sky is never truly dark. Above the clouds, there was still blue. It was a comforting thought, knowing that someday it would clear.

"You guys want to go see a movie?" Mom asked me and Ollie. We were playing video games in my room.

"Not really," I answered.

"Oh, come on. Let's get out of the house for a little. Dad's away for work, so now's our chance." Dad hated the movies. He said it didn't make any sense to pay good money to have other people annoy you for two hours.

"Is there anything good showing?"

"We'll find out. I was thinking we could buy tickets when we get there for whatever movie's about to start. It'll be fun."

I looked at Ollie, but he just shrugged. Apparently, the fate of our evening rested on my shoulders.

"Let's go."

In a flash, Mom shut off the Xbox and bounced out of the room. Ollie and I both yelled at her that we hadn't saved the game, but she was long gone.

"What's her deal?" I asked Ollie.

"Not sure, but I overheard her on the phone with Dad saying that the nursing agency has some people for you to meet."

"Really? She didn't say anything to me."

Ollie took the controller from my hand and moved the chair he'd been sitting on back to the corner. As I watched him, I remembered how Zander had said I never asked questions or took an interest in other people. There was probably a lot I could ask Ollie. For starters, I wondered why he thought all his teammates sucked. Maybe he was just as friendless as I was. But at least I had someone with me all the time, even at school. It felt like Ollie was truly alone; I saw it in the way he walked and how he spent every weekend with his parents and his little brother.

Ollie had always been like that. He never partied or got in trouble outside the house. He was the son and brother he was supposed to be, but I had never been much of a brother to him. I guess I thought that was more his responsibility than mine.

I opened my mouth to start asking the questions I should've been asking for years, but then Mom called for us.

• • •

We'd been to this movie theater a few times before. It was one of those large chain cinemas that oozed the scent of burnt popcorn and synthetic butter. It was definitely the place to be for bored teenagers and the elderly.

As soon as we parked, the rain started pouring again. For ten minutes, Mom contemplated the pros and cons of getting wet and seeing whatever random movie was playing or just going home. Ollie didn't care either way, while I argued that we'd already taken the time to drive to the theater and going home wouldn't stop us from getting wet because we'd still need to get out of Black Hawk and into the house.

"Let's just wait a few more minutes to see if the storm passes," Mom said.

"It hasn't passed in five days," I told her. "Let's just go."

She finally agreed on one condition: I had to wear my rain cape. As you can imagine, water and motorized wheelchairs are mortal enemies.

Mom climbed into the back of the van with me and draped the polyester poncho over my chair, making sure all the vital parts were completely covered. I looked like E.T.

"All right, make a run for it!" Mom said.

I drove as fast as I could toward the theater, but the wind was strong and pushed back against my hand on the joystick. Ollie jogged next to me to hold the cape and keep it from flapping up in front of my face.

Despite our valiant efforts, all three of us were soaked by the time we got inside. There were puddles in the metal footrests of my chair, dripping onto the thick theater carpet. It was sort of awesome how totally unprepared we were for the rain.

We got in line and purchased tickets for some animated movie. It was the closest to starting while still giving us the chance to see the previews (which we all agreed were the best part). The theater was practically empty, even after we'd wasted time buying candy and drinks. A lone older woman sat behind the wheelchair seating area.

"Do those green lights turn off?" she yelled, referring to buttons on the back of my wheelchair.

For the record, the green light isn't very bright, but I hated feeling like a nuisance, so I quickly parked in the empty spot next to my brother and had him turn off my wheelchair. I think the lady was just mad she couldn't obnoxiously chew on popcorn anymore, now that the theater wasn't empty. Oh, wait, she did that anyway.

"I'm going to the bathroom before the movie starts," Mom said.

Ollie and I nodded, and I realized this was my chance to ask him about Ridge Prep. I felt oddly nervous.

"How's school?" I whispered, like I was some random aunt you see once a year.

"Why?"

"I don't know. You never really talk about it."

"There's nothing to talk about. It's school."

"But the other day, you said all the guys on the team suck. Why do you think that?"

Ollie shrugged and sank into his seat. "Because they do. I already told you guys why. Can we not talk about this?"

I was going to drop it, but something wasn't adding up. Ollie usually got along with everyone. "Why don't they pass you the ball? Is it because you're new, or because you're better than they are? Either way, that's stupid."

"Yeah, it is."

Mom returned. "What are you guys talking about?"

"I'm trying to figure out why Ollie's teammates hate him and why he doesn't have any friends," I said.

"Oh my God," Ollie half shouted, "I have friends! I just don't hang out with the jerks on the lacrosse team."

"Harris is right," Mom said. "You never invite anyone over to the house."

"Most of the guys live too far away."

"What about the one guy who lives near us?" I asked. "The guy whose barbecue you went to?"

Ollie fidgeted in his seat. He looked at me, and I could see in his eyes that he was hiding something. "There's a girl at Ridge Prep who's in a wheelchair, though I don't think she has the same thing as you. Anyway, at the beginning of the year, the guys on the team started making fun of her. I sort of kept an eye on her for a while, and everything kind of died down, and I figured they'd moved on. But then it got worse, and they started touching her chair and asking her how she has sex. I couldn't take it anymore, so I told them all to fuck off."

Mom stared. "Christ, Ollie." Then she put her hand on his knee. "We're lucky that Harris never had bullying issues, but I'm proud of you for sticking up for her the way I know you would for your brother."

"Yeah, well, those assholes were relentless. I had to walk with her in the hallways for a few weeks until they stopped."

"You should ask her to come over. We'd love to meet her, and she can get into our house, of course."

"No, Mom, it's not like that. We barely talk to each other. I just watch out for her. That's all." Ollie sighed. "What I can't stop thinking about is whether I would've done the same thing if Harris wasn't my brother."

Mom rubbed his back. "I think you would have. That's the type of person you are."

I agreed with her, but so much of who we are is the life we've lived. If I hadn't grown up in a wheelchair, I wasn't sure if I'd have ended up the same person. I hoped Zander would still be my friend in that parallel life and that I'd still like the color blue.

• • •

By the time the movie was over, the rain had stopped, and a hazy yellow light covered all the cars in the parking lot. "You guys want to grab dinner?" Mom asked.

Ollie and I were up for it. Besides having nothing better to do, we were both hungry. And even if I'd said no, I'd still be stuck with Mom. Ollie could have ditched us if he wanted.

"Harris, you should use the bathroom before we go," Mom said.

"I'm fine."

"You haven't peed since this morning, and you drank a lot during the movie."

"There's no single bathroom here," I argued. "Where am I supposed to go?"

"Ollie can take you. He's capable."

"What? No."

"Harris, I can't take you into the ladies' room. You're too old. Ollie has helped you before and seen me do it a thousand times."

I looked at Ollie, who shrugged. "It's not that complicated," he said.

I strongly disagreed, but I followed him into the men's room. Only my mom and nurses ever helped me in the bathroom. Dad did it occasionally, but he always fought with my seat cushion to get it at the right angle for the urinal. He definitely made it more complicated.

Like all public restrooms, the wheelchair-accessible stall was in the back, which meant we had to walk past every guy taking a shit. Ollie knew the routine, though. He reclined my wheelchair and placed the jar in the proper location. At least I thought he had.

But I couldn't go. I was too distracted.

"You could still hang out with people who aren't on the lacrosse team," I said.

"What?"

"I mean, if you wanted friends, there are other students at Ridge Prep."

"Dude, I honestly don't care. All the kids live far away, and I'm only there for a few more months."

"Yeah, but it has to be lonely—"

"Can we not talk about this while I'm helping you pee?"

Finally, I was able to go, and Ollie did everything right. But I guess the urinal was pushed too close to me, because when he pulled it away, I sprayed pee all over the wall. I'm not joking. We both stared at it dripping down to the floor. We were lucky none of it had sprayed on us.

We couldn't stop laughing for a few minutes. I wondered what the other guys in the bathroom thought we were giggling about. I was sure their imaginations were running wild.

Ollie grabbed a wad of toilet paper and tried to wipe off the wall as best he could. Then he zipped my pants, sat me up, and we bailed as fast as possible.

"Everything okay?" Mom asked when we exited. "What took so long?"

"We're fine," I said, speeding past her. "Let's just get out of here."

IT'S OKAY TO NOT KNOW

THE DAY AFTER DAD GOT HOME from his business trip, Zander rode with me and my parents to Ollie's lacrosse game. It was the first time Zander and I had hung out since making up. Do guys make up? I mean, we were not talking, and then we were talking again. There wasn't a special hug or anything.

But either way, it felt good to have someone by my side again besides my mom. For months, she'd been the only person I talked to every day, and most of our conversations had involved her parenting me or telling me to go talk to Zander. At least her nagging had worked.

"Ms. Clare, are you going to be hanging with Harris the rest of the school year?" Zander asked.

"Why? Are you getting sick of me?"

"Nah, you're pretty cool."

"I like to think so, though I'm not sure Harris would agree. I'm like Vegas—whatever happens at school stays at school. That's why I haven't told your mom that you haven't been doing your homework."

Zander tipped an invisible hat. "Much appreciated."

"Ollie told me the nursing agency might have someone new," I said. "He overheard you on the phone."

"They did, but she can't work the hours we need. I called our insurance to see what other agencies we can use, since this one doesn't have anyone; we haven't had a meet-and-greet in months."

We still had thirty minutes until we'd arrive at Ridge Prep. We spent most of the time explaining lacrosse to Zander, who had only seen a documentary about the Native American origins of the game. He wasn't able to understand it any better than football, but I think that's why we're friends. We complement each other.

. . .

The Ridge Prep Raiders won yet again, thanks to Ollie's four goals and three assists. I didn't know if the guys were still pissed at him or whatever, but at least they passed him the ball, so the opposing team never had a chance. But in no way did their loss compare to Zander's—Ridge Prep didn't have a concession stand. Needless to say, he couldn't get gummy worms, which he complained about to the school's athletic director, who was sitting next to my parents.

After the game, we got something to eat at a restaurant right by the school. It was some random bar and grill in the center of a dilapidated strip mall, but the burgers were decent, and I was just happy that my family seemed close to putting all its broken pieces back together. Maybe it was because I'd repaired things with Zander and they all felt that too, or maybe it was because New Jersey was starting to feel like home. Either way, I didn't mind.

"Zander, it's good to have you around again, buddy," my dad said.

"Thanks, Jay. I guess Harris finally realized that his life is incomplete without me."

"You don't complete me," I said. "This isn't *Jerry Maguire*."

"Who's that?" Zander asked.

"It's unfortunate that I know your favorite movie and you don't know mine."

"You guys are like an old married couple," Ollie said. "But it's pretty funny. I missed you, Zander."

Zander nearly fell out of his chair. "Ollie, that's the nicest thing you've ever said to me. I missed you, too."

"Never mind. I take it back."

For the first time in a long time, I wasn't thinking about Miranda. I was closing the distance between who I'd been and who I wanted to be. And even though it felt like I was leaving something behind, that was okay. That's how it had to be.

Miranda had made my world exciting, adventurous, and colorful, but she'd also left it so unbalanced that I'd almost slipped over to the wrong side. Now the ground was finally starting to even out again. But there was still one thing missing.

"We need to get you back together with Nory," Zander said as if he was reading my mind.

"Dude, we didn't break up. There's no getting back together."

"You and I got back together."

"No, I brought you a bag of candy, and you leaped with joy."

Zander nibbled on his chicken fingers. "Then give her a bag of candy."

"Thanks, but I think Nory Fischer is a little less basic than that."

"Ouch," Zander mumbled.

"I can't believe I'm going to say this, but I agree with Zander," Ollie said. "You can't give up on Nory. You need other friends besides this nerd."

"Jeez," Zander moaned. "I don't just tag along for the free food, you know. I also like you guys, and I'd appreciate some reciprocity."

My mom leaned over to give Zander a hug.

"I think you are here for the food," my dad joked. "Every time I see you, you're eating something I paid for."

"Fair point."

Dad took care of the check, and we all piled into Black Hawk for the drive home. I stayed silent for a long portion of the drive, thinking about Nory and how to make things right.

"So, how do I do it?" I finally asked the van.

Mom turned to look at me from the passenger seat. "Do what, honey?"

"Get Nory back." I couldn't make eye contact with anyone. I guess I was feeling pretty vulnerable, asking for advice about a girl in front of my parents and my brother.

"Just apologize and admit that you're an asshole," Zander said.

"I tried that. She wouldn't hear me out past 'hey.'"

Zander made a face. "This is pretty bad, dude."

Talking to Nory wasn't going to work—at least not as a first step. I thought she was over hearing words come out of my mouth. I knew I was. What I needed to do was show her that I'd been listening.

"How do guys get the girl?" I asked Zander. "I mean, in the movies you watch?"

"I don't know. They do something small but grand like standing outside her house with a boom box."

That wasn't something I was capable of doing, but Zander's point got the wheels in my head spinning.

And just like that, I had a plan for winning back Nory Fischer.

SIGNS OF A ROM-COM

MY LIFE ISN'T SOME SAPPY ROMANCE flick where the main character knows exactly where to find the embittered love interest. They're always at some park or on the top of a cliff, waiting to be saved. Nory wasn't waiting to be saved by me. If anything, I needed to be saved by her, and it took a great deal of effort to find her in the sea of students at East Essex Central.

Of course, I would see her in class eventually, but I wanted to say what I needed to say first thing in the morning so I wouldn't be freaking out all day.

Like I said, though, my life isn't a movie, and Nory was practically the only person I didn't see before homeroom. Zander was even helping by running around the halls like a chicken with its head cut off, sending me a false-alarm text every time he saw a girl with brown hair in a ponytail. His defense was "All cute girls look the same."

Nory walked into homeroom late, and the first thing I noticed was that her hair was down. I decided that was a good sign. But the bell rang before I could talk to her. In our classes, I mostly just stared at the back of her head while she took notes, wondering if an entire day would slip by before I had a chance to make my move.

Then—and I don't say this lightly—a miracle occurred at lunch.

The spring air was starting to break into early summer heat, which meant more people were eating outside. Zander refused to leave our table out of paranoia; he thought it would somehow disown us if we ate anywhere else. I didn't argue, since I'd never liked eating outside anyway and an empty cafeteria was easier to survey. Case in point: I noticed right away that Nory wasn't sitting at Kelvin's table.

She was hunkered down alone at the far end of the patio overlooking the school's parking lot. It wasn't quite as romantic as a twinkling city skyline, but it would work for what I needed to say.

"Can you put my hand on the joystick?" I asked my mom.

"Where are you going? You still have half your sandwich left."

I nodded toward Nory, and nothing more needed to be said. Zander popped up from the table to follow me to the exit so he could hold the door.

For once, I didn't hesitate. I had a clear path to Nory, and I didn't need to waste any valuable lunch minutes contemplating what to say. The words were ready.

But as I got closer, I started to have second thoughts. I mean, she was probably sitting by herself for a reason. I watched her for a moment, debating whether I should go ahead with my plan or leave her alone.

I started to turn back, but Nory must've heard my wheelchair, because she asked, "What do you want, Harris?"

"Oh, s-sorry," I stuttered. "I can come back if you want to be alone."

"No, it's fine." She sighed. "You can stay."

I'll admit, inside I was smiling, but I remained calm. I drove around to the other side of the bench so Nory could see me.

"Do you remember the day we met?" I asked.

Nory shrugged.

"You pushed right past me to get to your locker, like you weren't at all fazed by my wheelchair."

"Harris, nobody cares about your wheelchair."

"I know. Well, back then I didn't, but I'm starting to realize that now. Before moving to New Jersey, I almost never had to deal with meeting new people my age. Everyone in my town had known me since kindergarten, and my chair was what defined me. At least, I thought so."

Nory sighed again. "What's your point?"

"My point is that moving here gave me a chance to start over. To be defined by something else. And then when Miranda came into my life, I thought she could make me into a different person."

"I still don't get what this has to do with the day we met."

"I'm getting there," I promised. "We were texting after school, and you'd forgotten my name and asked me to tell you again. That honestly crushed a part of my soul, because I'd already told you, and I already liked you so much, but at least you cared enough to ask. And it wasn't until a few days later that you asked about my disability. You saw me before you saw my wheelchair. I should have realized then that I didn't need to become someone else. Not for you."

Nory finally looked in my direction. "You know, this isn't much of an apology."

"I know. I've been practicing in my head all day, but I guess I'm doing a pretty shitty job." I took a deep breath. "I'm sorry I disappeared—and I have a lot more I want to say about that. But first I want to give you something. Can you reach into the pouch on the side of my chair?"

Nory pulled out a book from my chair and started turning the pages.

"That's every meal you cooked and sent me a picture of. I saved all of them. Even the gross one where you said the potatoes exploded."

Nory smiled—just barely. "You know, for a long time, I thought food was the only thing that would help me remember my mom. But then you showed up. I saw the way you were with your mom, all the little moments between the two of you and how much she loves you." Nory sniffled. "I know it sounds silly, but I really liked being around that."

I saw my mom and Zander watching us through the windows. I moved closer to Nory so I could speak quietly. "That's not silly. I'm sorry I took that away from you. I'm sorry for being a terrible friend. When I got sick, it reminded me of all the times when I was younger and would miss months of school and when I would get back, everyone always seemed to have moved on from the person they were before I left. I didn't want to come back and see that you were different. It was easier for me to just move on by myself. That's why I disappeared."

Nory nodded but didn't say anything. She just looked across the school parking lot to the neighborhood at the base of the hill. It was clear that her mind was somewhere else. Somewhere more important. And so I waited.

"You know, today's the anniversary of my mom's death."

"I'm sorry, Nory."

"It was two days before my ninth birthday." She was quiet again for a while, then she turned and looked at me. "She used to say I'm a roller coaster and all the boys should watch out."

"You definitely are. But I'm not afraid." I smiled. "Not anymore, at least."

She smiled back. "You haven't asked me about my favorite color in a while."

"I don't care about that anymore. I want to get to know *you*, not who I think you are."

Nory reached over to hold my hand, and my heart sped up.

"Thanks for making the book," Nory said. "I love it." She gave my hand a squeeze.

"Do you want me to leave?" I asked, my eyes on our hands. "So you can be alone?"

"No. Stay."

And so I stayed.

ARRIVE

I LIKE YOU (YOU LIKE ME, TOO)

TWO DAYS LATER, we threw Nory a sixteenth birthday party. Her preferred location was a karaoke bar way out in the middle of nowhere. My mom drove us and Zander, and thankfully it was almost summer, so it stayed light out late into the evening, which helped her navigate the one-lane roads past farms and old churches.

New Jersey's geography baffled me. You could start in the suburbs, drive for fifteen minutes, and somehow end up next to cows. I liked it.

"Have you guys picked out your songs?" my mom asked.

Zander reached for a wad of paper in his back pocket. "Got a list right here. I think I'll start with Britney and close the night with George Michael."

"Seriously?" I asked.

"Hey, 'Careless Whisper' is the perfect song to say good night with. Did you come up with something better?"

"I'm not singing."

"Harris, you have to," my mom said. "Your voice is great, especially when you break out a little Sinatra."

"First off, my voice *used* to be good when I was a kid. Then I hit puberty. Second, I can't hold the microphone."

"Karaoke isn't about being good," Nory told me. "Just have fun, and I'll hold the mic for you."

I wanted to kiss her. The problem was, I didn't know how to tell her. So I just smiled.

* * *

The karaoke bar was appropriately dingy and virtually empty. There were a few locals sipping beers by the TV and playing pool. We didn't belong in the slightest, but Nory was beaming.

The DJ was the cliché overweight old man with a ponytail who couldn't wait to go home so he could watch Japanese game shows. I mean, he literally told us that.

"Is your dad meeting us here?" my mom asked Nory.

"No, he has to work. But he wanted to thank you for taking us."

"My pleasure. I'll order us some food."

Zander was already at the DJ table, flipping through the binder of titles. I guessed nothing on his list was available.

"Are you having a good birthday so far?" I asked. "It kinda sucks that you had to take a trig test today."

"I didn't mind. Birthdays are always weird for me. My dad's usually working and doesn't get home in time to do anything, so I just treat it like any other day. This is actually my first party in a long time."

"Well, you had to go big. Nothing screams wild sweet sixteen like karaoke."

"Speaking of wild, look at Zander."

He was fighting with the DJ, who was trying to stop him

from taking off his shirt while he sang "I'm Too Sexy." We hadn't been there ten minutes, and Zander was already close to getting kicked out.

Nory laughed. "I think he's having a better time than anyone else in here."

"That's because everyone else has to hear him sing."

"Should we intervene?"

"No, I want to see him get beaten up by a hippie."

Mom returned with sodas and chicken fingers and potato skins. She then removed Zander from the stage and ordered him to take a seat. He was completely unfazed by singing half-naked in front of a room full of farmers. I think he actually enjoyed the attention.

I decided to let go and have fun, too. After eight months, it was time to accept my new life and the friends who came with it.

"It's a little weird that it's just the three of us at your party," Zander said. "Plus Ms. Clare."

"You're the only ones I wanted to celebrate with," Nory answered.

"You have other friends at school," I said.

"True, but I don't hang out with them much."

"You could have at least invited Kelvin. I wouldn't have cared."

"I know. It's my birthday. But I'm not that close with him." She winked at me like all the torture she'd put me through had just been for the fun of it.

Zander burped, then threw his napkin on the table. He was a real gentleman. "Are you two lovebirds gonna sing tonight, or is this place ready for my encore?"

"We weren't even ready for your opening act," I said.

I really didn't want to sing, but Nory hijacked my wheelchair and drove me right to the DJ booth. We chose some sappy duet—I don't remember which one—and she stood next to me holding both of our microphones, one in each hand. Nory swayed to the rhythm of the music while I moved my head to follow the mic she held. It must've been a sight to see.

LOOKS LIKE RED,
SOUNDS LIKE SORRY

THE DRIVE HOME WAS SHOCKINGLY BEAUTIFUL, lit by the flaming red sunset. After we dropped off Nory and Zander, I just stared at it the rest of the way.

It wasn't until we pulled into our driveway that I looked down from Black Hawk's sunroof and through the windshield. Then I saw more red. It was Miranda's Mustang, and she was leaning against the driver's-side door.

My stomach dropped. I wanted to tell my mom to turn around and never come back. I wanted to be anywhere else. I wanted to cry until I'd permanently drained my tear ducts and all the words I'd ever wanted to say were in a puddle in front of me.

"What are you doing here?" Mom asked Miranda. She wasn't mad; just confused, like me, I think.

"I just have some things I need to say to Harris."

My mom looked at me, and I nodded to let her know I was all right. She walked away but watched us from the garage.

Miranda looked exactly the same as the last time I'd seen her. Maybe her hair was shorter, but she was the same person. I was different.

"Where were you guys?" she asked. "I've been waiting here for a few hours."

"I've been waiting for a few months."

Miranda sighed. "I'm really sorry, Harris."

"You're sorry? You fucking disappeared. What the hell happened?"

"I know. I really am sorry." She paced around my driveway, her eyes on the ground. "I was so scared after you went to the hospital. I thought I had really hurt you, that it was my fault again. I thought another person I loved was going to die."

"We didn't blame you for anything. Not me or my parents."

"I know, but I was so ashamed. I mean, I gave you my vape. I almost killed you!"

"I don't think it was the vape, really. I had a bacterial infection; I would've wound up in the hospital eventually. But then you just bailed. I thought you were in trouble. You wouldn't answer any of my calls or messages. I thought Brad came back and locked you in his house or something."

"Brad had nothing to do with it. I haven't seen him in months." She looked at me. "I've made so many mistakes in my life, and abandoning you has to be one of the worst."

Miranda started to cry. She leaned against her car and put her head in her hands, and I remembered the tattoo on her arm: THIS TOO SHALL PASS. I knew it would. Miranda would leave again, but for now, she needed me. I'd already stopped needing her.

"I won't lie: there were days when I truly hated you for

what you did to me and my mom, to my whole family. But we got through it. And now I have other people I can depend on."

"Nory and Zander?"

I nodded.

"Good. Those jocks didn't deserve you."

Miranda and I didn't say much after that. We didn't have to. We watched the sky turn black, waking up the stars. My dad returned home with Ollie, and they looked at us but said nothing. My mom was sitting on the front steps.

Miranda opened her car door, but before she climbed inside, she said, "I still have some time during the day, if you want me to come back."

"I loved being around you, Miranda. For a while, I loved it more than anything. But I don't think that's a good idea. Both of us should start fresh. I know that nobody cares about my wheelchair and that I shouldn't be afraid to take risks. That's all because of you, and I know you're going to be a great nurse. Just not with me."

Miranda couldn't hide her disappointment, but she nodded. "I understand. But I would like to be friends again."

A few months ago, I would've accepted that offer to have Miranda back in my life. But I didn't like the person I became around her, and I was just starting to figure out the person I wanted to be.

"Maybe someday," I said. It was a gentle lie, but so was everything else I'd thought I once had with Miranda.

She held my eyes for a few more seconds, and I knew it would be the last time I ever saw that exact color again. Finally, she got in her Mustang and started the engine. It really was the perfect car for her.

DIFFERENT IS BEAUTIFUL

NORY TURNING SIXTEEN CAME WITH the gift of a learner's permit. She'd logged all the required hours, and from what I witnessed in the school parking lot, she was a pretty good driver. We begged my mom for weeks to allow Nory to drive Black Hawk. As you can imagine, my mom had her own test that Nory needed to pass.

First, she had to learn how to let down the ramp, which was automatic, and ensure that I was safely locked into the van. Then my mom took her on the road and pointed out every pothole and bump in the neighborhood that absolutely had to be avoided.

Then, on a Sunday about a month later, my mom handed over the car keys. Unfortunately, she still had to come with us, but even so, Nory and I felt free. We raced out the door with no specific destination in mind. Nory had been at my house studying, and Ollie had just finished his lacrosse season two days earlier. The Ridge Prep Raiders had won State on the back of Ollie's five goals and six assists. You should have seen the look on Coach Lemieux's face.

"So, where are we headed?" I asked.

"I'm not really sure."

"A soccer mom minivan isn't really the coolest look, huh?" I said.

"I don't care." Nory clearly meant it. "I kind of like driving Black Hawk. It's like I'm behind the wheel of a tank. Let's see what this bad boy can do."

Nory stepped on the gas, sending us speeding down the highway. She was in control, and my body tingled every time she peeked at me in the rearview mirror to see if I was okay.

We finally arrived at a park behind Nory and Zander's neighborhood. My mom took back the driver's seat and said she'd pick us up later. Zander was busy helping his mom around the house, or else we would have invited him. At least that's what we told him, but there was an unspoken agreement that we wanted to be alone.

"Do you want to hold hands?" I asked.

Without hesitation, Nory grabbed my non-driving hand, and we moved side by side along a dirt trail to the top of a cliff overlooking the park. Maybe my life was a movie after all.

I wished I could've reached out to hold Nory's hand on my own, but I don't think she minded. Our relationship was going to be different.

Nory sat down on a bench, and I pulled up next to her. Without missing a beat, she slipped off her flip-flops and stretched her legs out onto my lap. God, what a time to be alive.

"I like to come up here when things aren't making sense," Nory said. "Watching the trees sway back and forth and the pond ripple makes everything seem clearer."

"Are things not making sense?"

"They are. That's why I brought you here. I wanted to share this with you in case you ever need it."

I could see for miles. "How long have you been coming here?"

"A long time. My mom brought me here first. I always felt like we were breaking some kind of rule, since no one's ever on the hill."

"Does your dad ever sit with you?"

"Not really. Not since she died."

We watched the geese pick at the growing grass and drink from the pond. Only a few months earlier, the grass had dried out and turned a pale shade of brown, leaving nothing behind for the geese to eat, and naturally they'd flown away. Winter had frozen the pond and dropped the leaves of the towering trees, and the land had become barren of life.

But Nory and I were there now, witnessing nature's new beginnings, and our own. It was beautiful.

I reflected on some of the other new beginnings in my life. We'd convinced Zander to switch lunch tables and told him that our original table had never belonged to us in the first place. It had been claimed years ago, and it was time to make our own memories.

Nory, who'd became part of our lunch crew, suggested that we shouldn't be confined to a single table. So we came up with a plan to sit outside when it was warm, and when it got cold, we'd move inside the cafeteria and sit at a different table each day. Some days it would be with people we knew, and other days it would be with people we wanted to know. The thought of meeting new people and them watching me get fed terrified me, but I knew that with Zander and Nory by my side, it wouldn't be so bad.

I also promised myself that next year I would stop eating a deli sandwich every day.

But in that moment at the park, I was just content with Nory next to me, touching me. Then she picked her feet up off my lap and leaned forward so our faces were almost touching. For a split second, the world froze. I had just enough time to note that her breath smelled minty as it intertwined with mine. And then we were kissing. Her lips were chapped and just as inexperienced as mine, but none of that mattered.

After a few moments, she eased back, and we both smiled. My heart was beating out of my chest, and for the first time, I actually felt like I was where I was supposed to be.

"Oh, shit!" Nory's eyes got huge. "We still have to finish our physics project."

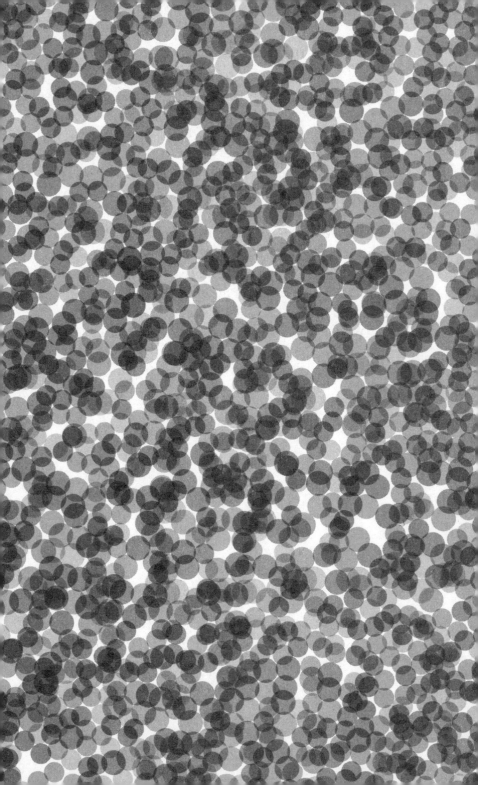

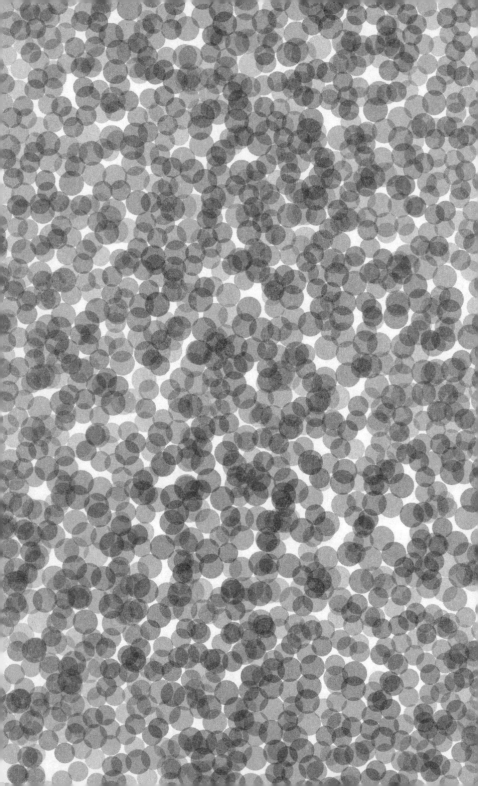

ACKNOWLEDGMENTS

I have written and deleted this opening sentence countless times in my head and on paper, not knowing how to start what can be such an interesting part of a book. So, I'd like to jump right into introducing you to some of the most influential and inspiring people in my life, each of whom left their mark on this story.

First, I want to thank every reader who decided to give this story a shot and welcome Harris, Miranda, Nory, Zander, and the Jacobus family into your life. I'm not sure I'll ever be able to comprehend the fact that my words are being read by people I don't personally know, but I'd like to think that now you know me in some capacity.

Thank you to my mom and dad, Sheri and Alan, for everything you do on a daily basis to keep me healthy so I can follow my dreams. You've never allowed me to say or think that I can't do something because of my disability, and that constant belief and encouragement is the main reason this book has come to fruition. I know my mom is reading this and thinking I'm being too serious and should've already cracked five jokes, but I don't care. So, hello, Mom! I've never said this, but you have always been the biggest reader in our family, and I think watching you absorb books when I was growing up definitely played a role in my passion for writing. I always wanted to write something for you. Plus, you gave me a cool name, which looks pretty awesome on the cover!

Thank you to my brother, Jacob, for being what a big brother should be: supportive, protective, and the right amount of aggravating. I love you!

My agent, Stephen Barr, undoubtedly deserves the next round of thanks and probably should've been the first paragraph because without him this book would not exist. I mean, maybe it would exist in a folder on my computer, but now it gets to be humbly shared with the world because he decided to give some unproven twenty-something kid a chance. Thank you, Stephen, for being such a champion of this story from the very beginning. Every time we email or talk on the phone, it's like speaking with a close friend who I've known my whole life. I hope you feel it, too, because there's nobody else I want on my side representing me except for you. Here's to you, good sir!

Huge thanks to my editor, Kaylan Adair. I knew you were the one when you said your favorite scene was Harris and Shannon in the bathroom. But seriously, my biggest fear going into this was that I would lose control of this story, and of course that never happened because you understood each sentence and character at its very core. It's kind of like at the end of the first *National Treasure* movie when they think they've found the treasure room but it's empty, and Ben (Nicolas Cage) is really upset but then his dad says, "You found what they left for us to find and understood the meaning of it." Anyway, that's a convoluted way for me to say that you're a killer editor who cares very much. Not to mention you're extremely fun and just a cool person to work with, although you really need to brush up on your pop culture and lingo.

And thank you to everyone else at Candlewick who has helped shape this story in some way. Thank you for allowing me to be a part of your family.

Thank you to my friend Michele Mesi. I know I joke around and say you'll get a small footnote, but you are so much more than that and truly deserve your own paragraph. You are such an incredibly fierce and empathic friend, and your passion for books is what I admire about you the most. Thanks for reading multiple versions of this story and telling me everything you hated . . . and everything you loved. Most importantly, thank you for being you and coming into my life, even with all your sarcasm. I really don't know how I ever lived without it.

Last, and certainly least (inside joke), I must thank Steve Stoma for giving me the power and energy to write every day.

And, with all of that, I will now say goodbye. Thanks again for reading! Maybe Zander will share a sour gummy worm with you if you ever see him around. Tell him you know me.

Much love.